THE PER

The Perfect Wife
and Mother

Nicola Thorne

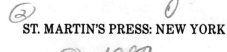
ST. MARTIN'S PRESS: NEW YORK

Library of Congress Cataloging in Publication Data

Thorne, Nicola.
    The perfect wife and mother.

    I.   Title.
PR6070.H689Pr   1981   823′.914   80-53084
ISBN 0-312-60077-1

Dedicated with affection to Jane Moonman who, although undoubtedly a perfect wife and mother, is not the model for this book.

Part One

Wife and Mother

1

Ruth Harrow knew it was none of her business, but she couldn't help wondering about the people who had moved into the house next door. Their arrival just after Christmas had seemed to disturb the peace of Lawnside, the quiet cul-de-sac carved into the green belt which surrounded Edgerton, once a country market town, but now almost suburban, being only twenty miles from London.

The neighbouring house was almost identical to that of the Harrows' – a fairly large, detached house mock-Georgian in style and set in about half an acre of ground. Invariably its drive was blocked by a van, sometimes two; or a huge pantechnicon would park by the kerb disgorging yet more old-fashioned looking furniture. It was hard to imagine where it would all go Ruth thought, as she stood behind the lace curtains in the sitting room sipping her coffee and watching a van reverse out of the drive next door. It had *TV Rentals and Repairs* on the side. Ruth couldn't work out whether they were getting a set or having it repaired. Surely they wouldn't have done without a television set for a whole six weeks?

Lawnside was a quiet, decorous, much sought after part of Edgerton where hardly anybody knew anybody well except to say 'good day', and it took a number of years to make friends. Naturally the Harrows made friends most quickly with other families who had children. The people who used to live next door had had none, and the Harrows hadn't even known their name though they had smiled across the hedge, or nodded in the street for at least ten years.

3

Nothing that Ruth could remember had ever quite disrupted Lawnside like the arrival of the new people. This frantic toing and froing had been going on for weeks. Most new arrivals – the few there were, for people tended to plant roots firmly in such a desirable part of the town as Lawnside – came with a van or two, put their net curtains up and that was that. They maintained the discreet anonymity with which they had arrived, gradually merging into the neighbourhood, neither holding back nor coming forward. But not the new neighbours of the Harrows at No. 44 Lawnside, who had made their presence felt. It was now nearly half term and every day vans arrived, plumbers' vans, painters' and carpenters' vans, and little men drew up on bicycles carrying ladders or were to be seen scampering agilely over the roof.

Unfortunately no one had yet been called in to attend to the garden. That was an eyesore as far as the cul-de-sac was concerned compared with so many neat and well tended gardens, paved forecourts or smooth neat patches of individual, well cut emerald-coloured lawn.

Ruth turned away from the window, feeling suddenly guilty and slightly ashamed. To be peering at her neighbours as often as she did was ridiculous, even demeaning. It meant that she hadn't enough to do, not enough on her mind. To be so curious about the people next door was absurd.

She took her cup into the kitchen, washed it and opened the oven door to look at the casserole. Then she glanced at the timer. Geoffrey would be home at twelve-thirty. He had lunch at home two or three times a week, particularly when he had an evening meeting and would have only time for a snack after work. Tonight it was the Edgerton Rotarians of which he was chairman, tomorrow the Conservatives of which he was treasurer.

Ruth went into the dining room and slowly, carefully, set places for two, the mats on the shining mahogany table, the second best silver correctly placed on either side, the serving

4

spoons, the condiments, napkins neatly rolled into the silver rings which bore the initials of each member of the family.

R.C.H. Ruth Catriona Harrow aged thirty-six; occupation housewife; colour of hair auburn; colour of eyes green; height five feet six inches; nationality British.

It was not much of a description. What else could one add? Ruth returned to the kitchen and salted the potatoes before setting a light under the gas.

Education: two years at university. Her degree interrupted to marry at twenty Geoffrey Vernon Harrow, aged twenty-two, articled to a solicitor, a friend of her brother's, also a solicitor. At twenty-one she had been a mother. Joe was born just ten months after the wedding. When he was three they had moved from Manchester to Edgerton where Geoffrey's elder brother had a successful practice in the expanding new town of Edgerton. Harrow and Harrow. They had done well.

What else? What else? Olivia was fourteen, born two years after Joe. Then there had been a miscarriage and finally George, now twelve.

Then what else? Ruth stood at the open back door looking into the sunlit garden. A few crocuses had come up under the row of ash trees which she and Geoffrey had planted to try and screen off the neighbour's back garden shortly after they had bought the house. She could just see the white, yellow and purple buds from where she stood.

Well, it was a normal quiet sort of life, not very much to say about it really. Geoffrey was prosperous, the children were happy and doing well at school. They had plenty of friends; they went out quite a lot and entertained often.

Ruth turned down the gas under the potatoes and glanced again at the timer. A little more seasoning in the casserole. Then she went upstairs to change. She went round the house in the morning in trousers; but she always changed for lunch with Geoffrey. She knew he expected it; that if she had opened the door still wearing trousers and jumper and without having made up he would have been surprised, maybe shocked. He expected it and she felt right doing it. If he was not home for lunch she always changed in time for the children when they came back from school. She felt that it was the image they had of their mother, someone who was always nicely dressed and properly made up. Ruth personally had no time for women who slopped around all day in jeans. She felt they had no pride in themselves.

Ruth went into the neat bedroom she shared with Geoffrey. It faced over the front of the house and gave a very good view of the drive next door. For a moment she stood behind the lace curtains looking down. For once there was no sign of activity, not a van, not a bicycle, nothing stirred; maybe the neighbours were settling down. She shrugged and began to cleanse her face.

She selected a paisley wool dress and as she washed and changed and carefully made up her face Ruth Harrow wondered why she was so preoccupied with thoughts about the past, and why she was so interested in the unnamed and unknown people next door. Somehow they appeared to go together. The answer to each question seemed the same though she did not know what it was.

As she patted on her foundation cream she glanced past her face to the room also reflected there. There was not a thing out of place. It was almost like a room in a hotel, impersonal. The four foot six double bed was covered in a deep gold dralon which matched the dralon curtains. The Axminster carpet was dark brown, the furniture polished mahogany. A lot of people these days had fitted contemporary furniture; but Ruth didn't like it, neither fitted nor contemporary. Everything in the Harrow house shone and could be moved about, not that it ever was. The bedroom had hardly changed since she and Geoffrey had first slept in it thirteen years before. George had been conceived in this very bed, in the same place then as it was in now, parallel to the window facing the outside wall. The dressing table with its deep panel and triptych mirror stood in front of the window, and the two large wardrobes faced the bed. Just by the door, as you came in, was a tall chest full of Geoffrey's socks and shirts. It had a lace doily on the top, a porcelain statue of a shepherdess and, usually, a vase of flowers. On either side of the bed were small mahogany tables, each with a shelf and small cupboard. On Geoffrey's side there was the alarm clock, a copy of the *Law Gazette* and *Whitaker's Almanac*. On hers a bottle of drops for her sinus and Mary Stewart's latest novel which Geoffrey had bought her for Christmas.

In the cupboard out of sight, she had the contraceptive pills she was careful to take every night. She continued to take the Pill regardless of the warnings about its possible dangers to women over thirty. She had a six-monthly check-up with the doctor every time she got a fresh supply, blood pressure, heart. She seldom smoked and she had no varicose veins. The Pill seemed to suit her. It had no effect on her mood, her libido or her figure. The doctor told her that as far as he was concerned she could stay on the Pill until the end of her reproductive life if she went on being as healthy as she was now.

Ruth outlined her lips with a strong pink lipstick, blotted them, gazed for a moment at her face and then got up and smoothed her dress over her hips adjusting the belt at her waist. Her weight had scarcely changed since she was twenty; her bosom was fuller, but she had had three children. She always had had rather a prominent bust, carefully controlled by a well fitting bra. She was never without it, except in bed. She had lines on her face that had not been there sixteen years before; but she regarded them as signs of maturity rather than age and her red-brown hair was unstreaked by grey, her eyes clear and all her teeth not only her own, but in excellent condition.

Ruth smiled at herself in the mirror, dabbed perfume behind

her ears and descended the stairs just as Geoffrey let himself in at the front door.

Even after all these years the sight of Geoffrey, the blurred outline of his head seen through the panel of frosted glass of the front door gave her a spasm of pleasure, a feeling of anticipation. She especially liked these lunches together because they were the only occasions on which they could have meals alone. They seldom went out to dinner together, it was usually in the company of friends or business acquaintances and at home all other meals were family meals.

He put down his briefcase, hung his coat on the hallstand, rubbed his hands together and looked up as Ruth came down the stairs, the welcoming smile on her face.

'It's still quite cold despite the thaw,' Geoffrey said. 'Thank God that snow has gone. We're having trouble with the central heating at the office. How are you, dear?'

Geoffrey put his arm around her waist in an intimate way and kissed her cheek.

'I'm fine, and there is a nice warm casserole for lunch. Rabbit.'

'Rabbit casserole? I don't remember having that before.'

'We have had it before; but rabbits became scarce with myxomatosis. Now they are apparently immune to it and are appearing in the shops again. The children don't like it.'

'I don't know that I blame them.' Geoffrey stood back for her to precede him into the sitting room, and then he went over to the drinks table and poured them each a sherry – pale Fino for him, Amontillado for Ruth.

'Oh darling, they are no health hazard I assure you! You used to love rabbit. I bought one as a special treat for us.'

Geoffrey gave her her sherry and kissed her on the cheek again.

'I was just joking. I adore rabbit. How soon can we eat?'

'In about ten minutes. Are you in a hurry?'

8

'I have an appointment at two-thirty, then all day until about ten tonight.'

Geoffrey sat on the sofa, crossed his legs and took up *The Times* which lay folded on a small table in front of him. He shook it out and went straight to the business pages frowning as he scanned the bleak items of news about the economy.

Ruth took her sherry into the kitchen and started to serve lunch, passing the dishes through the hatch into the dining room.

She went back into the sitting room and, looking over Geoffrey's bent head, saw that another large van had backed into the drive next door. She went over to the window and stood behind the curtains looking at it.

'My goodness. It's *another* furniture van. Where can they be putting it all?'

'All what, darling?' Geoffrey didn't lift his head from the paper.

'They just seem to have masses of furniture; yet their house is the same size as ours.'

'Did you count it?'

'Count what?' She turned in surprise and looked at him.

'The furniture. The pieces that go in.'

'Don't be silly, Geoffrey; but there is an awful lot of activity next door.'

'It is simply that we have never had neighbours leave or move in since we came here. You notice it more.' Geoffrey got up and came and stood behind her. 'That rabbit smells awfully good.'

'Do you know anything about the new people?'

They were half way through their meal, Geoffrey having had a second helping of rabbit stew. He looked up. 'No. Why should I?'

'I thought you might have done the conveyancing or something for the house.'

'Oh no. I don't touch that kind of thing now. It may have

9

been handled by our firm; but I don't think so. If you're so interested why don't you pop over and introduce yourself?'

Geoffrey reached for a piece of bread and mopped up the gravy round the side of his plate. He always enjoyed his food and ate with gusto. It showed in his figure; he had a definite paunch, but it seemed to go with his profession and his prosperity.

'Oh I couldn't do that, dear. We didn't even know the name of the people there before. I can't just pop over like that!'

'Why not?' Geoffrey looked at her in his direct lawyer-like way and reached for the cheese. 'That was excellent. I shall have to watch my waistline. Do you think we should cut out potatoes, dear? No, really, why don't you make yourself known if you are that interested.'

'Oh I'm not *that* interested!'

'But you talk about them a lot. Nearly every day you make some mention of the people next door. You seem obsessed by them.'

Ruth got up and, taking their plates, put them on the sideboard. Geoffrey always liked a glass of port with his cheese and she poured one for him and put it by his side. They only ever drank water with their main meal at lunchtime, or indeed their dinner. Wine was strictly for guests, birthdays or Christmas. She sat down again, the colour on her cheeks pronounced. She folded her hands under her chin and leaned on them.

'Geoffrey I am *not* obsessed by the neighbours. It is a very unfair, a silly thing to say.'

'This brie is awfully good.' Geoffrey smiled at her. 'Ruth, I think you *do* talk about them a lot. Have you ever thought of taking up some kind of occupation, dear, voluntary work or a part time job? Lots of women do it at your age, you know. Children off your hands, that sort of thing.'

The colour on Ruth's cheeks deepened. 'Are you suggesting that I am menopausal, Geoffrey, something like that? I am only thirty-six.'

'Darling, I'm suggesting no such thing!' He put down his knife and leaned back in his chair. Yes, he was getting too fat she thought looking at him critically, something she seldom did. It never occurred to her to appraise her husband as one did other people, but now his waistband was very tight and his stomach, encased in its expensive pink striped shirt, bulged over the top. Also, as he leaned back, she saw a very pronounced double chin, his jowl sank onto the knot of his tie. 'But I do think that to be so absorbed by the neighbours is maybe a symptom of not having enough to do.'

'I have *plenty* to do thank you, Geoffrey.' Ruth poured a glass of water, aware of the burning sensation on her face. 'I only have two days in the week when I don't have lunch to get. Do you suggest that to fill my time those two mornings I should go and work in a shop? They are, in fact, the days on which I do the bulk of my shopping to keep this house and feed its five inhabitants for a week. When you come home for lunch I spend at least half the morning preparing it, that is after I have washed up for five and made four beds, hoovered and dusted throughout. Mrs Grange comes twice a week for three hours. She concentrates on the kitchen and the stove, the stairs and the corners, under the beds. She . . .'

'Oh all right, all right.' Geoffrey got up and went to the french windows patting his full stomach and thrusting back his shoulders. 'I'm sorry. You have plenty to do; but still . . .'

'Yes Geoffrey?' Her voice was steely.

'Not enough on your *mind* darling. Your mind is not fully occupied, even if your time is.'

Ruth gave a sarcastic laugh and folded her napkin neatly into its ring. 'Empty little bird brain, all she has on her mind are the trivia of domestic life while her husband and children occupy theirs with intricate points of law and developing their education. I must remind you that I nearly got a history degree, Geoffrey Harrow. It was because of *you* I didn't.' She got up and thumped the napkin down on the table, seizing

11

the side plates as though they were discs that she was about to hurl across the room.

'Oh Ruth, for God's sake. I didn't mean to start a brawl . . .'

'Well that's just what you did isn't it?' She held one of the plates threateningly, shaking it in front of his face. 'I have spent sixteen years breeding children, bringing them up, keeping a nice house, providing food that was not only wholesome but interesting, shopping, cleaning, packing for holidays, washing, ironing, and now I am told that my mind is vacuous, possibly empty . . . Just because I happen to be interested in what is going on *next door!*'

She went over to the hatch and shoved the plates through; one fell to the floor on the other side and broke. The noise of shattering crockery had a sobering effect and she paused. She knew she was behaving irrationally, uncharacteristically. Her eyes were full of tears.

Geoffrey's hands gently clasped her shoulders. 'I'm sorry.'

She closed her eyes and let him hold her for a moment, then she shook herself impatiently and turned to face him. 'But you meant it, Geoffrey, didn't you? Am I boring? Is my conversation banal? Are you tiring of me? Would you like a mistress? Have you perhaps already got one? Am I having a bad effect on my children's education by being so stupid? Should I read John Updike instead of Mary Stewart? Is my mind in a trough? Does it, in fact exist at all?'

'Oh shut up,' Geoffrey shouted. 'I said I was sorry! Now you are making a stupid speech. Of course I don't think any of these things. If you are happy staring at the neighbours all day then go on staring at them. If that makes you happy, for God's sake *do* it. I shan't ever open my mouth again.'

Geoffrey walked into the hall and, taking his coat and briefcase, slammed the front door behind him.

Slowly Ruth followed him. Her tears had gone; self-pity replaced by anger. She folded her arms and, walking into the sitting room, stood behind the lace curtains while Geoffrey got into his Rover and backed out of the drive. She watched him round the crescent, the well tended circular patch of green that gave Lawnside its name. She saw him pause at the end before turning into the main road, thick white smoke, caused by the cold, coming out of the exhaust. With a puff he vanished.

It looked like a puff of anger, an expression of rage. Still with her arms folded she turned her attention to the drive next door. The furniture van had gone.

2

Twelve-year-old George was considered the most extrovert of the Harrow children. He did not have the fierce competitiveness of his elder brother, or a suspicion of the intellect of his sister. Consequently his father, not wishing to waste money on someone who was clearly not going to achieve much in life, had sent him to the town's huge comprehensive school, while Joe went to the former boys' grammar school that had gone independent and Olivia to the corresponding girls'.

His father was a loving parent as well as a severely practical one and it was, of course, understood that if George suddenly sparkled or was unhappy he would be moved to a school where his father considered he would get an education that was better than the one he was getting now.

Geoffrey Harrow firmly believed in the Conservative values of self help and hard work. He thought the grammar school system was the backbone of the country. It had produced him, after all. Like him, his parents had been solidly middle class, his father a businessman in Manchester who had sent him to Manchester Grammar and then to the University there.

Geoffrey was disgusted at the Socialist system of education that had scrapped the grammar schools and deprived bright children of the chance to ease themselves above the rest. Comprehensiveness meant uniformity; it meant equality and, in Geoffrey's view, people were not equal.

He accepted the fact that his children were not equal either.

That Joe was clever and ambitious and would go to university, hopefully eventually come into Harrow and Harrow, and Olivia might do the same; but that George would go into the lower ranks of business or maybe the Civil Service. Hence he was not going to throw away money on educating George who had never shown the least aptitude for scholarship.

As it happened George was quite delighted to be thrown into the whirlpool that his father considered the state system represented. A large informal school suited his temperament admirably. He disliked uniform and rules and regulations and Edgerton Comp with its progressive headmaster, its 1700 children was this sort of school. You either sank in it or you swam. It was up to the individual child, aided or impeded by its parents.

George Harrow now stood in the doorway of the kitchen, his patched jeans showing below his black and orange anorak, his dark tousled head wet with rain, his spectacles steamed over. Ruth was preparing tea.

'Shut the door, darling. It's very cold, and do take your shoes off if they are muddy. Mrs Grange has done the floor so thoroughly today.' She carefully eased a cake onto a plate and dusted it with icing sugar. Then she turned round. Behind George stood a tall, rather good looking youth of about his own age. The boy had a thin intelligent face, his cheeks almost cavernous, large blue eyes surmounted by thick brows and black curly hair. If anything he looked more unkempt than George, his jeans more patched, his anorak more threadbare, his trainers more scuffed and stained. It was a matter of some pride among the boys in George's class as to who could look the least well cared for. In Ruth's opinion the newcomer maybe had a slight edge over George in this respect.

'Mum, this is Chris,' George said removing his shoes and beckoning to the boy behind him. 'He's just come to our school. But he is in a class above me as he's a year older.'

'How do you do, Chris?' Ruth said brightly, giving him a

warm friendly smile. 'Come in, but do you mind taking off your shoes . . . .'

Chris mumbled something and started to kick off his shoes without untying the laces. His socks had holes in both toes. At least Ruth ensured that whatever George looked like on top his underthings were always clean and in good repair, underpants and socks changed every day. She somehow doubted whether Chris's mother, whoever she might be, felt the same about her son.

'There, I made a jam sponge this afternoon. Would you like some tea, Chris?'

Chris mumbled again and George looked at him.

'Yes he would thanks Mum. He's come to hear my new Abba disc.'

'Your what?'

'Abba. The pop group.'

'Well don't have it up too loud. Joe says he can't get on with his homework because of the noise you make.'

'Joe won't be home until supper. It is his philatelic night.'

'Oh so it is. And Olivia has got choir practice. I quite forgot. But don't make too much noise. There, sit down and have your tea.'

Ruth put the newly baked cake on the kitchen table together with mugs, a teapot and a plate of freshly cut bread. The boys sat on either side and she poured the tea into mugs for them, a china cup for herself.

'And where does Chris come from? Sugar?' She looked at him interrogatively, still with the bright welcoming smile on her face that was meant to put him at ease. There was no doubt that the children from the grammar schools were better mannered, more articulate than those from the comp. One had the impression that the grammar school children still wanted to please, that they had some respect for their elders. It was quite obvious that those from the comp, at least the ones

16

brought home by George, could not care less about the niceties of social intercourse.

'Next door,' George said pushing up his glasses and seizing a piece of cake with a dirty hand.

'Next door?' At first Ruth didn't understand. They knew ... 'Oh next *door?*' She felt a little thrill of excitement, a pleasurable but slightly guilty feeling of anticipation. 'The new people next door?'

'Mum the ones on the other side don't have any kids,' George said patiently. 'Chris's people moved in next door just after Christmas. You know you are always talking about all the vans bunging up the drive.'

'What nonsense!' Ruth said looking at Chris defensively. 'I can't ever remember mentioning the people next door.'

'Oh Mum ...'

She gave George a look that was meant to incorporate a warning, a threat and the prospect of actual physical punishment if he failed her. George stopped talking. He knew the look well and was not unused to having it translated in practice. He shut his mouth very tight and rolled his eyes. Chris giggled and reached out for a second helping of cake. Ruth tensed her face muscles with exasperation and played with the single string of pearls on her plain angora jumper.

'Where did you come from Chris?'

Chris looked at her rather like a sheep about to be penned in its fold and mumbled something into his cake.

'I beg your pardon?'

'He says London, Mum. They came from London.'

'Oh what part of London?' Ruth fixed the bright smile, determined not to be deterred. She was quite used to the mono-syllabic behaviour of her younger son's friends. Those from the grammar could be relied on to spell out chapter and verse in polite, staccato if rather bored tones. She sometimes despaired of state education as a grounding in good manners whatever its scholastic merits or demerits.

17

'Swiss Cottage,' Chris said at last, as if reluctant to part with the information. Ruth was rather relieved to notice that he had a good middle class unaccented voice – no London whine there, so far as she could determine.

'Oh how interesting. Almost in the heart of London. Were you sorry to leave?'

Chris shook his head and stuffed half of his cake into his mouth.

'Whatever did you have for lunch today? You boys are starving.'

Both made grimaces of acute disgust.

'We had spaghetti and rissoles and cabbage and . . . urrrh. It was horrible.'

'And soggy pudding.' Chris's face crumpled with laughter. 'It was so soggy we . . .'

Ruth held up a hand and poured a fresh cup of tea.

'Thank you. Spare me the details.'

'I left it all,' George said.

'Me too.'

Ruth passed the bread and butter and went to one of the cupboards, returning with pots of jam and honey. 'There, you had better fill up. Does your mother cook an evening meal for you, Chris?'

Chris shrugged, ignored the bread and butter, the honey and jam in dainty pots made of Doulton china set on a stainless steel stand, and grasped a third piece of cake.

'Depends.'

'On what?'

'Pardon?'

'I said on what does it depend?'

'On whether she feels like it.'

'Oh.'

Ruth pursed her mouth. That phrase seemed to sum up what she'd instinctively felt about the people next door.

'C'mon.' George got up and reached over to Chris.

18

Chris stuffed the rest of the cake in his mouth, grimaced at Ruth and belted out of the room after George.

The next week was half term for George. The grammar schools insisted on having different holidays from those of the state schools as though out of an instinctive desire to lessen the chances of casual contact between the children of the state and the independent sector. For parents who had children at both kinds of school it was very irksome.

As Ruth cooked and baked and cleaned, entertained George's friends, or rather put up with them, as there was little they needed in the way of entertainment, knowing that she'd have to do exactly the same the week after for Joe and Olivia, she reflected bitterly on Geoffrey's accusation that she had not enough on her mind. How could the mind drift off into rarefied atmospheres when the body had so much simple physical slogging to do?

She had carefully avoided any mention of the people next door ever since Geoffrey had made his hurtful remark. She hadn't even told him about Chris.

'Would it be nice to go to London tomorrow?' Ruth asked George over lunch in the middle of his half term.

'Nah.'

'I thought we could have lunch, go to a museum.'

'Nah.'

'George, please answer me properly and take your elbows off the table.'

'Well, I don't want to go.' He looked at her and a sudden idea apparently burst through his boredom, illuminating his face. 'Unless Chris comes.'

'The boy next door?'

'Yep.'

'But I don't know him.'

'You do. He's here almost every day. Oh Mum I'd love to

go if Chris came. Maybe we could go to the War Museum?'

'The *War* Museum? I was thinking of the Victoria and Albert or the Science Museum.'

'If Chris comes the War Museum or nothing. If he doesn't come nothing.'

Ruth angrily got up, took the fruit juice from the fridge and poured another glass.

'I can't possibly ask someone I don't know.'

'But you do know him.'

'I don't know his mother.'

'Then go and meet her.'

'I can't just walk in.'

'Why not, Mum?'

George finished his jelly and cream and pushed his plate away. Ruth noticed that his hands were still grubby despite the number of times she had told him to go and wash them. The thought of dragging her sullen son and his equally appalling friend round London suddenly filled her with dread.

'Oh forget it.'

'*No* Mum. I want to know *why* you can't welcome his mother to the area. Just pop over and say "hello". Ask if you can help. Other people would. You are just so . . .'

'Yes? So?'

The warning look came into Ruth's fine green eyes and George picked up the spoon from the empty plate and licked it, avoiding her gaze.

'Well, standoffish. His mother is very nice. They're a very warm sort of casual family. I like them. The mother asks about you.'

'She asks about *me*?' Ruth looked, and felt, astonished.

'Yes, what you do – that kind of thing. I wish you'd go over and say hello. Ask her if Chris can come to London. Anyway, I'm going to get Chris now. Can I say you'll pop over?'

'Certainly not.'

Ruth got up and carried the plates to the draining board.

'I think you're unreasonable, Mum.'

George stood beside her, with the tea towel. His freckled face was crestfallen and his glasses were halfway down his nose as though they were a bad fit. He looked so grave and serious, so troubled, that feelings of love and remorse assailed her at the same time. He was her youngest, her baby and they were always opposing each other just because she was so conventional and George was not.

'Ask his mother if it would be all right if I came round and said hello.'

'Oh Mum, thanks!'

George clasped her round the neck and hugged her. For a moment she held his sturdy body tight, aware of his vaguely unwashed small, not unpleasant – rather like a nice friendly dog.

'I suppose I *should* have thought of it,' she murmured. 'One is so constricted by convention.'

George was frantically tugging on his shoe. 'How do you mean?'

'Oh keeping oneself to oneself. It's what we're used to. It's how we are.'

'It's Dad, Mum. Being so stuffy.'

'Oh darling,' Ruth cried, appalled. 'Your father is *not* stuffy.'

George got up and put on his anorak pulling a face. 'He is rather. I get ragged an awful lot at school about him being a Tory Councillor. All my friends' parents are Labour. Having a father who is a Tory *and* a lawyer is a big disadvantage for me. I try and play it down.'

'Well if that is how you feel maybe we should think of taking you away from the school. It is certainly not how Joe or Olivia feel.'

Ruth suddenly felt very upset as though she were going to find it hard to control her emotions. To hear George criticise his father like that seemed unsupportable.

'I think Olivia feels that Dad's a bit stuffy. I don't know how Joe feels at all about anything; and I don't want to be moved from the school, Mum. I'd run away if you moved me.'

George looked at her defiantly and Ruth's feeling of tearful resentment suddenly crumbled and she wanted to laugh. His bespectacled, eager little face looked so serious.

'Oh darling, let's stop this serious talk. Run across to the people next door. What is their name?'

'Lazar.'

'Lazar? That's an unusual name.'

'It's Hungarian.'

'They are Hungarian?' Suddenly all the disorder was explained. Foreigners.

'The father is. The mother is English. I've never met the father. He's often away.'

'Well go and ask Mrs Lazar if I may pop in in about an hour.'

'I know she'll say "yes". She's that sort.'

'Not like me. Not my sort he means,' Ruth thought as she slowly climbed the stairs to tidy herself to meet Mrs Lazar.

3

The boys had disappeared almost as soon as they got to the Imperial War Museum and, after a desultory and apathetic look round Ruth and Isobel Lazar decided to seek refuge in the cafeteria.

'They'll find us here,' Ruth said noting the two kinds of cream cakes that Mrs Lazar had put on her tray.

'Oh I never worry about my children. They have tongues in their heads as well as brains, I hope, and know how to ask.' Mrs Lazar looked across at Ruth and smiled.

She had the lined, used-looking face of a mature woman whose experience of life had seen more of its disasters than joys. She was attractive rather than pretty with large grey eyes and a wide, well shaped mouth. Her black hair, carelessly combed and in need of attention, waved slightly and was streaked with grey. She was marginally taller than Ruth but her figure was thin and undeveloped rather like an adolescent boy's. This was a careworn, world-weary woman who yet enjoyed life, had not been completely defeated by it. Her looks were cosmopolitan, not especially English, and Ruth suspected that she was younger than she looked, maybe not much older than her.

'How very sensible you are.' Ruth put a Sweetex into her coffee and gazed at the froth whirling round. She felt rather out of her depth with Mrs Lazar who was like what she had expected, yet at the same time unlike. So far she seemed to resist strict categorisation.

'But you are not a worrier are you, Mrs Harrow? You seem so sensible. Such a practical woman I thought as you walked into my house. How I envied you.'

'Envied me? Good gracious.'

Ruth smiled again and nervously put her cup to her mouth. Mrs Lazar's gaze was frankly admiring.

'Well you see, I'm hopelessly impractical. You noticed the house? No doubt you tried not to. We had a flat in Swiss Cottage which was far too small – the children had to share rooms. A three-bedroomed flat for six people. However, we endured it until my husband did well enough in business to enable us to move. I thought "Ah at last, a roomy house". But we have the same problem. We fill every available space just the same as before. Only my weaving, thank goodness, goes into the garage. That drives everyone crazy.'

Mrs Lazar bit into one of the cakes and a thick ring of white cream around her mouth made her look rather grotesque. She licked it carefully with a long pink tongue but blobs remained at each corner of her mouth. When she raised her cup to drink Ruth noticed that her fingers were cracked, her nails grubby and worn down, not bitten, as though she was used to a lot of hard manual work.

'I hope you didn't mind me coming with you, Mrs Harrow; but I haven't been out of that house for weeks. I'm trying all the time to create order and space but I can't. I told Antal we shall have to move again. He already has to leave his car outside the house because I use the garage. I told him it wasn't big enough when he bought it; but he seldom asks my advice or opinion.'

'Why did you move to Edgerton?'

'Because Antal found a warehouse and suitable office premises there. It is not too far from London. He has that big new building just behind Woolworth's on the High Street. He was working there all last year and commuting. Of course I hardly saw him; but I didn't want to leave London. We had the school there, all our friends, my weaving commune, art classes and so on. It was a terrible wrench.'

'I can imagine.'

'But of course one can't afford to live in London these days. One can't find premises there. Anyway Antal decides. There's not much I can do.'

'He sounds a bit like my husband. Would you like another cup of coffee, Mrs Lazar?'

'Oh do call me Bella. Isobel really. But when we were courting – it was very romantic Antal being a Hungarian – he would call me "Bella, Bella". So it stuck.' Mrs Lazar reddened a little and shrugged her shoulders apologetically and suddenly Ruth dropped her veneer of reserve, that deliberate air of apartness she knew she maintained as a kind of defence, and decided to like her new neighbour.

It was difficult to imagine her ever having qualified for the pet name of 'Bella'. Both in looks and temperament she seemed unsuited to such a pretty, intimate diminutive.

It was the first new friend Ruth had made in years.

Bella seemed to divine the change in Ruth and smiled holding up her cup. 'I'd love another one. But let me pay.'

'No, let me.'

After lunch they left the boys at the War Museum and took the bus to the Army and Navy Stores in Victoria. They would have liked to go to Regent Street but felt they had not enough time. They sat on the top of the bus as it edged its way through the traffic jam around Parliament Square and up Victoria Street.

'Do you miss London?'

'Terribly,' Bella said her eyes misting over. 'I'm a Londoner. I always lived in north London; my mother still lives in Finchley. I though I would have a breakdown when Antal insisted. But really we had no choice. We rented our flat and our lease was expiring. We didn't want to buy it and there were various other complications. We just had to leave London

25

and that was that. We can't afford a large family house in the city any more. You?'

She looked at Ruth who was once again aware of the warmth and sincerity of her smile.

'Oh I'm a Manchester girl. You can probably tell from my accent.'

'Well it's very slight. I think it's attractive.'

'Thank you. My parents still live just outside Manchester in Cheshire. I met Geoffrey at university there and we decided to get married before I'd taken my finals. He was articled in Manchester to a firm of solicitors and after qualifying he joined his brother, Simon, who had established a law practice in Edgerton which had just been made into a development area. George was born in Edgerton.'

'In Lawnside?'

'Well, in the general hospital but, yes, we lived in Lawnside.'

'And you like it?'

Ruth looked out of the window at New Scotland Yard and the grey solid office buildings of Victoria Street. Ahead was the scaffolding of the new Army and Navy Stores that was being erected on the site of the old one.

'Yes, I do. Well it's home. It's our life. I don't suppose we would ever move now. We are established there. Geoffrey is on the Council. I think he hopes that one day he will be Mayor.'

'Oh dear!' Bella laughed and nervously clasped her hands. 'I see you are *very* established indeed.'

'This is our stop,' Ruth got up and moved down the bus.

'The store isn't what it used to be,' Ruth said as they moved about the departments. 'I used to love wandering round the old Army and Navy. Did you know it?'

'Oh yes, I used to work in Victoria before I was married. It was so huge, so old fashioned. I'm sure it will be very nice when it's finished.'

Ruth was gazing at a frilly evening dress that she had taken from a rail.

'That dress would look lovely on you,' Bella said with enthusiasm.

Under her well worn tweed coat Bella Lazar had a long skirt made out of thick material that she had woven herself. It was quite attractive; but it didn't fit well and on Bella's scraggy frame looked like a sack. With this she wore a thick turtle neck sweater that she had knitted and a waistcoat of the same material as the skirt.

In contrast Ruth wore a plain camel hair coat, very slim fitting, with a double row of buttons and a neat rounded fur collar. Her long brown boots had high heels and she carried a matching bag. An elegant little Robin Hood style hat sat neatly on her well coiffured head.

Ruth held the evening dress against her, and performed a half pirouette so that she could see herself in the mirror from all angles.

'Try it on.' Bella was looking enviously at the dress.

'I don't think I will. My sister-in-law has a boutique and can get me almost anything I want at cost price. Still . . .' Ruth thoughtfully swung round with the dress against her then put it back on the rail. 'No. Geoffrey would be furious.'

'Does he exercise *that* much control?' Bella was also looking at a dress, rather severe and plainly cut and she held it against her thick tweed coat with a grimace before putting it aside.

Ruth said nothing and they wandered across the passage that connected the old building with the new and into the furniture department. Bella clasped her hands.

'Oh I would love to refurnish the house completely with new furniture. Just think of it! We bought our stuff when we were married and most of it was second hand then. Imagine a new house and new furniture!'

'Well, have a new bedroom suite for a start,' Ruth said.

'Oh no. Nothing new. The expense has been enough already.

Moving, and the mortgage. Antal can't sleep some nights for worrying.'

Ruth glanced at her watch. 'Let's have a cup of tea and then go and get the boys. I think we'll have to take a taxi. I simply must get the five forty-five. There's a function at the Town Hall tonight.'

'Is that why you were looking at the dress?'

'Oh no. It was pretty. I've already decided what to wear this evening.'

They queued at the self service counter for their tea and sat down in a corner near the entrance to the bedding department. Ruth observed that once again Bella had two cakes lavishly filled with cream.

'I see you looking at me,' Bella said. 'I have a passion for sweet things. I think it is a form of compensation.'

'For what?' Ruth said lightly, emptying the low calorie sweetener into her cup.

'Well what do you think?'

Ruth didn't reply. She didn't really want to know, although she could make a shrewd guess as to what Bella meant. If Bella started revealing intimacies at this stage she felt she would be cagey about continuing the friendship. Instead she said. 'You asked me if Geoffrey exercised that much control over me when I was looking at the dress. The answer is no. I have my own allowance and an account here. But with Eunice, my sister-in-law, having a boutique Geoffrey would think I was extravagant if I were to appear with a new evening dress which I had paid £90 for at the Army and Navy. I just have to tell Eunice the make and she can get it for me at cost. We have to be careful too with two children at private schools.'

Bella shrugged. 'Well that's your affair, my dear. Personally we . . .'

Ruth held up a hand and shook her head. 'Please don't let's get on to education, Bella. I have enough arguments with George. It is something about which I am completely

28

detached. It is Geoffrey's decision and I leave everything like that to him.'

'Like what?' Bella sank her teeth into the second cake.

'Well, like education. Big decisions are always taken by Geoffrey.

'Don't you discuss them?

'Oh we agree. He knows I concur with his wishes.'

'It sounds terriby humble.' Bella looked shrewdly at her across the table.

'Not at all. Geoffrey is a very strong minded man. I knew when we married that he would always have to be the boss. And he has good sense. He is usually right. If we differ it is about trivial things. I feel he takes on too much, too many civic duties and doesn't give enough time to the children. But then he leaves a lot of that to me. Like today. Next week when Olivia and Joe are at home I will do things with them, if they wish. We feel in every family the man and woman have definite, realisable functions – a masculine and feminine role, maternal and paternal. I am the mother, the wife, the cook, the housekeeper. I have special care for Geoffrey and the children. He is the breadwinner; he controls the money; he makes important decisions. It is a perfect partnership.'

Bella had forgotten about her cake and was looking at Ruth – whose little speech quite surprised even herself. It was rarely that she had the occasion to summarise their marriage in this fashion. Bella put her elbows on the table and clasped her hands.

'I envy you,' she said. 'You sound like the perfect wife and mother. How I wish I could be like you.'

When they were younger, Geoffrey and Ruth used to play a good deal of bridge. It was a useful way of getting to know people like themselves, to start swimming in the social circle of the increasingly prosperous Edgerton.

For people did well in Edgerton. It had not the vulgarity of a completely new town; it had old traditions as an ancient market town with a charter given by Edward IV. It was an Assize town with the full, archaic panoply of local government. Its mayor was a Lord Mayor and, in addition, the centre of Edgerton had retained an ancient rustic charm. The Planning Council had been very careful to ensure that the new industries which came to Edgerton and the new people who followed them would conform to the image the town wished to preserve – a university town with ancient foundations.

There were no massive housing estates of the kind that attracted dissatisfied dwellers in inner urban areas – the sort who drank, threw stones or worse, stabbed one another and generally caused no end of trouble. Edgerton's police force, with its distinctive helmets, its old traditions, was not up to coping with that sort of thing.

No, it was the prosperous middle class who swelled Edgerton's ranks, moving into desirable specially built estates like Lawnside with decent grounds and a bit of space around each house; with lots of trees and shrubs and grass banks and verges to disguise drains and pipes and sanitary devices of an unmentionable nature. Lawyers did well in Edgerton, and so did doctors, dentists and schoolteachers who were welcomed in the many private schools that still abounded.

Edgerton comp was *faute de mieux*. It had come about as the result of a continuing war between the local council and the Westminster authorities dating back to the previous Labour Government. And, of course, a good number of Edgerton's prosperous citizens supported the Labour party. These were largely to be found among the professional classes (though not lawyers or doctors) and solidly among the members of Edgerton's university which had a foundation almost as old as Oxford or Cambridge, but had remained small and relatively unknown. It specialised in the humanities, had a small press and was well thought of in academic circles throughout the land.

The young, aspiring lawyer Geoffrey Harrow and his clever, pretty young wife were welcomed when they came to Edgerton, and they were soon well regarded because they did all the right things. They joined the tennis club, the Conservative Party and many societies that had to do with the history of Edgerton. Geoffrey did all the things that men were supposed to do. He played rugger, until he got too old, and squash, tennis in summer, darts in the pub. He had a small boat on the river and even belonged to the angling club. He rose rapidly in the ranks of the Tory party and headed the poll in the council elections.

They owed much of this to bridge, meeting the right people at the right time. It was like a pebble cast in a still water whose circles grew wider and wider until they embraced the entire pond.

In the pond that was Edgerton, the Harrows grew into very big fish indeed.

Due to his many commitments Geoffrey scarcely ever played bridge these days. When he was able to relax from formal duties he liked to go up to London for a theatre, or to go out with friends to one of the many excellent restaurants in the area, a county of civilised habits so close to London.

When one applied the word 'friends' to the Harrows one was usually talking about people they knew through business or civic affairs. They had hardly any close, intimate friends at all. Almost the only people who came into this category were Geoffrey's brother Simon and Eunice his wife.

Eunice Harrow was a tall very elegant woman who had been a successful London model before her marriage. It was understood that she had sacrified herself for Simon and he was rarely allowed to forget it. She had had her picture on the cover of *Vogue* when she was nineteen and few were ever allowed to forget that, even though it was all of twenty years ago.

Yet once one penetrated this awful, scaring superficiality of Eunice it was possible to detect a very nice person underneath. It was not easy, but it could be done. And Ruth had done it very successfully. She hardly ever heard about the *Vogue* cover at all.

Eunice was a paragon for Ruth. The older sister-in-law married to the older brother with older children, living in a bigger house in an even better part of Edgerton – all these were factors that influenced the young woman with two babies who had come south thirteen years before. Now the senior Harrows lived outside Edgerton altogether, in the heart of the countryside in a large house with a tennis court and a small swimming pool. This was considered very chic indeed.

The younger Harrows' neo-Georgian house with its portico and corinthian pillars was nothing compared to the mock-Jacobean mansion that graced five acres of wooded country-side between Edgerton and Upper Warford, the next town of any size.

Eunice, who tended to do everything well, was, naturally, a skilled bridge player. It was through being taken under her protective wing that Ruth had become so quickly integrated into Edgerton society and had so many friends, or almost friends, because most of the women tended to be like her and Eunice – to consider their homes and marriages very important and to maintain rather a detached view of the outer world. To keep aloof from it.

Eunice laughed and ruefully spread her cards on the table, her gold bangles clanking, her very long highly polished nails shining in the light of the candelabra over the table as she did.

'I knew I had a lousy hand. Sorry partner.'

Ruth glanced at the cards and frowned. She pursed her mouth and started to play.

In the end they won the rubber. Ruth was such a skilful player; she could turn the meanest hand to her advantage. People liked playing with her because she had such an even temperament. She lost as cheerfully as she won.

Eunice could only play because it was half-day closing. She took her business very seriously although she had a manageress. But on Wednesday half-days she usually played bridge. She regarded it as her chief relaxation.

'You should play more often, Ruth.' She crossed an elegant leg and sipped carefully at the hot tea. 'No thank you darling, no sandwiches for me. I put on a *pound* last week!'

Heather Leadbetter, who had long ago stopped counting pounds, cheerfully made a selection from the tempting sandwiches laid out before her. The bridge table had been moved to one side and the trolley wheeled in by Mrs Grange who always helped out on bridge afternoons.

'My dear Eunice, if I had a figure like yours I would be showing it off in a bikini in Bermuda or some such place, all the year round.'

'Well, who would pay for that I'd like to know?' Eunice smiled. 'I'm a hard working woman.'

'Without any need to work.'

Ursula Schmidt had a good figure, but could eat as much as she liked. Perpetual anxiety kept her slim.

'I have a need to work, Ursula. Oh not a financial need. But a need here.' Eunice pointed to her head. 'I must be mentally stimulated. Business stimulates me. I would have gone quite cracked long ago if it was not for the shop.'

'Oh don't call it a "shop",' Ruth said. 'It sounds so vulgar.'

'It *is* a shop.' Eunice smilingly held out her cup for more tea. 'Shop, shop, shop. I am a shopkeeper. We British are a nation of shopkeepers. The leader of the Conservative Party is the daughter of a shopkeeper. Geoffrey must surely approve of *her*.'

'I think Geoffrey is rather disgusted by the whole thing,' Ruth murmured. 'He is quite terrified in case Margaret Thatcher should ever become Prime Minister. Only he thinks that as long as the Tories have a woman leader they haven't a chance in the polls.'

'I knew Geoffrey would think that.' Eunice brushed an imaginary speck off her cream woollen dress. 'He is such a frightful male chauvinist pig.'

There was a little silence broken only by the polite munching of jaws. Ruth stared at Eunice and began stacking the plates on the trolley.

'What a curious thing to say, Eunice,' Ruth kept her voice under control. 'You know perfectly well Geoffrey is *no* such thing.'

'Oh the loyal wife!' Eunice laughed, but her beautifully matt complexion had slightly reddened. 'Darling, you know I'm joking.'

'Something in your tone made me think you weren't.' Ruth sat down, but remained on the edge of her chair as though poised to spring in defence of her mate. She continued to gaze unsmilingly at Eunice. The muscles in her chest had tightened with irritation and she could feel the slow regular thump of her heart.

'I thought you sounded serious Eunice, I must say.' Heather put her two feet on the ground and stared at her sensible shoes. Her husband was the head of the biggest group medical practice in the town and everything about her was sensible. 'I thought you were making some sort of point.'

'Well maybe I was,' Eunice said lightly. 'One never says anything without a purpose. I love Geoffrey of course; but I do think his attitude to women is very rigid. He keeps Ruth here like some sort of slave.'

'I am not a slave. What perfect nonsense.'

Ruth could feel her face flaming. 'I don't know what has got into you, Eunice. Or, if one never says things without a purpose, why are you saying all this? I do not want to have a shop, a boutique. I am perfectly happy as I am.'

'But are you? Geoffrey says you spend all your time standing behind the curtains looking at your neighbours. In fact he suggested you might like to come and work for me. I must say I thought that was most enlightened until I realized he didn't mean it.'

'And when did this interesting conversation take place may I ask?'

The pace of Ruth's heart had definitely quickened. It was no longer that slow thump, thump.

'Oh one day at lunch last week. I forget when. Geoffrey said, jokingly of course, that, apart from spending your time watching the neighbours, he thought you were perfectly happy, but maybe the obsession with the people next door was a symptom of boredom. Maybe you should get a job. It was all said very lightly, I assure you, Ruth.' Eunice looked anxiously at her sister-in-law and sat up in her chair. 'We all love and admire you darling, the perfect wife and mother. We would never dream of making a cruel joke about you.'

Ruth looked past Eunice, a thoughtful expression on her face. 'That's very odd,' she said.

'What's odd?'

'That expression you used, the perfect wife and mother. I never heard it applied to me in my life before, and now two different people have said it in the space of two weeks.'

Eunice laughed and, her eye on her watch, got up and straightened the fine gold belt around her waist. 'Well, there you are. It must be true. I must go, Ruth. We are going to the rep tonight. They are doing *The Second Mrs Tanqueray* which I must already have seen half a dozen times. But Paget is in it, and one must support one's children. You should get

35

Olivia interested in the rep. It would help her to meet MEN.'

'Olivia is not at all interested in men, thank goodness. After all she is only fourteen.'

'Oh my dear, that's rather old these days. No you two, don't get up.' Eunice smiled at Heather and Ursula. 'I know you like a glass of sherry before you go. I'm sorry I haven't time for another rubber. Oh thank you.'

Ruth had brought in Eunice's wild mink coat and held it out for her. She was still angry but she tried not to show it. However the lines around her mouth were more pronounced and Eunice knew she had offended.

She kissed her in the hall and held her arm for a moment. 'I am sorry. I was clumsy and silly. It was, I assure you, the most harmless fun. I thought you'd be so amused to hear it. By the way, who else called you the perfect wife and mother?'

'My neighbour,' Ruth said without a smile. 'You see, if you watch them long enough you eventually get to know them.'

4

Bella Lazar was the sort of neighbour given to 'popping in' a lot, just the thing that Ruth disapproved of. Or rather she had disapproved of it, but there was something so wholesome and unaffected about Bella that she found this informality essential to her personality. Bella was a very natural person, and one could be natural and unaffected in return.

Bella had no car and it was a good brisk walk to the shops. One of the reasons why so many vans called, Ruth discovered, was because Bella ordered nearly everything – the groceries, the meat, even the bread. Ruth enjoyed her bi-weekly shopping trips to the High Street. She parked the car in the big parking lot by the new Woolworth's and progressed along the High calling at shops where she was known, seeing any number of people she knew and stopping for a gossip. It was a distinct adjunct to social life. Occasionally she went to the large supermarket in the new shopping precinct on the edge of the town, but although it was cheaper and more efficient it was not like the small shops that had existed in the High Street for years and where she was known and had accounts and received a good deal of deferential treatment.

But Geoffrey supported the shopping precinct as an example of Tory enterprise and initiative. Bulk shopping helped to encourage thrift. It was where his ideas as an upholder of the nation's heritage conflicted with those of a progressive member of the Conservative Party whose philosophy approximated to the law of the jungle – the ability of the fittest to prosper and survive.

Ruth met Bella Lazar outside the kitchen door as she moved towards it, her arms full of parcels.

'Oh let me help you!' Bella ran to the car and scooped up more parcels from the boot.

'Oh thanks, Bella. I went crazy today. We now have a deep freeze and I went to the shopping precinct to stock it.'

'Oh how *sensible*. Now that is just what I could do with and then I wouldn't always be running out of things. I don't know where we'd put it, though.'

Bella placed a large box full of groceries on the kitchen table and tugged back a wisp of hair. She had on very old faded jeans and a sort of fisherman's smock. 'Oh dear, I wish my kitchen was like this. It is absolutely the model of what a kitchen should be.'

Ruth laughed and went to plug in the electric kettle. 'Bella you are always knocking yourself! You make out that you are a complete flop.'

'But I *am*! We have been in that house over two months and Antal said last night it is worse than when we moved in.'

'I'd love to meet Antal. He sounds full of criticism, but no practical help.'

'Oh that's Antal. He says the house is no concern of his. But he runs his business very efficiently. Yes you must meet him. He'd like you. I'd ask you and Geoffrey for dinner but . . .' Bella gestured vaguely as though to demonstrate the absurdity of the proposition.

'Oh there is plenty of time. I don't think Geoffrey has a free night for a month. We'll fix something for later on. Anyway, you must come here first. Now, coffee?'

'Well, a quick cup. I actually came to ask you if you would like to meet my daughter Anna. She is the eldest you know, at LSE. She just popped down for the day. I've knocked together a salad and some cheese for lunch.'

'Oh that would be nice, but . . .' Ruth glanced at the clock. Why not? Geoffrey was not due for lunch today. There was really no earthly reason why she shouldn't accept, yet Ruth always had that vaguely uncomfortable feeling that there was lots to do and she should be very busy even if she wasn't. 'Yes I'd love to meet her. Shall we say one o'clock?'

Bella bent double with laughter, hugging her arms across her flat chest. 'Oh you make me die, Ruth. It sounds like a *formal* lunch engagement. We are simply having salad and cheese off the kitchen table.'

Anna Lazar was a tall dark girl, as neat as her mother was untidy. She had dark eyes, olive coloured skin and black hair scraped back like a ballerina. She wore jeans and a tee shirt, high cowboy boots and a denim jacket. Her bustline was firm but obviously bra-less. Her nipples seemed very prominent under her tee shirt.

'This is Ruth Harrow,' Bella said holding the door open for her, pointing to Anna who was shredding lettuce. 'She is everything that I am not, Anna. The perfect woman.'

'Oh what rot. How do you do.'

Ruth went over to Anna and shook hands, aware of the younger girl's appraising look. Ruth had not changed and still wore the herringbone tweed suit she had gone shopping in with the brown shetland sweater underneath, a green scarf loosely tied round her neck showing the solitary row of pearls. A large cameo surrounded with tiny rhinestones glinted in her lapel. Her springy chestnut hair, secured by a plain velvet bandeau, lifted gently over her ears and on her feet she wore flat, sensible but stylish calf shoes made by Bally.

'Mother is certainly not perfect,' Anna said taking her hand. 'But I don't think any of us are, do you Mrs Harrow?'

'No I certainly don't, and your mother is a very warm, sincere person, qualities that make up for a lot.'

'Mind you this house *is* like a pigsty,' Anna said glancing round the kitchen. 'The carpets are not even down. Mother spends all day long weaving while the house tumbles about her. I am going to come and sort her out during the vac.'

'You're at LSE?'

'Yes.'

'And what are you doing?'

'Anthropology.'

'How fascinating. Will you make a career out of it?'

'I don't expect so. My boyfriend is a lecturer at King's and pretty ambitious. I don't expect he will want to see me off to the Andaman islands.'

'Oh?' Ruth raised her eyes and sat gingerly on an upright wooden chair after removing a pile of dusty cookery books from it. 'It is as serious as that?'

'Oh yes, the pair bonding sets in early these days, Mrs Harrow. It is all to do with Liberation – only it makes us less liberated than before.'

Ruth was aware of a bitter note in Anna's voice.

'Anna has just had an abortion,' Bella said apologetically. 'She's a bit tense.'

'I am *not* tense, mother,' Anna said tensely and threw the shredded lettuce in a bowl. Ruth saw with dismay that it was not lettuce but cabbage. It was going to be one of those awful raw vegetable meals.

'Well darling, not *quite* yourself.'

Ruth wanted to hide the fact that she was shocked. She gazed at the curtainless window which was covered with grime both inside and out by the look of it. She saw Anna glance at her.

'Are you upset, Mrs Harrow?'

Ruth shifted in her chair. Any moment she felt that it might give way; it creaked in an alarming manner every time she moved. 'Well . . . maybe surprised, and sorry for you. It can't be pleasant to have an abortion at your age – or any age,' she added quickly.

'Well how old do you think I am?' Anna disconcertedly turned right round to face her, peeling a carrot.

'I should have thought nineteen.'

40

'I'm twenty-two. I am a post-graduate student of anthropology.'

'Oh I'm sorry. I didn't think you could be as old as that, because . . .' Ruth twisted awkwardly in the dangerously creaking chair. 'Well I thought your parents were only married . . . I mean your mother said twenty years . . .'

'My parents weren't married when I was born. It was a trial marriage wasn't it, Mum?'

'Darling,' Bella said with a little worried frown creasing her brow. 'Not everyone is like you. There is no need to tell Ruth the story of our lives.'

'But you told her about the abortion.'

'Because you told me to speak of it naturally, as one of life's experiences like birth and death.' Bella's face was pained. 'I'm sorry, dear, if I said the wrong thing.'

She went to the fridge and emerged with a plate of tired looking cheese which she set on the table, expertly brushing everything extraneous to eating on to the floor with the side of her arm.

'I'm not ashamed of my abortion, or sorry I had it. Dieter and I have no wish to have children yet.'

'Aren't you on the Pill, though?' Ruth said. 'I thought all that kind of thing was so unnecessary these days.'

Anna raised her eyebrows and brought the shredded cabbage together with the plate of raw carrots to the table. 'Mrs Harrow, don't you know all the doubts there are about the Pill? It is very old hat. I wouldn't dream of letting it interfere with my metabolism and Dieter agrees with me. No, *rhythm* is the thing, but unfortunately we miscalculated.'

'Rhythm?'

'You know the thing the Catholics use – the safe period. It has worked for us for three years, but I don't know what went wrong. Anyway, Dieter was very supportive about the abortion and it made him very sad.'

'I should think it would,' Ruth said.

'I see you *are* disapproving, Mrs Harrow.'

Anna sat down and poured, for herself, a glass of red Algerian wine from a litre bottle which stood open on the table.

'I am against taking life, especially when there are so many safe methods of contraception. I've used the Pill for years with no ill effects.'

'You're lucky . . . so far.' Anna gave a malevolent grin. 'They're all saying that no woman over thirty should be on the Pill and, if you ask me, no woman under it either. It is quite shocking the way the Pill has been developed by men with so little regard for women's welfare.'

'But then what can people do? You can't just use abortion as contraception.'

'I agree,' Anna said, spreading margarine liberally on her wholewheat bread. 'It is a great dilemma we are all in, men and women. Dieter is very conscious of both our responsibilities in this matter, especially after the abortion. No, I have had a cap fitted.'

'But the cap is terribly old fashioned!' Ruth screwed up her nose in an expression of disgust.

'It is *not* a hormone Mrs Harrow, it is a barrier. It does not interfere with our metabolism. If I were you I'd go off the Pill this very day. If I may say so, you are far too old still to be taking it. You've a young family haven't you?'

Ruth swallowed. She began acutely to dislike the complacent, accusing girl sitting opposite her looking so in control of everything – the cabbage, her life, her mother, her womb. 'Well, youngish. I don't want to leave them if that is what you are saying.'

'Then I'd forget about the Pill. Throw it away. Have some of this wine?'

As though pleased with the confusion she'd caused, Anna held up the bottle and passed it over to Ruth with a friendly smile, showing her large, even teeth.

Geoffrey's thirty-eighth birthday had been carefully prepared well in advance like almost everything that happened, or was about to happen, in the Harrow household. That is, diaries were opened weeks beforehand, erasures made and notes pencilled in.

He was to lunch with Ruth, have tea with the children; and Simon and Eunice were taking Ruth and Geoffrey to dinner at the Angler's Arms, a trendy hotel that stood on the river not far from where Geoffrey had his boat.

A few years before, the Angler's Arms had been a seedy pub patronised mostly by artisans from neighbouring villages, and local fishermen. But as the interest in eating out grew in the late sixties and early seventies it had not taken long for an enterprising entrepreneur to spot its possibilities and turn it into one of the most fashionable places to eat between Edgerton and London. A restaurant had been built onto it, furnished with heavy antique refectory style tables and chairs padded with chintz. Brass and pewter urns and ornaments hung from false oak beams and a great fire roared in the inglenook. Naturally a spit turned there too, although its function was purely ornamental and a large iron cooking pot that looked like one of the cauldrons in *Macbeth* swung from a hook in the chimney embrasure.

Oil lamps shone from nooks in the walls and candles guttered on the highly polished tables. In the summer there were always fresh flowers and in the winter tasteful assortments of twigs and red berries artfully arranged on the tables.

Yes, the ambiance was good and the food excellent; but not the least of the attractions of the Angler's Arms was that it was terribly expensive, and to be seen eating there was a sign not only of status, but fortune. Consequently it was always crowded.

On Fridays and Saturdays a small band played in a corner and a tiny square of the floor had been cleared for dancing. By clinging so closely together as to appear to merge, half a dozen couples could manage to gyrate, but not by any means dance, at the same time.

Simon and Geoffrey were safe eaters and had the pâté and steak, but Ruth had prawns marinated in white wine and grilled on a skewer followed by wild goose stuffed with chestnuts. Eunice had coquilles St Jacques and veal cordon bleu. Champagne was drunk throughout the meal in honour of Geoffrey's birthday.

'Thirty-eight!' Simon said raising his glass.

'Shh!' Geoffrey pretended to duck his head and glanced furtively around.

'My dear boy, you are a youth. A stripling.'

'But the *next* birthday is a milestone,' Eunice said. '*That* is what's worrying him.'

'Exactly,' Geoffrey said still pretending to mind. 'Nearly forty.'

Simon leaned back and raised the tulip shaped glass to his lips. 'Well, we have both passed you there, haven't we Eunice?'

Eunice shrugged her slim shoulders, bare except for the thin straps of her black evening dress. 'Why deny it? They say the best is yet to be.'

'Well, I hope that's true,' Simon said, 'although I can't grumble. Life has treated us well. Eh Geoffrey?'

Geoffrey bowed his head. 'Mustn't grumble, mustn't grumble.'

'We have a fine business, two beautiful wives and let me see two, four, five excellent children between us.'

'You mean you had forgotten how many children we have?' Eunice glanced at him, her heavily mascarad, false eyelashes looking like fringes around her clear blue eyes.

'No darling, how could I? I had forgotten how many we had *in toto*. And we are to expand our business.'

'You're opening another office?' Ruth said looking at Geoffrey. 'You didn't say . . .'

'No, when I say "our" I mean mine and Eunice's, or rather strictly speaking Eunice's. She's opening another boutique in Upper Warford. Didn't you say anything, Eunice?'

'Not yet.' Eunice produced a small silver cigarette case from her evening bag.

'But it is all settled.'

'Well I forgot to mention it.'

'To Ruth? But you are buddies.'

Eunice glanced at Ruth and smiled.

'Well it really was only finally *settled* last week, Simon. I mean we actually completed the purchase of the shop then and . . . I had already slightly offended Ruth so I didn't want . . .'

'How had you offended me?' Ruth demanded, pushing her cheese away.

'Well you know the silly thing I said at your bridge afternoon.'

'What silly . . . ? Oh.'

'Stupid of me to bring it up now.'

'What is this, girls?' Geoffrey signalled to the waiter. 'Don't say you two are quarrelling?'

'Oh no of course we're not. I just was very stupid and said . . . oh forget it.'

'Could you bring the cigars, please?' Geoffrey, red-faced, looked up at the waiter. 'Now let's get to the bottom of this. You've quarrelled. Why?'

'We did not quarrel.' Ruth began to fiddle with the rings on her hands.

'Oh yes you did.' Geoffrey roguishly wagged a finger. Geoffrey habitually drank more than anyone else on these occasions. By the time they came to the port and cigars it showed.

'Come on,' he persisted in that silly, slightly drunken way. 'I want to know. Why did you girls *quarrel?*'

'Eunice said you thought I should take a job. It wasn't a

quarrel, except that she said you told her that all I did all day was look at the neighbours.'

'Ah thank you.' Geoffrey looked gratefully at the waiter. 'Simon? A Corona? Come I insist this is on me. No it is my treat! Choose which one you want.'

Geoffrey waved expansively in the direction of the tray and Simon, pretending to be a prey to vast misgivings, took a lot of time selecting his cigar. By the time they were pierced, lit and drawing well minutes had passed. Geoffrey leaned back, exhaling.

'A cigar is a beautiful thing. You women don't know what you miss.'

'There is *no* reason we shouldn't smoke cigars if we choose,' Eunice said. 'I often have a little Panatella.'

'I don't think it's very feminine, I must say.' Geoffrey half closed his eyes and drew heavily.

'Oh Geoffrey, you and your masculine views . . .' Eunice flicked back a heavy strand of her gleaming hair and took a cigarette. Simon leaned over and lit it for her.

'I am not ashamed of having masculine views,' Geoffrey said. 'I want men to be men and women women and Ruth knows it.Of course I don't want her to take a job. She doesn't want one either. Do you, darling?'

'It was all a *joke*,' Eunice said again. 'I know she doesn't want a job.'

'Ruth is perfectly happy as she is,' Geoffrey said as though he hadn't heard. 'Aren't you, darling?'

'Come on Ruth,' Simon said, 'dance with me. Let's join the scrum on the floor.'

Ruth got up and gratefully allowed her brother-in-law to lead her from the table.

The couples bumped and jostled into one another on a tiny patch of polished floor. Simon, perspiring heavily, clasped Ruth tightly to him. He still had his cigar in the hand that held her back. She thought he was a bit more drunk than

46

Geoffrey. However he was a lot slimmer, a tall, fair, feline-looking man and drink seemed to have little effect on him. They wove skilfully in and out, managing to keep moving but that was about all.

'It's not dancing is it?' Simon breathed into her ear.

She could feel the prickle of his well shaved skin. 'Well it's something,' she murmured aware of his mouth still pressed to her ear.

'You look bloody attractive tonight,' he said, and she felt the wet impress of his lips on her ear. She wriggled away, almost breathless with the effort.

'Simon!'

'Just joking.' Simon drew his head up and winked at her.

They cannoned into another couple and Simon turned round indignantly. 'I say . . . Oh I beg your pardon. Mr Lazar isn't it?'

Ruth raised her head at the name, a ready smile on her lips. She looked into the eyes of a man of medium height with olive skin, blue eyes and black slightly wavy hair just receding a little from his forehead. His eldest daughter resembled him.

'Ah, Mr Harrow!' The man's face broke into a good tempered smile showing excellent even teeth with a slight gap in the middle. He wore a blue dinner jacket and he was the sort of man who would always have a five o'clock shadow.

The crowd began to part them.

'We must meet soon, Mr Harrow. I'll call you.'

Simon nodded and smiled. 'This is my sister-in-law. Ruth . . .'

But the crowd came between them and all Antal Lazar did was raise his hand and smile.

They decided, after being stationary on the dance floor for several more minutes, that trying to dance was futile and returned to their table.

'Hopeless,' Simon said holding back Ruth's chair. 'Let's have another drink.' He beckoned to the waiter.

'I won't have any more,' Geoffrey said. 'I have to go to town tomorrow for a meeting with Counsel over the Berry-bridge affair. I . . . you seem very absorbed, darling?' He glanced at Ruth who was staring past his face into the darkened room.

'I've just been introduced to our neighbour,' she said.

'*Our* neighbour? I didn't want to say anything when you mentioned it earlier in case it caused another row, but darling *have* you got neighbours on the brain?'

'I thought that would provoke some response. Antal Lazar. I know his wife.'

'You know her?' Simon looked surprised and followed Ruth's glance. 'She didn't seem to recognize you.'

'That is not his wife.'

'Oh.'

'Oh Lazar, the man who has bought the High Street warehouse. Very capable they say.' Geoffrey too turned to stare.

'Please don't look.' Ruth lowered her gaze. 'He might be embarrassed.'

'Why should he? He is a client of ours.'

'He is not with his wife.'

'Well he is in some sort of party or something.'

'No, he's alone with her. He is sitting in the corner, and any moment he will see us all staring at him. Please don't look.'

'He didn't seem very bothered to see us.' Simon relit his cigar.

'Why should he? He doesn't know me. He doesn't know that I know his wife.'

'Oh it's all *very* involved,' Geoffrey said impatiently. 'You know I don't like gossip, especially about clients.'

'We're not gossiping.' Ruth took her compact out of her bag. 'My, my nose *is* shiny. I'm sure there is a perfectly inno-cent explanation.'

'You and the neighbours,' Geoffrey said.

48

'Please don't start that again,' Eunice pleaded. 'I'm going to the little girls' room. Ruth?'

Ruth smiled and got up. On the way to the powder room she passed very close to Antal Lazar. You could hardly have put a hair between his face and that of the young, very young girl opposite him. He was trying to kiss her across the narrow table. He didn't notice Ruth at all. He was so absorbed by his companion that she doubted whether he would have noticed anybody, even his wife.

5

The interior of the boutique was almost finished. Like its counterpart in Edgerton it had hand-blocked William Morris wallpaper and looked like a comfortable lounge rather than the inside of a shop. The clothes were all in closed cupboards except for one or two gowns in the window, and customers went to discuss their needs with the owner or her manageress rather than to point out anything that they fancied.

Workmen were fixing the lights, rehearsing them rather like a stage show, and the painters were putting a second coat onto the woodwork.

'It's very charming,' Ruth said. 'It feels so intimate already and yet you have no chairs and no stock.'

'It is my knack,' Eunice fingered some curtain material that lay on the new carpet. 'I can create ambiance.' She turned and looked at Ruth, her streaky blonde hair falling chunkily across her forehead, partly concealing one eye. She wore a three-piece outfit in light wool: sweater, skirt and three-quarter coat. It was just right for March and the warmer weather. Eunice seemed effortlessly to fit into the seasons as though she had a built-in barometer. She never wore unsuitable clothes, was never too cold or too hot. 'I'm not boasting, you know.'

'Oh I know that. You *can* create ambience. You . . .'

'You could too you know Ruth, if you let yourself go.' Eunice drew out her cigarette case and selected a menthol filter-tip, lighting it with a small silver lighter. 'I'm saying

50

that I really would like you to join me in the business, and I don't mean any funny stuff about the neighbours. That *canard* has got vastly out of hand.'

'There was obviously some truth in it for it to have lasted so long,' Ruth said lightly.

'Maybe you do have a need to do something, as I do. Why not admit it?'

'But I don't *feel* a need to do anything. Honestly.' Ruth picked up her coat and flung it over her arm. 'Shall we have a snack next door?'

'Yes, do let's. Then I can come back for the afternoon. What are your plans?'

'I'm doing a monumental shop for the holidays. Joe and Olivia break up tomorrow and George next week.'

'It's Paget's last term. I can't really believe it. My daughter is grown up.'

Paget Harrow, very beautiful, wanted to be a model like her mother. Her father had insisted on A levels first. Eunice had a few words with the workmen and followed Ruth to the coffee bar next door. As it was only noon it was still empty.

'Ah, this is nice. You know, I've worked terriby hard this week.'

'I can imagine.' Ruth was studying the menu. 'I'm going to have the antipasto and coffee.'

'No wine?'

'Not at lunchtime.'

'Oh have a glass with me.'

'No thank you. I don't, really.'

'But your figure's lovely.'

'I'm not thinking about my figure. It's my head. I always want to go to sleep after drinking wine.' Ruth ordered a glass of Valpolicella and a salad, and coffee and antipasto for herself. 'I'm paying,' she said. 'You treated last time.'

Eunice smiled at her fondly. 'You're always so fair, Ruth.

You never forget a thing. I don't think I've ever known such a well ordered person.'

'You're very well ordered, too. You run a large house, two teenage daughters, a husband and a business.'

'I don't run them. They run themselves. All I have to do is make sure that the wheels are kept oiled. Don't forget I have a housekeeper *and* a daily, and a manageress. I believe in paying people to work for one. Don't you think that work would add just that little extra bit of interest to your life? I mean I admire you. I value your qualities. I'm not offering you a job out of pity. It's not as though you are at a loose end; but I would like you as my manageress either here or at Edgerton. Mrs Carlisle wouldn't mind starting off the new shop.'

'But that would be a full time job! I couldn't *possibly* consider a full time job.'

Ruth felt irrationally indignant and took a sip of too hot coffee which made her choke. 'Anyway I am not at all interested in the fashion business. I know absolutely nothing about it. Please don't mention it again, Eunice, but thank you for asking me.'

Eunice sipped her wine and watched the spiral of smoke rise slowly from her cigarette burning in the tray. 'I promise not to mention it again.'

'*Did* Geoffrey put you up to it? I just want to know.' Ruth realized that her tone was belligerent and Eunice looked mildly surprised.

'Good Lord no. But he gave me the idea. I was looking for someone and there was you. Why should Geoffrey put me up to it?'

'I wondered if he finds me dull.'

'You dull? What nonsense. We all know that you are the cleverest member of the family, and pretty too.'

'But I don't use my mind. I read novels from the library and the *Daily Mail*.'

'I don't read at all.'

'I watch chat shows on TV, the women's programmes in the afternoons and all the corny serials.'

'Does it bother you?'

'But you just said I was clever, and I say I'm not. I'm rusty. I do absolutely nothing except see to the house and my family. I play bridge once a week, golf a few times a year, tennis sometimes. I belong to the WI and the Women's Conservative committee. I think Geoffrey finds me empty.'

'Oh Ruth, you are being quite ridiculous. I must have another glass of wine. These asinine remarks are driving me to drink.'

'I think I find myself empty. My new neighbour is so busy that she can't find time to get the house straight.'

'Well I don't think that's so very admirable.'

'I do. She puts other things first – she weaves and paints and reads. She doesn't let herself be bogged down by the trivialities of keeping house. She has all she needs delivered – and what she forgets she borrows from me. Her mind is alert and active.'

'You don't mean that very odd looking woman who blew in when we were playing bridge one day?'

'Yes.' Ruth nodded. 'Bella Lazar. Why did you think her odd?'

'Well, not like us.'

'She's not at all like us; but she's not odd.'

'I'm sorry. You're obviously friendly.'

'No not exactly friendly; but she is different. She is so completely unlike me that I find her rather fascinating. She always has something of interest to talk about. You and I talk about trivialities.'

'Well I don't think we do. You're making me feel uncomfortable. Should we discuss the economic situation? We never have, so why begin now? We talk about our families, our friends, the business. Our talk is very normal if you ask me. I'm sorry you don't find it stimulating.' Eunice consulted the small brooch watch on her lapel.

'I didn't mean to offend you Eunice.' Ruth reached out a hand and lightly touched that of her sister-in-law. 'I mean I think of you more as a sister than an in-law. You know that don't you.'

'Of course I do.' Eunice pressed her hand. 'And it must always be like that.'

'Eunice, do you mind if I ask you something very intimate.' Ruth was glad she had her back to the light so that her sister-in-law wouldn't see her faint blush.

'Oh dear. That sounds very frightening. Fire away. Be as intimate as you like.'

'Well we never have discussed this sort of thing very much. In fact I don't remember discussing it at all; but I have no one else I can ask.'

'Oh my dear, what is it?' A look of anxiety replaced the smile on Eunice's face.

'It's nothing dreadful. I just wondered if you used the Pill?'

'The Pill?'

'The contraceptive Pill.'

'Oh that? Oh no.'

'Is it because of your age?'

'How do you mean my *age?*' Eunice screwed up her nose. 'I thought I had overcome that awful hurdle rather well.'

'No, I mean they are now saying that women over thirty shouldn't use the Pill. There is a lot of controversy about it.'

'Is there? Well I don't, so that's all right.' She looked at Ruth, understanding dawning. 'Oh you mean you do?'

'Yes.'

'And you wonder if you should go on?'

'Yes. The doctor thinks it's marginal; but it does worry me. It was the blasted girl next door that gave me the fright in the first place. Anna Lazar.'

'The neighbour?'

'No the neighbour's daughter. She's only twenty-two and *she* is frightened of it.'

'I'd be guided by Doctor Marlow,' Eunice said.

'Then what do you use if you don't use the Pill? If you don't mind me asking.' She thought it was because their husbands were brothers that she had always avoided intimate conversation with Eunice. But now she was curious. The barrier was broken and she wanted to know.

Eunice was playing with her lighter, her eyes rather bright. 'I was sterilized years ago.'

'Oh. I didn't know.'

'No, you didn't.' Eunice flicked the lighter open and shut it again several times, the flame each time showing her pupils dilated with nervous excitement. 'As you say we never discussed these things, why should we, though sometimes we probably both yearned to confide in each other.'

'You wanted to tell me about that a long time ago?'

'Well it was five or six years, I can't quite remember when.' Eunice looked at Ruth, appearing to be trying to choose her words carefully. 'I discovered Simon was having an affair. I was so disgusted and furious that I resolved I would never have sex with him again. One does react like that. I stopped using the Pill and consequently I became pregnant because one never does keep a vow like that, something made in a rash moment. I had an abortion which disgusted me, and I was sterilized at the same time. Fortunately either that or the knowledge that Simon was still carrying on, despite the fact that he said he wasn't, seemed to dampen my sexual urge. I was never very interested in sex afterwards. They say sterilization can have that effect, or maybe it was knowing Simon had other women. It was a very bad time. The whole thing was revolting.'

Ruth felt as though she had opened a floodgate. 'And all this has been going on for years without me knowing?'

'Geoffrey knew about the girl – Rosa Morris. She was one of the secretaries in the office. It's a wonder he didn't tell you. It provoked a terrible storm at the time. I nearly left Simon and it was only Geoffrey who patched the whole thing up.'

'And he never said a word to me.'

'Well let's face it, darling, the Harrow men are rather taciturn. English stiff upper lip at its uppermost and all that.'

'How did you find out?'

'About Rosa? In the usual corny way. I was driving along in my car and Simon passed me, driving in the other direction with a woman in the front. When I asked him who it was he said it was a client. I didn't believe him, I can't say why. He's such a bad liar. But this was a very pretty young woman and there was something about their position in the car – she was sort of huddled up close to him. Anyway it all came out eventually about Rosa and Geoffrey paid her off and found her a job elsewhere. I think Simon still sees her or maybe it's somebody else. I don't know and now I don't very much care. That's why I threw myself into my business.'

'Yes six years ago you started your business.'

'Well now you know why.' Eunice got up and started fastening her coat. Her face was slightly pink and her eyes were still unnaturally bright. 'I didn't lose Simon because I didn't like sex. I did, and so did he – too much it seems. I don't think people can be faithful. I think it's contrary to nature.'

Ruth looked solemnly up at Eunice as though some new aspect of life had been unexpectedly revealed to her. 'Do you think Geoffrey has ever had an affair?'

Eunice tugged her tie belt tight. 'I don't know, dear. I wouldn't imagine so. He was very upset about Simon. He believes in the good old traditional virtues, you know. He really saved our marriage, though whether it was worth preserving is a thing I sometimes wonder about.'

Geoffrey reached for Ruth in the warmth of their bed sliding his hand between her legs. Ruth was half asleep and, at his touch, she opened her eyes and tried to focus her thoughts. Geoffrey moved closer to her and slipped his other hand through the opening in her nightie fondling a breast.

'Geoffrey what are you doing?'

'What do you think?'

'But it's Monday.'

'Well?' His finger manipulated her nipple. She felt too drugged with sleep to feel desire.

'We only did it yesterday.'

'Oh Ruth.' Geoffrey impatiently pulled away from her breast but left his hand between her legs. 'You are so conventional.'

Conventional. That word. Read 'boring' she thought.

'I'm sorry.'

'Our lovemaking should be spontaneous, not a habit.'

Ruth felt frozen in the dark. She imagined the goose pimples standing up on her flesh.

Geoffrey switched the light on at his side of the bed and looked at the clock. 'I can't get to sleep.'

'Make love if you like.'

As Ruth opened her legs in a conciliatory gesture, Geoffrey removed his hand altogether. 'One o'clock. If you say it like that I don't feel like making love.'

'How? Like how did I say it?'

'Well, *if* you like. Take it or leave it.'

'I'm sorry Geoffrey but I'm sleepy.'

'Then go to sleep.' Geoffrey lit a cigarette. Ruth wished he would stop smoking. Suddenly their lives seemed alive with little hidden dangers. There was the Pill; its possible threat to her life. In her mind's eye she saw Geoffrey and the children weeping over her grave. Geoffrey was thirty-eight. He smoked too much. A sudden heart attack. The picture changed and she and the children were weeping over *his* grave. Either

57

way it seemed a pretty bleak outlook. Neither of them obviously had very much longer to live. She transferred the children to an orphanage. Their faces were pressed to the window while the rain poured down. No of course there were Simon and Eunice, that dependable . . . *Dependable?* Why, their marriage hung on a thread.

'I know about Simon and Eunice.'

'What about them?' Geoffrey lay back exhaling smoke.

'The affair.' Geoffrey was silent. 'I know about Simon's affair.'

'Which affair?' Geoffrey tipped ash into the tray.

'You mean Simon has had more than one affair?'

'I suppose you mean the affair with Rosa Morris. When Eunice found out.'

'And there've been others besides Rosa Morris?'

'Simon was never faithful. He has to prove himself with women over and over again.' Geoffrey stubbed out the cigarette and sighed.

'I only knew about it today, Eunice showed me the new shop.'

'How did she tell you?'

'It came out in the conversation. I asked her . . . well I asked her if she used the Pill. She said she had been sterilized and then she told me everything.'

'Oh well, now you know. It doesn't make any difference. They'll stay together.'

'But Eunice is so attractive, so . . . well I would have thought so sexy.'

'Yes and she's a good wife and mother.'

'Then why?'

'I don't know.' Geoffrey yawned. 'In all my years as a lawyer I have never discovered the answer as to why some men wander and others don't. I only know it causes a hell of a lot of trouble when they do.'

'Has Simon got someone now?'

'I expect so. He never tells me.'

'And what about Rosa?'

'Oh she got married to someone. That was all years ago.'

'Does Eunice know he still has women?'

'I expect she guesses. You never stop that kind of thing. You're either the type or you're not. Simon is and I'm not.'

Ruth felt tender towards Geoffrey and moved closer to him in the bed. 'You never have been?'

'Of course I haven't. I don't want anyone else but you. I don't need anyone else. We have a good sex life and you're everything I could want as a wife and mother. I think the best thing a woman can do is to do her job in the home well. That is if she has chosen it. I'm not against women having jobs and careers, but from what I've heard, from what I know in my practice, I think it damages the home. Why should I be unfaithful to you and risk our marriage?' He looked at her and took her hand.

'You think our marriage is good?'

'Of course I do.'

'And I am not boring or dull?'

He leaned over and kissed her cheek. 'Oh darling, that is absurd. Why should I think that?'

'Well I never *do* anything. You just said I was conventional about sex. I am. I'm conventional and boring. I like everything to be predictable.'

'So do I. That's why we suit. We're a very good team.'

'What am I going to do about the Pill?'

'Why should you do anything?'

'They say it could be dangerous in an older woman.'

'Really? Then you must stop using it. You have checks and everything don't you?'

'Yes.'

'Then is there any danger?'

'Dr Marlow says it is really up to me.'

Geoffrey sighed in an exaggerated manner. 'Well what will we do? I couldn't bear going back to the old condom.'

'There's the IUD. The cap.'

'Oh Christ.' He put his arms around her and hugged her. 'They're always finding something wrong aren't they? Just when you have something that makes you happy they go and find something wrong with it.'

'I wish you'd stop smoking,' Ruth said.

With an angry exclamation Geoffrey put his mouth on hers, preventing further conversation.

Afterwards she couldn't get to sleep. Suddenly life seemed to have become less certain, more complicated and perilous.

6

'But women really *don't* choose,' Bella said kneading the wholemeal dough and pummelling it fiercely. 'It's all very well for your husband to say they do, but they don't.'

'How do you mean?' Ruth watched Bella attacking the dough fiercely, slamming it about the table.

'They are conditioned to marry and have children. They feel something is wrong if they don't. Afterwards when they realize they've made a mistake it's too late. Even now if a woman says, "I will not marry but will have a career", she's considered odd.'

'But she can do both?'

'Have you known many women brain surgeons?' Bella glanced at Ruth sitting on the rickety chair clutching her cup of decaffeinated coffee. 'Many top women lawyers? One or two, yes, there are in any profession. They are the exception that proves the rule. There. The children like my home baked bread.'

'How's Anna?'

Bella sighed and started to divide the bread into three, preparatory to plaiting it. 'Oh, she's all right I suppose. I don't think she really got over that abortion, though she won't admit it.'

'Did she *want* to have it?'

Bella scratched her head with a floury finger. Her jeans and shirt made her look like an old young man, her figure was so slight. She had no bust to speak of. 'Who knows what she wants? Does she? Do any of us?'

'Oh that's awfully negative, Bella.'

'Well you know what you want, I'm sure. The perfect wife . . .'

'*Please* don't say it again. Beside, it's not true. My husband thinks I'm conventional.'

'Isn't he?'

'Yes I suppose he is. But in me it's a fault.' Ruth got up and poured herself more coffee from the pot. It was gritty, rather like Turkish coffee, but the taste was all right.

The breakfast dishes hadn't been washed; nor she thought had the dinner things from the previous night. On the stove were a mass of half filled pots some with wooden spoons still stuck in them. The pots looked very old with black sides and bottoms. Upstairs she knew the beds weren't made and the lavatory would smell very slightly and perhaps be out of toilet paper.

'Why does he think you're conventional?'

'Well he suggested to my sister-in-law I should have a job. They both say it was meant as a joke but I'm sure it's true. Then . . . well it's something rather personal. No I'll tell you.' Ruth looked directly up at Bella. 'He wanted to make love last night and I was surprised because we usually have certain days.'

'And last night wasn't one of them?'

'Yes. I was surprised and because I showed it he minded.'

'Yes, he probably takes the initiative in lovemaking.'

Ruth felt herself redden. 'I never see much point in a woman doing it if a man doesn't feel like it.'

'Ruth you are very *submissive*. I think you relish the feminine role.'

'If you say I'm subservient I'm not.'

'It's not the same. There.' Bella finished plaiting the bread and put it into the oven. 'Come into my weaving shed, or will it be too cold?'

'It depends how cold it is there.' Ruth looked round the

kitchen aware of a sense of outrage. To think that anyone could leave the place in this mess to *weave!*

She could see the point of the weaving. The sun shone through the dirty garage windows on the neat piles of finished woven material, the spindles of wool and the polished wood of the old shuttle. Surprisingly the place was clean and tidy and there was a peace and harmony about it that was lacking altogether in the house. There were books stacked on shelves on the wall and a table against the window with neat piles of paper and assorted biros and pencils.

'Do you write, too?' Ruth asked looking at what appeared to be a manuscript.

'Didn't I tell you? Nothing interesting. Text books for schools.'

'Text books?'

'Economics. I was also at LSE you know. In fact I was there when I met Antal. He was a post-graduate student, just like Anna's Dieter. History repeating itself.'

'But Dieter isn't Hungarian?'

'German. Very bitter about the war and full of guilt.'

'Oh dear.'

'Antal and I lived together and then Anna was born just before the Hungarian Rising. He tried to get back and fight the Russians but thank God he couldn't. Antal never really recovered after the failure of the rising. He became very bitter and cynical about everything. He said he wanted to be rich and went into one disastrous business enterprise after the other. Now he seems to have made it. You haven't met him have you?'

'No.'

'You must. He'd like you.'

'You've said that before. Why should he like me?'

'You're his type. He likes pretty women. I know Antal would like you.'

'Don't you mind?' Ruth thought of Antal leaning over in

the resturant kissing the very young blonde girl opposite him.

'What is the point of minding?' Bella shrugged and sat at her frame. 'I don't know what you can do to make a man stay faithful if he doesn't want to. Minding doesn't. What is infidelity anyway? Do you expect people to stay faithful for ever?'

'I'd be very unhappy if I knew Geoffrey wasn't faithful.'

'Are you sure he is?'

'Pretty sure. Yes I'm sure. But I just found out that his brother wasn't, which surprised me a great deal.'

'That is the husband of the sister-in-law you like?'

'My only sister-in-law. Geoffrey only has one brother. This is very confidential you know, Bella.'

'Who should I tell?' Bella said with surprise. Ruth had remembered that Antal was one of Simon's clients. The web of deceit was growing wider, because Bella didn't know that Ruth in fact had met Antal.

'Well, your husband for instance.'

'Oh Antal and I never talk about anything like that. In fact we don't talk much at all.' Bella got up from the frame and went over to the tidy desk by the grimy window. 'You know, ours is a marriage that in many ways is over, Ruth. He is not faithful and I do not care. We overcame the barrier where infidelity and suspicion provoked terrible rows all the time, largely because of the children. The constant fights were having a very bad effect on them and both Antal and I care very much about our children. Even now I think Anna was deeply affected because she was that much older and I told her when I first found out about her father. That was silly and wrong. Anyway I adapted to Antal. I didn't want to leave him and set up as a single parent with four children. He was content to come home every night, or almost every night, to maintain the semblance of a marriage. He didn't want to marry anyone else, so that was it. We live together yet go our own ways.' Bella gestured at the unexpectedly tidy tranquil room. 'This is my sanctuary, my salvation. You will have noticed it is very tidy and the rest of the house is not. You will already have marked me down as a slut. This is me, you see, the real me – creative, beautiful, important. The house is a shell for my fragmented family and our disordered lives. I don't care about the house really so that's why it is such a tip. This is *me*. What is important you care for and I care for my work.'

'But your family is important to you?'

'Yes but they have their lives too. Anna and Robert no longer live at home. Robert is at Aberdeen University and hardly ever comes home. Christopher and Irena have their own lives too. They like the comp immensely, by the way.'

'Yes I know. George is very pleased with Christopher. Your younger daughter I don't know at all. She must come over and meet Olivia.'

'Does Olivia have many friends outside her school?'

'Not many; but she's a very friendly girl. Maybe next week when they're all on holiday?'

Olivia Harrow was a pretty girl of a sunny disposition and equable temperament. She did everything calmly and neatly and one had the feeling that it would take a lot to disturb the even tenor of her life. She was a good all-rounder, playing games with as much enthusiasm as she applied to her studies. She thought she wanted to be a teacher when she grew up and was particularly good at French and German. Olivia never gave any trouble, never had ever since she had been a contented baby.

In fact, Ruth thought to herself as she prepared the lunch for the children, she was very lucky to have two such normal, polite, well adjusted elder children. Not that George was abnormal; he was just a cheerful, nice rather naughty boy. Yes she was lucky with all her children.

She was lucky with her life. She finished laying the table

with the heavy Denby plates and tableware that were kept for everyday use; put a litre bottle of Coke in the middle of the table and then went to the stove to check the Bolognese sauce she was making. She wouldn't cook the spaghetti until the children had arrived back from their various occupations.

Joe had been practising for the opening of the cricket season, Olivia rehearsing for a pageant in honour of the Queen's Jubilee and George had gone off for the day with Bella and Christopher Lazar while Irena Lazar was coming to lunch.

Everything in the kitchen shone. Mrs Grange had been and together they had changed all the beds as they did every week, putting the top sheet to the bottom. Ruth had been busy all the holiday, never a moment to spare, very little time to think or even to do everything she wanted to do. This week alone, as well as mountains of shopping, she had had two committee meetings, a Conservative women's lunch and it was only Wednesday.

She had plenty to do and she was happy. Happy.

Irena Lazar arrived early, tapping timidly on the kitchen door and looking like a shy gazelle as she came in. They had only briefly met once.

'Come in, Irena. Olivia won't be long. Are you interested in drama?'

'Not particularly.' Irena tossed her dark curly hair and looked at Ruth out of her very blue almond shaped eyes. Except for her hair she was very like her elder sister, maybe fractionally taller but with the same well developed elegant figure. She was fifteen, a year older than Olivia, but she could have passed for a girl of eighteen or so.

'Would you like some coffee, a glass of Coke, while we're waiting? Olivia shouldn't be long.'

'Coke would be nice, thank you.'

'It was kind of your mother to take George off for the day.

He gets so bored. Where have they gone, do you know?'

'Oxford. Dad ran them to the station. Mummy's publishers are in Oxford and she thought she would combine that with a day's sightseeing for the boys.'

George hated sightseeing. He loathed anything cultural. Well, maybe in the company of his beloved Christopher it wouldn't be too bad.

'You must be very proud of your mother.'

'Why?' Irena took the Coke and looked curiously at Ruth over the rim.

'Well because she writes books. She is such an active person. She weaves and paints and . . .'

'She's an awful housekeeper. You see what sort of a tip we live in.'

Ruth salted the boiling water and took the spaghetti out of the large glass jar. 'Maybe you could help your mother. She must have so much to do,' she said carefully.

'I do what I can but it's hopeless. She has little interest in anything domestic. It annoys my father terribly. His mother was so house proud. Continental women are. Your house is beautiful. Everything is warm and gleaming as you come in. As soon as you go into ours you want to go out again.'

Ruth felt embarrassed. She was glad when the door was flung open and Olivia bounced in, her duffle bag over her shoulder. She was singing but stopped when she saw Irena.

'Hello.'

'You know Irena don't you, darling?'

'We met the time she came here with her mother.'

'I invited her for lunch with us because her mother has taken George to Oxford with Chris.'

'Good Lord whatever will *he* do in Oxford?'

'I'm sure he'll enjoy it. Mrs Lazar has gone to see her publisher. I was saying to Irena how lucky she was to have such a clever mother.'

'And I was saying . . .' Irena began.

'Really Irena, do you think . . .' Ruth began anxiously, faltering as Irena ignored her.

'I was saying that it must be nice to have someone who looks after the house like your mother does.'

'This house?' Olivia looked around with surprise.

'Well compared to ours . . .'

'If a thing is out of place here Mummy has a fit. It's like living in a glass house.'

'Oh really Olivia!'

Olivia went up to her mother and briefly hugged her. 'I knew that would get you. But it's true Mum, you are too house proud. It seems to come before everything else. If you had other things to do I'm sure you wouldn't be so fussy about the house.'

Ruth stiffened and stirred the spaghetti to stop it sticking on the bottom. Then she looked again at the sauce and added a little more spice. 'What sort of things do you think I should do?'

'Oh I don't know.' Olivia sat at the table and reached out for a piece of bread in the basket in front of her. 'I don't know what you could do really. You're not trained for anything are you? I suppose you could learn to type.'

'And then what would I do?'

'Work in an office. A charity? No?'

'No.' Ruth kept her voice level but she felt angry. Angry and resentful. 'I'm sorry you find me so lacking in stimulation.'

'I don't, Mum. That is not the point at all. Anyway who brought this up?'

'I think you did. You said I had not enough to do which was why I was so fussy in the house. I happen to like a nice well cared for house. Funnily enough I was just thinking this morning how happy and contented we all were. Now I wonder. Ah, that sounds like Joe.'

She looked through the kitchen window and saw her eldest

68

son lean his bicycle up against the garage and undo the clips on his trousers. His cricket gear was strapped on the back of his bike and as he undid it he whistled. Ruth went to open the door for him.

'You're just in time. Hungry?'

'I'm starving, Mum. Uh hello.'

Joe paused at the door and looked at Irena, his face non-committal. As far as anyone knew Joe had no interest in girls. Coming from a boys' school he maintained an attitude of self-conscious indifference to them that might have been defensive. At sixteen he seemed almost fully grown with a tall sturdy figure like his father, his thick ash blond hair flopping engagingly over his face. He was like a youthful Geoffrey, handsome and self confident, with an almost arrogant air that was probably shyness.

'How was cricket?'

'Good.' Joe nodded and poured himself some Coke. He still wore his cricket whites, his school sweater over his open necked shirt. Irena was gazing at him appraisingly whereas he studiously avoided looking at her.

Ruth put large blobs of butter on the dish of steaming spaghetti and brought it to the table. She served the Bolognese sauce separately, spooning it over the mounds on the plates.

'Only a little for me please, Mrs Harrow,' Irena said quietly.

'Oh dear, don't you like it?'

'I do; but I must watch my figure.'

Ruth stared at her. 'I wouldn't say you had a problem.'

'I don't want one either. About half the girls in our class are overweight.'

'But I would have thought, constitutionally, that you were unlikely to develop a weight problem. Neither of your parents are fat are they?'

'No. Mum's like a skeleton. But I have a different temperament and a different figure. My Hungarian grandmother was huge.' Irena made an expressive gesture, holding her hands yards apart. Olivia was looking at her with interest.

Ruth suddenly realized that the girls were separated by a mental gulf that could almost be measured in years not months. Irena at fifteen looked eighteen and had the mentality of a much older girl. At this stage Olivia would never be self conscious of her figure. On the whole her tastes were still those of a fourteen-year-old schoolgirl, as Ruth's had been at her age. She had only the most casual interest in boys, and then as friends, none in make up or clothes, and her tastes were intellectual and sporty.

No they had very little in common. On the other hand Joe's naturally and healthily rubicund face was redder than usual and now he was taking surreptitious looks over the table at Irena. She kept her eyes coyly but rather calculatedly fixed on her plate except for the casual, very direct and provocative glance straight into Joe's eyes.

Ruth had a feeling that she was progressing down some slippery slope towards she knew not what at the bottom.

'Now, what are you children going to do this afternoon?' she said brightly, spreading low cholesterol margarine on her Ryvita. 'Would you like to go to a film?'

'There's nothing on.'

'I've got cricket practice again,' Joe said looking at his watch. 'I said I'd be back just after two.'

'Well then, you girls . . .' Ruth, sensing a lack of rapport between the two, searched desperately in her mind for something that they could do. 'I . . .' she began.

'Oh I would *love* to watch cricket!' Irena clasped her hands together and looked at Joe. Joe went even redder and shovelled the rest of his spaghetti into his mouth.

'You *like* cricket?' Olivia said unbelievingly. 'It is the most boring . . .'

'No I really like it.' Irena crumbled her bread feverishly on her plate. 'But I don't mind if you would rather do something else. I'm quite easy.'

'There's no need for you to do something together if Irena would rather go with Joe, and Joe doesn't mind. I do know Irena that, though on the whole Olivia likes sports, she does detest cricket.'

'I've plenty to do,' Olivia said shortly. 'My words for the Jubilee pageant are decidedly shaky.'

'I can hear you darling, if you like. Joe, do you mind if Irena comes to watch cricket?'

'Not at all,' Joe mumbled. 'But I've got my bike.'

'Well I'm sure you would not mind *walking* with it, darling. It's nice to have some support.'

'Well we'd better go then.' Joe got up abruptly.

Irena rose too, patting her pert little behind in her tight fitting jeans. Her eyes were sparkling. Ruth looked at her, trying hard to conceal her dislike. The crude sexuality of the girl irritated her. She was much too young to be setting her cap at the Harrows' studious, protected son. Sixteen. Was he vulnerable?

Joe put on his blazer and held the back door open for Irena.

'Thank you so much for a lovely lunch, Mrs Harrow.'

'It's a pleasure,' Ruth said tersely. 'I hope you enjoy the match.' She was careful not to ask her back for tea.

Olivia helped her clear away in silence, putting the plates down on the draining board with that extra emphasis that seemed more a measure of her anger than words. It was unlike Olivia to be so put out and after a few moments, stirring the suds in the sink, Ruth said, 'Did you mind, darling?'

'*Mind?* Mind what?'

'About Irena going off like that.'

'I didn't mind at all. She's not the sort of girl I like. I don't like her mother or her brother either. I think they're a horrible family.'

Ruth rested her wet hands on the side of the sink and looked at her daughter. 'Olivia, that is not a fair thing to say. I'm surprised at you.'

'Look how Christopher is having a bad influence on George. They are always laughing and giggling and I feel they're up to something furtive all the time.'

'That's funny, so do I. George is usually so direct and straightforward. He does skulk a lot lately now that you come to mention it.'

'And the mother . . . my goodness. Every time I come in she's sitting at our kitchen table having a cup of tea or coffee, her arms full of borrowed goods, never to be returned I'll bet.'

'Well she has no car. She's always running out of things.'

'She's the sort of person who would be begging and borrowing even if she lived next door to the shopping precinct.'

'I think she wants company. I quite like her, actually.'

'Really Mum, I just don't know how you can say that. She's so unlike the people we know.'

'Maybe that's why I like her. She's unusual.'

Olivia stared at her mother, her lips tightening into a retort. 'Mum you *are* bored with life aren't you? If you really find Mrs Lazar interesting maybe you *do* need something to do. Maybe your mind is too closed, too empty . . .'

Ruth spun round and shook a wet hand at her daughter. Olivia backed away looking rather frightened, a few tiny soapy suds glistening on her pale cheeks.

'Mother! Whatever have I said?'

'You said my mind was empty.' Ruth advanced on the cowering Olivia. She knew if she had something in her hand, a tea towel or a dishcloth, she would probably have thrown it at her. 'I've heard so much of that recently that I am beginning to think it must be true. Your father says I'm conventional, Aunt Eunice thinks I need a job and you have said several times that I was closed, empty, lacking in something to do. Well maybe I should get something to do and then you, you children, can see what it would be like to come home to a house like the Lazars' with unmade beds and dirty crockery in the kitchen sink; cupboards full of half rotting food and the lavatory smelling of stale urine. See how you would like that!'

Ruth sat at the table aware that she was shaking. She poured what was left of the Coke into a glass and drained it down. Olivia leaned against the bench that ran alongside the wall.

'I'm sorry, mother.' She only ever called her 'mother' as a formality when they quarrelled. 'I didn't realize you'd take it so badly. It was a kind of joke.'

'And *that's* what everyone says too. There should be no need to explain a joke. Was it a joke, Olivia? Was it really? Do you not find me dull and boring, the house too tidy, your father stuffy and old-fashioned?'

'No Mum, really not.' Olivia took a few steps forward in a tentative gesture of reconciliation. 'But you know a lot of kids have working mothers *and* a nice well kept home. The mother of Patricia Boulé in our class is a psychiatrist.'

'Oh yes? And how many mothers are psychiatrists?'

'Well only her . . .'

'Presumably she didn't just decide to become a psychiatrist like that! I mean Mrs Boulé one day and Dr Boulé the next!'

'No, she always was.'

'Then she was a career woman when she married. I'm not.'

'But the Boulés have five children *and* a lovely home. Mrs Boulé goes up to London every day and they entertain a lot. Then Catherine Hudson's mother is a dentist and quite a lot of the girls' mothers work in shops and offices.'

'Are you ashamed of me because I don't work?' Ruth got up and fetched a packet of cigarettes from the dresser. She hardly ever smoked except at times of crisis. She felt such a time was now.

'Of course I'm not ashamed of you, Mum. You've got the whole thing out of proportion. It all started because I said I didn't like the Lazars.'

'No, it has been said before in this house. Too often for my liking. You children take too much for granted. I suggest this particular bit of venom today is because you're jealous that Irena Lazar has gone off with your brother instead of staying with you!'

'Oh that is absolute rot!' Olivia threw the kitchen towel on the ground and walked to the door. 'That is rubbish. I didn't like her because I don't find anything in common with her. I hate those girls who have nothing but sex on their minds. She was flirting with Joe, all right, and that kind of thing doesn't happen to interest me. You want to watch out she doesn't get Joe into trouble that's all. I know her type. The comp is full of them.'

'What type?' Ruth shakily lit her cigarette.

'Really Mum. I try and keep *some* schoolgirl innocence but you know there are limits. I've heard of two of the girls at the comp who have had abortions and one of the boys responsible was from the *grammar*.'

'Oh you disgust me.' Ruth found that the smoke was making her feel dizzy. She could hear the heavy thumping of her heart.

'Well that's it, Mum. Life is disgusting and you appear to know so little about it. Yes, your mind *is* closed and shut and barricaded. No wonder Dad has so many things to occupy him outside the home! What on earth can you have to talk about? All those committees of Dad's are absolutely nonsensical. There must be a reason for them. Did you ever think of that?'

Olivia ran through the door and slammed it behind her. Ruth stubbed out the cigarette, shaking her head to try and clear the muzziness that both befuddled and alarmed her.

74

7

'Well, smoking and the Pill are certainly not a good combination, I can tell you that,' Dr Marlow said. 'You can put on your things now, Mrs Harrow.'

Dr Marlow went to his desk and started making notes. 'Blood pressure, heart, everything is good. But I must say there are strong contra-indications to a woman of your age taking the Pill. I didn't realize you smoked.' He looked at his card. 'Yes it says here "non-smoker".'

'But I don't smoke.'

'Yet you told me just now you had a spell of dizziness while you were smoking a cigarette.'

'I hardly ever smoke, except when I am overwrought.'

'And you were overwrought at the time?'

'Yes.' Ruth fastened her skirt.

'Well I think that's what made you dizzy. Also if you don't smoke and had a cigarette that might induce dizziness temporarily. Why were you overwrought?'

'I had a row with my daughter.'

'Olivia?' Dr Marlow looked up. 'I thought you got on well.'

'We do, usually. Oh I don't know, everything seems to be going wrong. I suppose the children are growing up.'

'Well they do.' Dr Marlow smiled ruefully and looked at his watch. 'I wouldn't have thought Olivia would give many problems.'

'I think it's me. Dr Marlow, are there many pregnancies among schoolgirls in this town?'

Dr Marlow stopped writing and stared at her. 'Olivia isn't . . .'

'Oh no. Not her. She was talking about somebody else.'

'No there aren't many. You must expect a few in a community like this.'

'Is it mostly girls from the comprehensive?'

Dr Marlow laughed. 'Oh no, on the contrary! It is the girls from single sexed schools that tend to go off the rails. The girls from the comp are much too canny. Many of them are even on the Pill. No Mrs Harrow, this is a mixed society. You cannot blame it all on education. Now what are we going to do about you? You have been to see me twice in a month. Usually it is for your check-up once a year. You're worried about the Pill aren't you? Isn't that what it's really about?'

'Yes I suppose I am.'

'Then come off it.'

'But what shall I do instead?'

'There is the cap, the IUD, the condom, vasectomy, sterilization.'

'I don't like the sound of any of them very much. My husband would certainly *never* agree to vasectomy. The Pill always suited me.'

'Well it doesn't seem to suit you now.' Dr Marlow held up a hand. 'I hasten to say not for any physical reasons that I can detect; but I think psychologically you are frightened. Why not give it a rest for a while until we see what the next report on the subject says. They are always doing them.'

'But what will I do instead?'

'Your sex life is regular?'

'Oh yes.'

'Good, good, that is what I like to hear. No problem there. How about the cap?'

'But it's terribly messy.'

'It need not be. The IUD then.'

'But don't people bleed?'

'Some do and some don't. It is very difficult to predict. It suits some women and not others; but it can take some time to settle down. Why not try it?'

'What do I do?'

'Telephone Mr Wrotham, the gynaecologist, and make an appointment. You do know him don't you?'

'Yes, he delivered George.'

'There you are. The best man. It's over in a jiffy, and if it doesn't suit you you can try something else.'

Ruth continued to look doubtful.

'Mrs Harrow. *I* will make an appointment with Mr Wrotham and my secretary will tell you when. Is that a good idea?'

'No, no I'll do it,' Ruth said hastily, getting up. 'I'll do it this afternoon.'

Bella Lazar sat twisting her hands anxiously in her lap. There was a thin film of sweat on her upper lip and every few moments she looked at the clock. 'I don't know what can have kept him,' she said. 'He promised to be home on time.'

Ruth, on her third gin, was feeling a little tight; but it seemed to take the edge off her irritation that the roast lamb would be a muddy brown colour inside instead of moist, succulent pink.

Everyone sat waiting for Antal Lazar to turn up for dinner. Geoffrey, who hated being kept waiting, who regarded it as a personal affront, kept leaping up from his chair to part the curtains and peer out of the window, making angry grunting noises as he did so.

Eunice tried to keep the conversational ball rolling while Simon did his best to pacify Geoffrey and be polite at the same time to Mrs Lazar. Ruth made frequent sorties to the kitchen to try and halt the cooking process of the lamb by turning down the oven.

77

The level of gin and whisky in their respective bottles sank lower and lower while everyone assured Bella that of course it was *perfectly* all right. Ruth came back from the kitchen for about the fourteenth time.

'I really think we will have to eat. The starter's cold so that doesn't matter; but the lamb is going to be very overcooked indeed.'

Geoffrey made a wide gesture with his arm and consulted his watch. 'It *is* after nine. We said eight didn't we?'

'Seven-thirty for eight,' Bella said in a small, crushed voice. 'I'm terriby sorry.'

'I do hope nothing . . .' Eunice began.

'Oh no,' Bella said quickly. 'I'm afraid my husband is not a good timekeeper; but I would have thought that on this occasion . . .'

They all trailed into the dining room. Even the floral decorations on the table seemed to have wilted and the butter pats that had been so crisp at seven had started to run into oily congealed messes in their respective dishes.

They were half way through the haddock mousse, keeping up a desultory conversation which consisted largely of Bella's apologies and the constant reiterations that it was really and truthfully *perfectly* all right, when there was a ring at the front door bell and everyone sat up on their chairs, like birds perched on a wire, heads in the air, eyes darting from side to side, ready to fly off. After a few minutes, during which desperate apologies could be heard in the hall, Mrs Grange opened the dining room door.

'Mr Lazar is here.'

Having waited so long for the offending guest whose absence had, so far, ruined the evening, everyone was immediately at pains, especially Geoffrey, to persuade him that he wasn't late at all, that they always ate at this time and anyway what did it matter?

'Now Simon, I think you know Mr Lazar best. Maybe you could . . .'

'Of course.' Simon got up and shook hands with Antal Lazar, clasping him on the arm. 'Do forgive us starting. But . . .'

'Please,' Antal Lazar said deprecatingly. 'It is entirely my fault. My car . . .'

Of course it was the car, or the traffic, or someone late at the other end. Bella eyed her husband with a tired expression, noting the effect of his charm, especially on the ladies, as he was introduced round the table.

'And finally this is my sister-in-law Ruth, your hostess.'

Antal Lazar bent very low over her hand and gazed into her eyes. 'Mrs Harrow, how can you forgive me? It is *absolutely* inexcusable . . .'

'No Mr Lazar, *please*.'

His deep blue eyes surmounted by thick brows had a magnetism that made Ruth immediately want to please him. His hair, receding from the temples, was sleeked back and his skin had an olive cast like his daughters'. He was not as tall as Simon or Geoffrey, yet his presence somehow dominated the room. He was well built and his grey suit sat easily on broad shoulders, evidence of a good tailor. His blue shirt and dark blue tie brought out the colour of his eyes.

Compared to Geoffrey and Simon he was like a neat, dark bird from a foreign country. A stranger, an alien, someone who went with diplomatic parties, important conferences and mysterious messages, not an Englishman. Ruth knew she blushed slightly as he held back her chair before sitting next to her. On his other side was Eunice. Opposite, Bella Lazar kept her eyes on her plate. Her mousse, previously delicious, now tasted like clay.

Mrs Grange bustled in and took the mousse from the sideboard for Antal to help himself. He gave her a glance of friendly gratitude, murmuring his thanks too as Geoffrey poured the hock. He was clearly doing his best to be placatory. It was very effective.

Everyone now wanted to relax Antal Lazar and assure him that he had not put them out at all. He settled down complacently to his food knowing that if he was charming enough and grateful enough people would react as they had, even the men.

'My car has clutch trouble; my goodness this mousse is delicious.' He took an appreciative mouthful and some brown bread and butter. 'Just outside Upper Warford. Luckily a garage was open; but it still took them an hour to fix it. British cars are really . . .' Antal shook his head. 'This is only six months old. I like to support Britain but what can you do?'

'I have just as much trouble with my Fiat,' Eunice said. 'I am sure you are not a chauvinist, Mr Lazar?'

'Oh no. I am a citizen of the world, naturally!' Antal smiled, and seemed to lean a little closer to her. 'So you have a Fiat?' He made his answer sound sexually responsive.

Ruth watched their heads together, the one fair, the other very dark. He had that smooth black shadow on his face and his lips were aggressively straight, without indentation, the upper one protruding over the lower. There was a dent at each side of his mouth which emphasised the sensuality of his lipline. There was a deep cleft in his chin. Eunice's eyes seemed positively to smoulder as she looked at him. Across the table Bella was preoccupied with her food.

In the event the lamb was not too overdone, though certainly not succulent, the vegetables delicious, the profiteroles exquisite, and the cheese perfect. All adjectives used frequently and profusely by Antal Lazar who exclaimed with genuine gratification as every dish was set before him. He was also knowledgeable about wines, commenting on the year, the colour and the quality of the grape, the grenache in the case of the red, the traminer in the case of the white, which he knew well.

At the end of the meal he had restored everyone to good humour and praised his hostess to the skies. What had been a very tense, anxious evening was now, because of his presence, a success. Bella Lazar said scarcely a word.

'Yes, I love a good cigar. Thank you so much.' Antal Lazar held it to his ear, looking gratefully at Simon as they sank into easy chairs in the sitting room. 'You know I can get the best Coronas for you virtually at cost price? No I assure you it will be a pleasure. Yes, a brandy please. I can get you the best brandy too at a fraction of supermarket prices.'

'What exactly do you do, Mr Lazar?' Eunice, her feet tucked under her, sat very demurely yet also provocatively next to him. She wore a velvet gown of a particularly alluring midnight blue, cut sparingly to emphasise her good figure and low enough for her large white bosom to feature prominently. From where he was sitting Antal Lazar could almost see right down her cleavage to her stomach, and he didn't have to peer either.

Antal Lazar waved an expansive arm, his cuffs a good two inches below his jacket sleeve, a slim expensive gold watch just showing on his left wrist. 'Oh Mrs Harrow, I do practically everything. Essentially I import and I export, mainly furniture, antiques, that sort of thing; but as I am in the business of transporting and shipping goods of all kinds I know all kinds of people. I can get almost anything for a fraction of what you would pay anywhere else. My contacts are enormous.' He looked across at Simon and smiled. 'All strictly legal, Mr Harrow.'

'Oh I am quite sure.'

'You must come and see my warehouse, Mrs Harrow. You know I have those large premises behind Woolworth's? Any day of the week you are most welcome and if there is anything you care to buy . . .' He waved a hand dismissively as though price was the least consideration. 'And you too, Mrs Harrow.' He looked at Ruth who, slightly bemused by the evening, found that he mesmerised her. Something as explosive, as potentially sexual, as unconventional as Antal Lazar had very seldom entered her life, the lives of any of them, she thought. He was like a force rather than a person.

'I should like that,' Ruth said. 'Do you do carpets?'

Antal Lazar dropped his head, as though he were ashamed. 'Ah. No. Carpets alas no.'

'Oh that's quite all right. I just wondered.'

'But I know someone who *is* in carpets. If you could telephone me tomorrow I could give you his name. My office number.' Antal Lazar produced a card and gave it to her, smiling. 'And one for you, Mrs Harrow,' he said to Eunice. 'I would not like you to call when I was not there to show you around personally. Please give me a ring beforehand.'

'All these Mrs Harrows are very confusing,' Eunice said lazily. 'I am sure we can all use Christian names.'

'Just what I was thinking. Especially as Ruth has been so kind to Bella.'

His deep voice with its foreign accent seemed much more versatile than the normal middle class English tone. It could be soft, winsome, placatory and now slightly hard, as he addressed his wife. It become more commanding and less conciliatory, as though challenging Bella to disagree. But Bella gazed at him unflinchingly, not cowed by him; yet there was something guarded about her attitude. Her chin tilted slightly as though she had to be perpetually ready to defend herself.

Bella had transformed herself for the evening. Her hair had been done and, though she did not tint it and it was streaked with grey, it looked very becoming waved casually about her ears and falling over her forehead in little curls without a parting. She wore lipstick and a trace of rouge on her cheeks; black mascara and green eye shadow subtly contrasted to enhance the arresting clear grey of her eyes. She wore a green kaftan with high neck and long sleeves, an attractive yet practical garment that looked particularly chaste when constrasted with the vamp-like nature of Eunice's evening dress. Ruth, whose auburn colouring made black suit her, had a short evening dress with a V neck, long sleeves and a rather cleverly layered skirt made of black organdy and silk.

'Yes indeed,' Bella said. 'She has made moving here a pleasure instead of the ordeal I expected it to be. I felt so lonely at first after knowing all the neighbours in Swiss Cottage.'

'I have so little time to be at home,' Antal stretched his legs comfortably before him – one could see he was a man used to making himself at home almost anywhere. 'My business has expanded at such a pace, which is why we had to move. I am most grateful for your help, Simon, in assisting me with the property.'

'That was a pleasure,' Simon said coming over with the brandy bottle. 'It is nice to welcome such a dynamic addition to our business community.'

'Darling, I thought you said you did not know Mr Lazar?' Ruth looked at Geoffrey. 'Apparently your firm *does* deal with him.'

'As we are a large firm we partners deal with different clients, dear. It is true that I didn't know Simon knew Mr Lazar until he was pointed out at the Angler's on my birthday dinner.'

At that moment Ruth caught Bella's eye. A guilty start had made her instinctively look at her. She lowered her eyes quickly knowing it was too late.

'I didn't know you had met before?' Bella said noncommitally, placing her hand over her glass and shaking her head. 'No thank you, Geoffrey. I have had plenty to drink.'

'We didn't *meet* exactly,' Ruth said. 'It was . . .'

'I was entertaining business friends,' Antal said with composure. 'We waved across the room. It was weeks ago.'

Bella lowered her head, involuntarily biting her lip.

'Well that's all sorted out,' Geoffrey said bluffly. 'You interested in community activities, Antal? I'd be glad to introduce you to any of our clubs.'

'I'd be delighted to partake in community activities,' Antal said, 'as soon as I have settled and can find more time. I hear you are a Conservative Councillor, Geoffrey. I would be very eager to take part in your activities.'

'Oh you support the Tories?'

'Of course. Am I not a refugee from Communism? The Tory party is a bulwark against Socialism. I am not a member of the party as such, but a supporter, very firmly, unlike Bella.' Antal gave his wife a frosty look. 'She persists in thinking the road to prosperity lies in Socialism. Of course we met at the LSE, a hotbed of radical politics. You would have thought my views would have influenced Bella but they don't.'

'They influence me all right,' Bella said, 'to vote Socialist. I am so tired of hearing about the evils of Communism. The evils that went before I think are a lot worse in many countries, particularly Russia.'

'But what about Hungary?' Antal was beginning to lose his cool. Clearly politics provoked him as nothing else did. 'You feel we are better off now than before? What about Czechoslovakia and Dubcek? What about Poland?

'I'm not saying everywhere.' Bella had the air of one who had had this argument many times before. 'I certainly think that the Russians are better off now than they were under the Tsars . . .'

'What about individual freedom?' Antal thumped the arm of the sofa, beginning to shout, and Ruth cleared her throat.

'Is it not that Russia is a country so peculiar to itself that we can hardly judge?' she said. 'It was governed by an autocracy for centuries. It simply changed one form for another.

I always think we forget this aspect, how the KGB is an extension of the Cheka.'

Geoffrey and Eunice looked at Ruth with surprise. Antal nodded and smiled, the sudden colour ebbing from his cheeks.

'You are clearly a peacemaker, Ruth. I can see that. Of course you do not want a political brawl in your drawing room. Yes you have a point and we, particularly we anti-Communists, forget it. But our opponents do not see carefully enough either. Tell me, are you involved in academic work yourself?'

'I?' Ruth gazed at him in astonishment. 'Oh no.'

'But you have such a clear analytical mind. I saw that at dinner. I thought you were probably attached to the university or something.'

'I'm a mere housewife,' Ruth's voice was tinged with sarcasm. 'As my family frequently remind me. Only a housewife.'

'Oh Ruth, that's not fair,' Geoffrey said. 'No one ever says that to you.'

'You all do,' Ruth persisted. 'My daughter said my mind was "empty" only a few days ago.'

'Then I will reprimand her.'

'Why? If it is how she feels.'

'Your mind empty?' Antal Lazar expostulated. 'What nonsense.'

'My family seem to think I should have a job.' Ruth realized that her tongue was loosened by drink. Even though she felt fully in rational control of her faculties she knew that she was being careless about what she said. She knew, in a way, that she was playing for sympathy. Antal's sympathy.

'I don't think you should have a job,' Antal said. 'But it might be nice for *you* to have one. Bella is very contented with her work. I say nothing about the state of the house because I am used to it and because things like that are unimportant to me. As long as my wife and children are contented I don't care what the house looks like.'

'The house isn't all that bad,' Bella began.

'The house is awful, darling,' Antal said fondly. 'When we return this marvellous hospitality we shall take the Harrows to the Angler's Arms.' He raised his hands and shrugged his expressive elegant shoulders. 'But I don't mind. I don't complain. You are very happy in your work and that is important to me, too.'

'What sort of work do you do?' Simon said curiously.

'She paints, she weaves, and she writes text books on economics . . .'

'For schools,' Bella said quickly.

'Schools, universities, lay people, what are the odds?' Antal went on waving his hands about in a definitely Balkan manner. 'You write books. You are fulfilled.'

'But *I* can't write books,' Ruth said.

'I suggested she should work in my boutique,' Eunice produced a cigarette from her evening bag. 'Do you have a light?' She looked at Antal with a smile that seemed to invite more than a flame for her cigarette. Her lower lip, with its thick layer of pale pearl lipstick, trembled slightly showing the gleam of her small, very even teeth.

'Alas I don't smoke. But let me . . .'

Antal made to get to his feet but Geoffrey forestalled him bending low to light Eunice's cigarette. Ruth thought how fat he was as he bent over, his quivering lower chin almost covering his tie. He was getting very flabby and now his face was bathed in perspiration. He was drinking and smoking too much. His hair was thinner too and a few stray blond strands hung across his eyes showing an area of his pate that was completely bald and shiny.

She suddenly compared him with Antal Lazar who she knew was older. Even though his hairline was receding he had a full healthy head of hair. Besides it made him look attractive, almost distinguished. His face was absolutely free from perspiration, his eyes not overbright like Geoffrey's with too much booze but intelligent and alert. His figure was taut and his waistline trim. His legs were long, elegant in well fitting trousers, black socks and highly polished black shoes. His legs were undoubtedly covered with fine black hairs like the back of his hands. She wondered why she was thinking of his body and started up guiltily to see Bella observing her with a slight smile on her face.

'Why not if she wants to work in a boutique?' Once Eunice's cigarette was drawing satisfactorily Antal returned to the subject, looking at Ruth.

'But I don't want to work in the boutique.'

'You have a boutique?' Antal looked sideways at Eunice.

'Two. Chez Estelle.'

'Oh I have seen the one in Edgerton. It is near my office. Where is the other?'

'Upper Warford. We've just opened.'

'Very expensive.' He smiled.

'Very.' She smiled back. Ruth resented the rapport their undoubted commercial success seemed to give them.

'So you are a business woman, and a mother, no doubt . . .' Antal opened his eyes wide, inviting confidences. His glance strayed to the not inconsiderable mound of her bustline. He shifted a little in his chair and momentarily, almost unnoticeably, a hand flicked at his groin as though he were easing some constriction.

Ruth felt that Antal was interested in Eunice and knew that she was jealous.

'Yes, I have two children, daughters, and a large house to run. But I do have help.' Eunice glanced at Ruth. 'Ruth simply feels she doesn't want to work.'

'No reason why she should.' Antal shifted his attention once more to his hostess, those blue attractive eyes with dark irises open very wide. 'I would have thought she was an intellectual myself.'

Geoffrey bellowed with laughter and spluttered on his

cigar. A globule of spittle trailed over his lip onto his chin and he wiped it away leaving a wet mark. Ruth felt a sense of unease as she looked at her husband that she had never known before. He suddenly seemed like an amiable buffoon compared to the urbane, elegant, intelligent, sexually attractive, sexually *most* attractive, Antal Lazar.

'Oh dear.' Geoffrey put his handkerchief away in his hip pocket. Even that bulged because his trousers were too tight. 'Ruth is no intellectual.'

'I actually completed two years of a degree course in history,' Ruth said icily, clenching her hands. '*Then* I left prematurely to marry *you.*'

'Nearly *twenty* years ago,' Geoffrey said meaningfully.

'Well.' Antal gave that charming inconsequential continental shrug. 'Twenty years ago. What is that? You have done your duty by the community, and your family, I doubt not. You have raised a family, kept a beautiful home. If that is enough, if it pleases you *why* do anything? But if it does not seem enough, if people taunt you that your mind needs developing – I do not think so myself mind you – why *not* develop it? Why not complete your degree, Ruth?'

'Complete my degree?' Ruth stared at him as though he were posing some conundrum.

'Go back to the university. Become a mature student.'

'Are you serious?'

'Why not?' Antal was half laughing, but the expression in his eyes was earnest. 'Here in Edgerton. I would have thought it an ideal thing for a woman whose family were partly off her hands.'

'But they're not off my hands.'

'How old is your youngest child?'

'Twelve. Nearly thirteen.'

'Bella has been working since our youngest was six months. You have given your children, your husband if I may say so, everything they could reasonably expect you to give. Now take something for yourself. Complete your degree.'

'Oh this is ridiculous.' Geoffrey eased himself forward in his chair, the smile gone from his face. 'That is the last thing Ruth wants to do. A job yes, a few hours in a shop or office; but the university . . .'

'Why not? I think it's a splendid suggestion,' Simon said 'I can't think why no one thought of it before.'

'Because Ruth doesn't want it,' Geoffrey said with determination. His voice was harsh and angry. His face was very red and his stomach bulged over his waistband, his legs were apart as though his thighs were too large for him to put them together. 'This is awful nonsense and I wish it would stop. It's making me very angry.'

'Why?' Ruth looked at him.

'Because . . .' Geoffrey began, the veins welling on the side of his neck.

'Because he doesn't know,' Eunice taunted, putting her knees neatly together. She got up, looking at Simon. 'I shall have to go to university myself in order to keep up with the high level of conversation that will undoubtedly be the norm at the junior Harrow household. Now we must go. It is after midnight.' She turned and kissed Ruth lightly on the cheek pressing her arms. 'Think about it, darling.'

'I shall,' Ruth returned the embrace, hiding her hot cheek against Eunice's cool white arm. 'I really think I shall.'

Antal Lazar bent low over her hand as he took his leave. His lips were very firm and even in that brief gesture he managed to transmit an urgent sexuality.

'It was a wonderful evening, Ruth. I am so happy we moved next door. Do consider that suggestion. Your husband will soon come round to it.' He put his arm round his wife's shoulder and pressed her. 'I am very proud of my wife. I like a woman who has brains.'

8

'What a fabulous man,' Eunice said tossing her coat on the chair. 'Of course the business about university was absurd. I think he was flattering you.'

'Why should he want to flatter me?' Ruth hung her coat behind the door. She had responded to a genuine emergency on Eunice's part. The manageress and assistant at the Edgerton shop both had the flu and Eunice had to go on a buying trip to London. Ruth occasionally did help out if Eunice was stuck.

'Oh I think he's like that with women, don't you? He absolutely *undresses* one all the time with his eyes. I must say it's a change from Simon's cow-like glances, not that he ever looks at me very much.'

'I thought Simon was looking at you a lot the other night.'

'Yes and in bed he tried to make love! Jealousy obviously turns him on.'

Ruth didn't like to ask if the attempt had been successful.

'That man is a *charmer*,' Eunice went on with enthusiasm, opening the till. 'There is some cash here; not that you're likely to want it. I'm hoping you'll be dealing in large cheques or banknotes in high denominations for those who want to spend cash. It's surprising how many do. That poor wife – Lazar's wife – looked absolutely browbeaten though. How dull she is.'

'She isn't dull. She just hadn't anything to say because her husband hogged the evening with all that steamy sexuality.'

Eunice giggled. 'Yes he did, didn't he? I think he is very naughty. I could imagine one could have a very nice time in bed with Mr Lazar.'

'Would you like to?' Ruth sat on one of the salon chairs and crossed her legs.

Eunice put a hand on her hip, a model pose, and considered her. 'I might. I must fly darling. I'm not taking the car because of that awful traffic in London. I . . .'

There was a tap on the window and both women looked up. The object of their conversation was beaming through the thick plate glass at them. It was almost uncanny. Eunice motioned to him enthusiastically and went to unlock the door, throwing it open.

'Well, *hello!*' She stood back and made an elaborate bow. 'Have you come to buy a dress Mr Lazar?'

Antal put his hat on the chair, a soft brown derby that toned with his camel hair coat. He had a thin expensive briefcase which he put on the floor. 'I was just going to my car when I saw you ladies coming in. Now, I thought, is my chance . . .'

'Alas, I am just off to London.' Eunice consulted her thin Cartier watch. 'I'll miss the train.'

'Train? You are going by train?' There was something in Antal's tone that made them both look at him.

'Yes. Why?'

'Because I am going by car. Let me give you a lift.'

'Are you going now?' Eunice's tone betrayed her suppressed excitement.

'This very moment. I was coming away from my office to the parking lot opposite where I keep my car.' Antal made a vague gesture through the window. 'I start work early you know.'

'My goodness you must start very early if you were leaving at this time.'

'Seven,' Antal said. 'My secretary brings me tea and toast

91

when she comes in a little after me.'

Ruth wondered if the secretary was the blonde pretty girl she had seen him with at the Angler's. 'You start as early as that?'

'Yes. Most days I go to London or one of the ports, Dover, Southampton. I can often give you a lift.'

'That would be marvellous. I must be in Great Portland Street by eleven. I was catching the nine-thirty.'

'No problem.' Antal took up his hat as Eunice resumed her coat.

'Ruth?' He smiled at her.

'No. I am minding the shop.'

'Then you have decided to work?'

'I just help out occasionally. Eunice thinks that you weren't serious anyway.'

Antal looked grave. It was difficult to know whether he was mocking her or not. 'It is a very important matter, a person's life and career. Very serious indeed.'

'Well, her husband is very cross with you.' Eunice mockingly wagged a finger at him.

Antal feigned dismay. 'Oh why?'

'He thinks you've unsettled her. He says she talks about it every day.'

'Then you do think it's a good idea?' Antal came closer to Ruth and bent his head, like a sympathetic doctor listening to one's woes.

'In a way. My family hate it. Especially my husband.'

'Oh dear,' Antal looked contrite. 'I must give him a box of Coronas and ask him to forgive me.'

'You shouldn't unsettle the marital nest,' Eunice said smiling.

Ruth watched them both walk slowly to the car park.

Britannia descended on a huge, round, very realistic looking

92

penny as it was lowered slowly on wires from the ceiling. Although this part had been rehearsed countless times Britannia nevertheless looked as nervous as she felt, perching astride on the huge penny, praying that she wouldn't fall off. The penny landed safely and the audience broke into thunderous applause. Britannia, visibly relieved, smiled and relaxed. The great historical characters of English history – King Alfred, King Arthur, Boadicea, Henry V, Shakespeare, Milton, Florence Nightingale and, finally, triumphantly, Elizabeth I in full courtly regalia, gathered round her.

The audience stood up roaring its appreciation as the curtain fell on the final tableau.

'Splendid, really splendid,' Geoffrey said, his round face gleaming with sweat.

The row full of Harrows and Lazars clapped vigorously. There was only one place empty in the row, almost in the whole auditorium.

'I do think Antal might have tried to be here for this,' Bella murmured still looking round as she had during the whole performance. 'What with Christopher being Drake and Irena Britannia. They'll be very disappointed.'

Ruth smiled sympathetically. 'It *is* trying. Does he work on a Saturday?'

'Every day. But he promised. We should all be used to it now.'

'There's going to be a most awful scrum for food.' Geoffrey put his arm around Ruth's waist and steered her towards one of the exits. 'I must say the comp did the Queen proud.'

'Did you recognize George?'

'No, which one was he?'

'He was one of the courtiers to Queen Elizabeth. He looked extremely solemn.'

'Ah yes I did see him, standing behind the throne.'

Olivia and Joe straggled behind talking to Simon. Eunice

93

came along with Bella Lazar and her soulful, difficult younger daughter Dorcas.

'Irena looked really beautiful as Britannia. You must feel very proud of her.'

'Thank you.' Bella glanced shyly at Eunice. 'She was very nervous.'

Eunice was looking around too. Antal's absence had rather agitated them all; they kept on shuffling in their seats and looking behind them all during the performance until the people behind got restless too and wondered if there was anything wrong so that *they* started looking round. It was like seeing a pack of cards collapse.

'Your husband will be sorry he's missed it. Has he always been a bad timekeeper?'

'Always.' Bella stepped carefully over an upturned chair. 'The thing is we never seem to get used to it. He always promises and we always think he will keep his promises. Then the children are disappointed, I feel let down and am resentful and Antal lectures us without being in any way contrite. He is a law unto himself.'

'It must be tiresome,' Eunice murmured. 'I'm dying for something cool.' She waved a hand across her face and smiled at an acquaintance.

The pageant had been held in the school hall, but outside on the lawn a huge marquee with red and white striped awning had been erected. Little tables and chairs and striped umbrellas helped to enhance the festive atmosphere. The sun kept on breaking in brilliant flashes through the clouds. So far it hadn't rained.

'All this on the rates,' Simon said. 'The thing must have cost a fortune. At the Royal the tickets cost us £2.00 each *and* we had to give a hefty subsidy towards the costumes.'

'And it wasn't half as good as this,' Eunice said looking at her younger daughter. 'Sorry darling but it wasn't.'

Dorcas Harrow draped herself against one of the tables

and studied a pointed toe with indifference. 'Mother, who cares? Who cares a rap for the Queen's Jubilee or anything else? It's all such a hoot anyway.'

Dorcas Harrow's main interest was young men. She thought everything that interfered with this serious pursuit a 'hoot'. Her parents had decided to take her away from school when she had her O levels. Any further study was a waste of time and money as she had no ambition other than to get married. Her father hoped that would be soon. She had very expensive tastes in clothes and make-up and collected number one hits with the seriousness that some people gave to first editions.

When Dorcas set off for school every morning she looked ridiculous in a uniform. She wore her hat on the back of her head and was regularly sent home for wearing mascara. Her headmistress hoped she would soon be off their hands too. Places in the independent schools were much sought after by those who wished to achieve more in life than young Miss Harrow.

Wherever she was she attracted young men. Her sexual quality was quite blatant. In no time after perching languorously half off and half on the table she had quite a few sniffing round.

Simon and Geoffrey went to the marquee to queue for strawberries and cream while Eunice and Ruth chatted to parents like themselves who had children at both the schools. Bella knew nobody. She felt lost in such a large crowd.

'Is Dad getting you strawberries?'

'Oh yes, Joe, thank you! You are all very kind.'

'It's a pity Mr Lazar wasn't here.'

'Isn't it?'

'Irena was smashing.' Bella was surprised to see him turn red. 'Is she coming out?'

'I believe so after she's changed. Oh here is my husband. Joe, can you see him over there by the entrance to the school? Could you . . .?'

Joe sped off and Bella watched half in anger half in relief as Antal, looking very poised and urbane, followed him across the lawn towards the marquee.

'Sorry . . .' Antal gave his charming apologetic shrug. 'Got held up.'

'You missed the whole performance.'

'*Please* Bella.' Antal's tone forestalled criticism. He wiped the perspiration from his brow. 'My goodness it is a hot afternoon.' He took off his jacket to reveal sleeves already rolled up. He was looking around and his eyes alighted on Ruth.

'Oh the Harrows are here.'

'They brought us, very kindly.'

Antal ignored the edge to her voice and went over to Ruth. 'Ruth!' He spread his arms. 'Can you forgive . . .'

'*I've* nothing to forgive, Antal. Your children might be disappointed you were not here.'

'But taking my family. It was so kind. I had an urgent business conference . . .'

'I thought everyone would be so busy today with the Jubilee celebrations?' Ruth looked at him with surprise.

'My work *never* stops, Ruth. Ah Eunice . . .' Antal bowed and kissed her hand. Ruth noticed that he held it for quite a long time. Eunice had that special moist look in her eyes that she seemed to keep for Antal Lazar.

'Hello, Antal. What a shame you couldn't see . . .'

'I was devastated.'

'You are a *very* badly organized man.' She gave him a look that pretended to be severe but which somehow conveyed intimacy. Ruth suddenly wondered if they were intimate. She had been so busy for so long with preparations for the Jubilee celebrations at the beginning of June that she had hardly had a moment alone with her sister-in-law. Not only were there the schools requiring parental attention and support, but all the organizations with which she and Geoffrey were concerned were celebrating too. The Conservatives had a gala ball this very evening, the Sports Club had an afternoon tomorrow, the council had had an official ball the night before, and the Yacht Club a gala the previous Saturday.

From the corner of her eye she saw Geoffrey and Simon emerge with huge trays bearing dishes of strawberries and cream.

'Joe darling, go and help Daddy and Uncle Simon.'

She knew Joe was looking out for Irena. He hadn't taken his eyes off her all the time she had been on the stage. Well she was very pretty . . . Ruth decided, on this fraught day and at this moment in time, not to start worrying about Joe who obediently crossed the lawn towards the marquee to assist.

'This is my younger daughter,' Eunice was saying detaching Dorcas from the crowd of admirers. Dorcas came rather reluctantly forward and stared rudely and pointedly at Antal. She was calculating his age. He bent low over her hand, his eyes on her face.

'A beauty,' he murmured. 'Just like her mother.'

Ruth saw Dorcas's expression change from boredom to interest. It was like the lifting of a veil. The girl preened herself as they all did in the face of this onslaught from the Balkans. Ruth felt ashamed of her sex, of her own susceptibility to Antal's quite unashamed sexuality.

'Neighbours of Ruth and Geoffrey,' Eunice was saying. 'Their daughter Irena was Britannia.'

'She was super,' Dorcas whispered. Some people thought Dorcas had a throat defect because she hardly ever spoke in a normal voice. Those nearest to her knew it was contrived, so had long since ceased to worry about it.

'How sorry I am to have missed it.' Antal sounded sincere.

'What do you do?' Dorcas moved closer to him.

Ruth saw Eunice wince with annoyance just as a diversion was provided by Chris and George who ran across the lawn still covered with grease paint followed at a stately distance, as befitted the star of the show, by Irena.

'Oh Dad you *were* here!' Chris called. 'Everyone said you weren't.'

Antal gave his by now familiar regretful shrug and held out his arms to embrace his daughter. 'Darlings, I missed it. My conference didn't end until . . .'

'Oh Dad, you promised.' Chris looked hurt but Irena had the same resigned look as her mother. She hugged her father and patted his arm.

'Never mind, Dad.'

'But I wanted to see you as Britannia!'

'You should have made an effort to get away,' Chris said. 'It's only once every twenty-five years after all.'

'Please don't criticise me, Christopher.' Antal's voice was stern. 'I am working for us *all*.'

'But other fathers are here. Why is it always you who can't turn up? What's so different about you?'

'Chris, don't spoil the day please,' his mother said quietly. 'I'm sure Daddy would have come if he could.'

'You always say that.'

There was a painful silence, palpable in the noisy throng. Antal didn't look the least ashamed of himself, only angry. He obviously belonged to the brigade of those who never apologized or never explained. Might was right, and the father of the family, the breadwinner, was mightiest of all. He turned his back on his son and resumed his conversation with Dorcas. Eunice moved to stand at his side.

'God in heaven, that man,' Geoffrey murmured to Ruth, wiping his face. 'I really can't stand him.'

'But you hardly know him.'

'Yes, but what I know I don't like. A greasy, oily foreigner. Christ he's so *smooth*.' Geoffrey lit a cigarette and started coughing. His face went purple. Antal Lazar's back, his sleek black hair looked by contrast so cool. He had on a blue shirt and carried the jacket of his dark blue suit on his arm. He wore sun glasses and his shirt was undone at the neck. His trousers fitted him beautifully, so neat over the hips and buttocks, his creases immaculate.

'Geoffrey, you'll have to lose weight,' Ruth said. 'That cough is getting worse.'

She turned away, feeling distracted with the noise and the heat, the beginnings of a headache.

'Shouldn't we look at the exhibition?' she asked Olivia. 'Have you seen it?'

'Yes, but I can show it to you again if you like, Mum.'

'That would be lovely, darling. I'm getting awfully head-achey.'

The assembly hall of the comp stretched from one end of the building to the other in order to accommodate its huge population. It could be divided into smaller classrooms by means of glass partitions; but on this day, the day of the Jubilee fête, they were all pushed back and the hall was given over to a vast exhibition displaying the many skills of the pupils of the school from the eleven year olds to the sixth formers.

'It's impossible to see it all,' Ruth said gasping at the numbers of people who clustered round the various tables and exhibition stands. 'Let's just look at George's class.'

'They're all bits of wire; very technical,' Olivia said derisively. 'Some of the sixth form stuff is first class; nearly as good as ours.'

'I must look at George's,' Ruth began to edge her way to the centre of the hall where the middle forms were exhibiting their drawings, models and handicrafts. Olivia was right. Boys and girls of twelve seemed mostly interested in intricate compositions of wire, string and balsa wood. There were some very nice drawings and poems neatly tacked upon the wall. There was nothing by George.

'I'll just look at the sixth form and then I'll have to go to the toilet to get some water for my Paracetemol,' Ruth said. 'I won't be able to go to the dance tonight, otherwise.'

'Poor Mummy,' Olivia tucked an arm through hers. She was a companionable child; her prop.

'The sixth form is really huge.' Ruth strolled round, glad that this part of the exhibition was given more space. It ran into one of the laboratories and there were various experiments displayed, their respective stages printed clearly on cards together with the names of the originators. The work looked accomplished, complicated, impressive.

'I don't understand it at all,' Ruth said, 'but I'm full of admiration. People seem to know much more now than they did when I was young. Look at that, for instance,' she peered at the card standing in front of a gigantic structure made of gleaming wires and coloured balls of different sizes which spun about at various speeds. 'And by a girl, too – Jennifer Hale.'

'Why shouldn't it be by a girl?'

'Well I was interested to see that it was. That's all.'

'Girls can do science as well you know, Mum.'

'Oh of course I know, Olivia! Don't let's have one of our little arguments.'

Olivia took her arm away and stood in front of her mother, lowering her voice so that those around would not hear.

'I don't want to argue, Mummy. But you always seem bent on diminishing women, as though they were rather stupid, automatically inferior to men.'

'That's a very silly and unfair thing to say, Olivia,' Ruth whispered, bending her head.

' "And by a girl too," ' Olivia mimicked her mother's voice. 'You can't really help it, can you? You're conditioned to think that there are certain things only men can do.'

'No, that's not true,' Ruth kept her voice steady and smiled at Olivia just in case anyone they knew was looking. 'But female achievement does impress me. It impresses me a lot.

It was certainly not as common in my day when girls either became nurses, teachers or, as most of them did, secretaries. Only the very few did anything exceptional.' Ruth walked slowly along the rows of benches, gazed at the drawings and paintings, many of them of undoubted merit, on the walls. Half of them by girls.

Could she really return to university? Could she slough off all the mental sloth of nearly twenty years and get down to the basics of academic learning? The young women of today had such an advantage over her generation. Might it not be exciting, challenging to try and catch them up? She turned round and grasped her daughter's hand, smiling at her.

'I'm glad we came,' she said. 'I'm glad we came together.'

Bella Lazar sat in the same green caftan she had worn for dinner with the Harrows with the same patient fixed smile on her face. She only drank orange juice explaining to anyone who was interested that alcohol had a most peculiar effect on her.

Ruth had ruthlessly suppressed her headache by almost overdosing herself with Paracetemol. She felt rather detached and very weary, guilty about Bella and yet enjoying the evening. It was ten o'clock and the Edgerton Conservative Party Jubilee Ball in honour of the Queen's twenty-fifth accession to the throne had gone well.

Geoffrey was always good in a crowd; fetching drinks, dancing with wallflowers, exchanging jokes with the men. He had a tendency on these occasions to drink too much but then so did everyone else.

Antal danced expertly, his feet almost doing the work for both of them. He swung her gracefully away and then drew her to him while the band went uptity-dump-dump and everybody did their own thing. A few elderly couples danced a stately kind of foxtrot, one-step-two-then-one-step, and some of the Junior Conservatives danced on their own. Those in the middle range did every variation of dance you could dream of and Antal and Ruth found themselves very much in harmony.

The number changed. This was definitely a slow foxtrot. Couples clasped each other and the younger ones practically entwined. Ruth could feel his breath on her cheek. The lights had been dimmed.

'It is a tremendous party, he said.

'I'm glad you're enjoying yourself.'

'Oh very much.' She felt the pressure of his hand on her back. 'We're very lucky to know your family, to be introduced to all the best people in the town.'

Ruth looked at him. 'I think you're joking.'

'I'm not. Honestly I'm not.'

'Maybe you're not.' Ruth continued to look at him doubtfully.

'It's very different from London, this sort of life. We lived in London for nearly twenty years and hardly knew a soul.'

'But Bella said she had a lot of friends.'

'Bella may have; but not both of us. We didn't have shared friends. Bella had so many activities that she knew a good many people, but there was no sense of community life as there is here. We hardly ever went out with other couples or in a group.'

'Oh we move around like that all the time. We scarcely go out together!'

'And you're very close to your brother-in-law and sister-in-law?'

'Yes.'

'Eunice is a very smart woman. Very clever.'

Antal turned his head and looked over to where she was sitting at the large table they all shared. All the elder children were there as well, though Dorcas and Paget Harrow were perpetually at tables with other young men, giggling all the time.

'You like her, don't you?'

Antal raised his head, not changing rhythm. 'Not especially.' It seemed to be a question rather than a statement. 'I mean I like her. I like you all.' His deep blue eyes, with the darker blue circles, looked very innocent. 'I think she is a very smart attractive lady. And so are you.'

He pulled her closer to him. His face was so near that his breath was quite warm.

'I find you very intriguing. You pretend to be the ordinary suburban housewife, but I know better.'

Ruth was glad it was so dark and he couldn't see her face properly. 'Oh do you? You fancy you know women don't you?'

'I do. Very well. Did you do anything about the university?'

'I had an interview with the Dean last week.'

'And?' Antal stopped dancing and looked at her eagerly.

'My husband is furious. The children aren't too pleased either.'

'But what did the Dean say?'

'He'll let me know. They're not quite sure how my previous studies will stand up to modern scholarship. I could concentrate on history for one year and do something else the other. It would be two years. They'd credit me with the first.'

'Aren't you pleased?'

'I haven't made up my mind.'

'I feel you're wasted. You know, I really approve of Bella having so many interests. It has saved our marriage. It might save yours.'

'There's just no question of my marriage being in danger. It is very secure.'

'You're lucky you can be so sure.' He twirled her under his arm.

'I am sure. Geoffrey and I are really quite a devoted couple.' She didn't like the way Antal looked at her. 'You needn't look so sarcastic.'

'I never take anything for granted. You just wait until the

103

children are older and your husband busier than he is now. You'll find you've nothing to do. You'll envy your sister-in-law and her busy career.'

'I don't know why you're so concerned about me,' Ruth said. 'You hardly know me.'

'I know you better than you think,' Antal very briefly touched her forehead with his lips. Ruth felt disturbed and backed sharply away. She tried to compose herself, keeping her voice steady and low.

'Is Bella enjoying the evening?'

Antal glanced once more at the table. 'Bella is never very happy at this sort of occasion. She doesn't drink you know and she's not awfully sociable. In London of course it didn't matter much but here I can see we shall have a good deal of socializing. She says she is happy but I know she isn't.'

'Olivia's a bit like that. A very serious girl. She didn't want to come; but Geoffrey is treasurer . . .'

'Oh quite, she had to come. I must say that Joseph and Irena seem to get on rather well.'

Too well. Joe's attentions to Irena had threatened to spoil Ruth's evening.

'I think he's a bit young to be serious about a girl,' Ruth said doubtfully. 'He's only sixteen.'

'But that is quite old. At his age I had had my first affair.'

Ruth looked at him again not quite sure whether he was serious or joking. 'I think you're a tease,' she said.

'Only one of our maids; but I knew what it was all about.'

'They say continental men are precocious.'

'Oh they are.'

'Well I don't want it to happen to Joe. He is just a boy.'

'You can't stop these things, Ruth.'

But she wanted to. She would.

'Excuse me.' Eunice tapped Ruth on the shoulder. 'This is an excuse me dance, Ruth.'

'Oh!' Ruth smiled and stepped away.

Antal, hardly pausing, immediately enfolded Eunice in his arms. She was a very snug fit.

Ruth made her way back to the table smiling at people she knew. Her headache was beginning to return again.

'Don't you think it is time I danced with my wife?' Geoffrey waylaid her so that she almost bumped into him. She looked up and he held out his arms with a rueful, appealing smile. 'You are so popular,' he said holding her very close to him and leading her onto the dance floor. His lips touched her hair.

'I try to please everyone,' Ruth said.

'You try to please that Lazar fellow.'

'Oh nonsense! All the men here have got an obsession about Antal Lazar.'

'Have they?'

'I think they're jealous of him.'

'Not jealous. Furious about the way he looks at their women. Look at him now with Eunice. Wouldn't that make Simon cross?'

As the lights went even lower she could see that Eunice and Antal were dancing very close indeed, practically merging. A bit too close for the Conservative Party Ball.

'It's just his style,' Ruth said. 'People like that are always quite harmless. They flatter the women, but that's all there is to it.'

'Simon said he'd knock him down after seeing him dance with Dorcas.

'Simon can't talk,' Ruth murmured. 'He's been dancing on and off all evening with Jordine Smith-Shaw. I would call that beyond the call of duty as a committee member.'

'She's a committee member too.'

'I still think . . .'

'I really can't *stand* Lazar,' Geoffrey said. 'I wish to God they didn't live next door. That sort of easy charm of his makes me sick. It's not English.'

'He's not English.'

'It's like an Italian waiter.'

'You *are* jealous, Geoffrey.'

'No, he's always offering to get me things on the cheap, do a deal in this, that or the other. Now it's property speculation. Simon thinks he's very sound commercially; but I can't stand the fellow. He's even turned his wife into a sort of drone.'

'She's O.K. on her own. I admit he does outshine her here. He's that type.'

'And that tramp of his daughter is eyeing Joe in a way I don't like, and George follows his son about as though he were god. I wish the whole bloody family had never come here. I really wish they hadn't.'

Part Two

The Student

9

Ruth hurried in, switching on the lights as she went quickly through the house. None of the beds were made and the dishes were still stacked in the kitchen. Ruth sighed in a resigned manner, dumped her books on the table she used in the bedroom to work on, and rushed rapidly again around the house. It was nearly six. At least if she made their bed that would be something. She flung the sheets over the pillows and then straightened up as she heard a car outside. She went to the window and saw Geoffrey parking his car behind hers. She had left the lights on, too.

She was in Joe's room when Geoffrey came into the hall and called for her.

'Ruth?'

'I'm here. Upstairs.'

Joe's bed was a terrible mess. From the tangled blankets it looked as though he'd had nightmares. Frantically she shook out the bottom sheet. She felt the presence of Geoffrey like a threatening storm as he came slowly up the stairs. She could hear his heavy breathing as he stood by Joe's door.

'This house is in a bloody awful mess. It looks a tip.'

He measured his words, heavy pauses in between as though he was presenting the case for the prosecution in court.

'I know, darling. Mrs Grange has had flu all week. I did hope she'd be in today. I had a lecture at nine. I haven't had a minute at all since.'

'Ruth, you say that the whole time. It's always some reason for the beds not being made.'

'Only since Mrs Grange has been ill.'

'It's *not* since Mrs Grange has been ill!' Geoffrey folded his arms and teetered on his feet. 'It is every time she is not here. I would never have believed that a woman like you would let the place go like this.'

Ruth shook the sheet in his face. 'Oh sorry. That was not intentional.'

'Making the beds at this time. The dishes are not done either.'

'You could always do them,' Ruth said smoothing down the blankets.

'I beg your pardon?'

She took up the bedspread and turned and looked at him. 'You could always do them. Or don't you know how?'

'Ruth!'

Ruth smoothed the bedspread and brushed past Geoffrey. In the doorway she stood and faced him. 'I can't remember you wiping up in seventeen years of marriage.'

'I was never asked.'

'Well I'm asking you now. The fact is you were never *taught*. You were spoilt by your mother and spoilt by me. Oh I see from the expression on your face that you still don't think it is the "man's job".'

'No I don't, frankly. We've always been partners in this house with our tasks and duties.'

'I was the perfect wife and mother and you the perfect husband and father.'

'Well not perfect, but . . . Ruth you know what I mean.' Geoffrey's tone was now placatory.

He followed her into Olivia's bedroom. There the chaos was worse. In Joe's room it was just the bed. In Olivia's it was everything. Her drawers looked as though they had been ransacked; her wardrobe was open, clothes lying half in it and half on the floor. There was a mound of records in the middle of the floor, the sleeves at the sides. Her dressing table was full of open pots and crumpled tissues were scattered about. The bed, though neat, was unmade as though she had jumped out of it into clothes and out of the house. The toothpaste was open on the shelf over her washbasin in which were a couple of wet facecloths. Ruth put her hands on her hips.

'I feel just like going right out of this and leaving her to do it. She is fifteen, Geoffrey. Fifteen.'

Geoffrey shrugged and rumpled his smooth hair. 'It is pretty shocking.'

'I've spoilt her too. I've looked after her for fifteen years and now she can't even make a bed or close a drawer. I've fetched and carried and polished and washed and cooked and . . .' Ruth paused, trying to find the right words. 'What hurts me, really hurts is that none of you seem to give a rap for my happiness; to be pleased that I have found satisfaction in resuming my studies.'

'Of course we care about your happiness . . .'

'Well you don't show it. All you do, all of you, is think about yourselves.'

'Oh Ruth shut up!'

Geoffrey lifted his fist and Ruth ducked. The gesture made them both stare at each other, breathing deeply.

'You were going to *hit* me?'

Geoffrey had gone very red and the sweat broke out on his face again. His well cut suit concealed the outlines of his figure which was even bulkier than the previous summer. The portion of anatomy between his stomach and his crotch looked like a steep cliff that had been cut away by a landslide. He now had a completely round bald patch in the middle of his head which the strands of hair, however strategically placed by the comb and greased into position in the morning, failed to cover. His large frame now quivered like a large piece of jelly.

'You'll give me a heart attack, Ruth.'

'*I'll* give you a heart attack? You'll bring it on yourself.

You can't stand the truth, can you? Well this is the truth. I have ruined this household rotten. It is my fault. Not one member of it is capable of looking after his or herself, let alone anyone else. And I blame myself. My house was my pride, my family my career ...'

'And what is so wrong with that?' Geoffrey shouted. 'You talk as though you were some kind of slave. Well you weren't. You were, still are, a free and independent woman with your own income, your own time, your own hobbies and pursuits if you wanted any. Well you didn't. You wanted children and you had them. You didn't even want to stop at three and if you hadn't had two miscarriages you would have gone on and on until the whole place was full of screaming kids. And I would have put up with it – paid and put up with it. That's what you wanted, Ruth. You never once complained. You said it was what you wanted, what you enjoyed until that blasted family came to live next door and persuaded you differently.'

'They didn't persuade me.'

'Put the idea into your head.'

'I wouldn't have found it so attractive if it hadn't been something I wanted. Yes I was ready for it. And why?' Ruth advanced towards him shaking her finger. 'And why? Because of you, my precious family whom I had molly-coddled and ruined. "Empty mind", you all told me. "Conventional". "Not a thought in her head". "Boring" ...'

'We did not!'

'You did. What wasn't said was implied, more than once. By the time Antal Lazar suggested university I felt futile and useless. I wondered what lay ahead.'

'Well you now know what lay ahead. Chaos. Dirt. This is only one step removed from the house next door.'

'It is not! They still haven't laid all the carpets. And our lavatory doesn't smell.'

'Thank God for that anyway. Oh Ruth.' Geoffrey sat on Olivia's bed and mopped his brow. 'Oh Christ, how did we get to this pass? What has gone wrong? Can you help me?' He looked at her so pitifully that Ruth felt her anger evaporating. The wild rage that had seemed to seize hold of her was there no more. She felt pity and sorrow, and a kind of guilt. She brushed her hair off her forehead and, sticking her hands in the pockets of her jeans, leaned against the wall facing the bed.

'I guess it is a mess. I'm sorry. When it started I never meant it to get like this because I am a very houseproud sort of person. But it's just that – ' She ruffled her hands through her hair trying to find the right words. 'It doesn't seem so important any more. I mean the house isn't basically filthy like Bella's. I do have a cleaner and she sometimes does come. It is simply that it isn't as tidy as it used to be, as you'd all got used to.'

Geoffrey gazed at his wife. It was like looking at a stranger. Her once carefully coiffured hair was screwed back behind her ears and inches longer than before. If she had make-up on it was only lipstick – no carefully blended mellow glow provided by Messrs Lancôme and Lauder.

The wife who formerly greeted him in a good skirt, twin set and pearls, with beautifully manicured nails, well groomed hair and a beauty-parlour complexion, looked like a rather old teenager who had somehow lost direction in life.

Of course she didn't always look like this. When they went out for a function or to dinner it was difficult to tell the new Ruth from the old. But he knew. He knew that whatever the appearance of the packet, the inside was different. *She* was different.

'I'll make up for it in the vacation,' Ruth said suddenly smiling as though she could read the expression on his face. 'I'll become the model wife and mother again.'

'And when for Christ's sake is that?'

'Only a couple of weeks. I'll organize Mrs Grange. Maybe she could come every day. We can afford it, can't we?'

113

Geoffrey nodded without speaking. He felt very tired and in need of a whisky.

The college cafeteria was full of mostly young people trying to grab a snack between classes or lectures. It was early, before the leisurely argumentative lunchtime crowd packed it to over-flowing. Ruth glanced at her watch.

'I have a tutorial at one. Another coffee?'

'I'd love to. Let me.'

'No, I will.'

Ruth got up and Bella watched her trim form moving along in the self-service queue. The change in Ruth in three months – no not quite three, two and a half – was extraordinary. She seemed to have shed years, become a girl again. Bella had never seen such a transformation in a person in such a short time. She told her. Ruth smiled.

'I know. My husband emphasised the finer points to me last night. Only he does not consider it an improvement.'

'He likes the twin sets and pearls?'

'Apparently.' Ruth sipped her coffee. 'No, I must do something, Bella. Geoffrey says my behaviour is destroying the family.'

'Surely that's an exaggeration? You are still the same person.'

'But not to them. They like someone to wave them off in the morning and welcome them home at nights. They like the beds to be made and the dishes washed, the smell of cooking in the oven upon their return. Hearth and home. It is what they are used to. I suppose they are the ones to lose by my new interest.'

'Doesn't Mrs Grange come?'

'Well, she's been ill but she only comes three mornings a week. After a horrible row last Thursday with Geoffrey I especially stayed at home the next day, missing a lecture, to ask her if she could come full time.' Ruth shook her head. 'She doesn't want to. She even intimated she wouldn't mind giving us up. "It's too much like 'ard work Mrs 'arrow, now that you are all day at the university." She wanted, nay expected, a clean house that she just had to wipe over – polish on top of polish, spruce on top of spruce. Now she has to get down to the basics. Anyway, my studies of Marx and Engels have shown me that cleaners are all wrong. I am having to rethink old attitudes.' Ruth smiled again and finished her coffee.

'And how does Mr Harrow like that?'

'Oh I would never mention Marx to either of the Messrs Harrow, nor to Mrs Simon Harrow. It is a word that would not pass my lips in their presence.'

Bella laughed and put a hand impulsively on Ruth's wrist. 'You know, you have a sense of humour. I only caught a glimpse of before.'

'No dear, I have become childlike. *Childish* according to Geoffrey. "You look like a teenager and behave like one." In his opinion Olivia is an improvement on a mother who has obviously entered her second childhood.' Ruth waved a hand at people passing. 'My philosophy class. We're doing Marcuse. My goodness he's difficult to understand.'

'But you like it?'

Ruth put her arms on the table and leaning on them stared at Bella. 'I love it. I am like someone who was dead and has been brought to life again. I didn't know it but now I do. I feel very very happy, stimulated and fulfilled. I only am sorry about the attitude of my family. They are making it very hard for me.' Ruth tucked her hair behind her ears and smoothed her hands down over her face. 'You see I do love them, Bella.'

'Of course.'

'But I'm making them unhappy. They are all seriously worried and disturbed.'

'Because their well ordered existence is threatened.'

115

'But isn't that my job? Aren't they maybe right? Geoffrey's point is I wanted domesticity from the beginning. And I did.'

'People can change.'

'He says he's never tied me down and has always given me what money I wanted. Never asked questions. It is quite true. He is the most bewildered of all. Olivia is resentful; Joe rather distant. George cares the least because he is not so well supervised as before. He rather likes that. But Geoffrey wants, metaphorically speaking, a warm fire to come home to, dinner on the table and slippers in the hearth. He is used to it. It is what he wants out of marriage and he misses it. Do you think he's right?'

Bella shrugged her shoulders. 'I can see his point of view now that you put it like that. It is as though he decided to stop being a lawyer and went on Safari to Outer Mongolia.'

'In a way,' Ruth nodded her head. 'Yes it's the same sort of thing. I have threatened our life style. Had I the right?'

'You're not having second thoughts? You're not going to leave?'

'Oh no, I'm not voicing doubts as serious as that, not yet; but I am questioning the morality of my behaviour. I am doing that. Antal said I would improve our marriage. I haven't. I certainly haven't.'

'When did Antal say that?'

'When we were talking about it at the Jubilee dance. I told him I'd had the interview with the Dean and still wasn't sure what to do. He said it would improve my marriage. I said it didn't need improving. That it was fine.'

'Is it not so fine now. Maritally speaking?'

Ruth raised an eyebrow. 'You mean sex? Well sex is sex. It's a habit; but I think our sex life certainly has deteriorated in the last couple of months. We don't do it twice a week regularly as we used to. For one thing I really do feel very tired. I am whacked at nights because after all I still cook when I get home even if not on a perfectly clean cooker. Sometimes I do most of the housework then too. The night Geoffrey and I had the blazing row I was making the beds; but that has improved. After a *conseil de guerre* it was decided the children should, rightly in my opinion, make their own beds and I would make ours.'

'You? Not Geoffrey?'

'Oh no. Not Geoffrey. Men's lib still reigns supreme at 45 Lawnside. Geoffrey will not make a bed or touch a dirty crock. It is not his place and never has been. He would rather die, so he informs me, than break such a time-honoured tradition. So our sex life is spasmodic and Geoffrey and I argue a lot. He complains and I make excuses. He's even started to eat at the Conservative Club. I bet there are a few tongues wagging at *that*.'

'I don't want your marriage to break up, Ruth,' Bella said solemnly look at her nails. 'I thought it was a good and a happy marriage. If I thought Antal's suggestion would really break up a home I would rather he had never made it.'

'Oh it won't break up our home.' Ruth laughed, checking the time again. 'At least I seriously hope it won't. But you know at the Jubilee party I would have said our marriage was as safe as a rock. Now I can't. I can see why marriages break up, and before I couldn't. I will try very hard for it not to flounder which is why I'm making adjustments. I'll go back into twin sets and pearls for the vacation, ensure we have a nice warm family Christmas and go regularly to the hairdresser. I will try and get daily help; but I am not going to give up my course or my life here, not unless I can see the marriage snapping in half. My mind wasn't being stimulated at all. I really had nothing with which to occupy myself except trivia. Of course I was very good at school, you know, and my tutor at Manchester University was horrified when I left. He even suggested an academic career, as though a First was a foregone conclusion. I don't know. We shall never know. I'm not sorry I married and had children or became part of the Edgerton community. I am sorry that I let it swamp me, the trivia of domestic routine, the coffee mornings, bridge parties, endless telephone conversations with "girl friends". That I'm sorry about, because I would have had a fuller life; but it is true that what you don't know you don't miss and, thanks to Antal, I found out in time. Thanks to my family too for making me feel so inadequate and therefore restless.'

'But Antal makes *me* feel useless too.' Bella cleared a space on the polished but stained table and studied what she could see of her reflection.

'But I thought . . .'

'Oh all that talk about my work? No, he makes me feel inadequate. I don't believe I've achieved anything. I was never domesticated, never interested in making a beautiful home. I thought it would all come naturally but it didn't. I learned nothing at boarding school and my mother, who was a university teacher all her life, of course never taught me though she did manage to run the house well. Mind you, you could get help in those days more easily. Of course I was passionately and wildly in love with Antal, the intriguing exile from Hungary and nothing like that mattered for some years. Then I realized he had other women and it did. I had small babies, a dirty house and nothing to do.'

'So you resumed your career?'

'Yes. Of course I had my degree. I took a doctorate. The whole place fell to pieces . . .'

'And the marriage?'

Bella looked thoughtful. Some sugar had spilled on the table and she started to play with it with her finger. 'Well that didn't fall to pieces at first.'

'You mean you didn't *mind* him having other women?'

'Oh no. I minded; but I tried not to know. I pretended he didn't and of course he always swore he didn't.'

'How did you know in the first place?'

'Oh I found a letter from a woman. He'd been very careless and just left it casually on our dressing table when cleaning out his pockets. Just like Antal! Too sure of his power. "It doesn't really matter if she does find it" would be his subconscious thought. He knew of his hold over me; strong bonds, strong sexual ties. I couldn't have given him up if he'd confessed to a thousand mistresses. But gradually I got worn at the edges like a well used woollen blanket. I became indifferent. My sexual urges diminished, which helped, and I was able to refuse him when I wanted to, knowing he wasn't completely dependent on me. I didn't feel I always had to please him. That was nice. I felt a lot freer.'

'Did you ever really talk about it?'

'The marriage?'

'The falling apart.'

'No. Some things are better not discussed. I thought if he wants a divorce, he'll ask for one. If he wants to marry someone else he'll tell me. But he didn't and he doesn't. It suits him, and it suits me. The children are O.K., two of them grown up. It's not ideal but it's how it is.'

'And sex. Do you ever have sex?'

Bella drew a pattern with the sugar. Her white face took on a slight tinge. 'Yes, occasionally.'

'Like us.'

'Oh no I would say not like you. Even if you don't do it regularly twice a week – "do it" is a horrible term don't you think but so is "have it"; "make love" is too serious to say all the time – I'm sure it is more often than us. I'm talking about a few times a year. I love him in a way, you know. We are very fond of each other. We are familiars. We can have sex if we want. We are much better alone than in company. We can talk and discuss things. I feel then I am an important person in Antal's life – someone who matters, to whom he gives attention. But when we are in public and he is so busy trying to impress the men and being charming to all the women I feel quite anonymous, an embarrassment. I am em-

119

barrassed. That's why I like to stay at home and why we so seldom go out to parties. I am absolutely at a loss in society.'

'We seem hardly to have seen you since the Jubilee. I think I've seen Antal about twice. I really must have a dinner party.'

'I don't think your husband likes him very much.'

Ruth returned her gaze. 'Why do you think that?'

'I can tell. He resents him. He tries to despise him because he is a foreigner, but he is jealous of his success with women. Antal likes you, for instance. It is obvious. He makes it very obvious when he likes someone. It doesn't mean he will go to bed with them, but he likes them and he shows it. Geoffrey is very English. He hates the continental charm.'

Ruth smiled. 'You're right; but then he has very little to do with him. I think Antal and Simon get on better.'

'But Simon is more of a womanizer, isn't he? He and Antal have more in common. Geoffrey is not a flirt; he does not have a "way with women".'

'He might if I go on like this.'

'I doubt it. I can see you looking at your watch.'

'Yes, I must go.'

Bella leaned back. 'I love the atmosphere here. It is an old place isn't it?'

'Its charter came from Henry VIII. But the new buildings are quite hideous and that is where I have my lectures.'

'No; they blend. They don't jar, on me anyway.' She collected her things together and then sat staring at Ruth unsmiling for some moments. 'I envy you, Ruth. I hope it works for you, this new experiment in living, I really do.'

10

As midnight struck for the end of the old year, the beginning of the new, Eunice raced to the front door and flung it open admitting a dark man.

'Welcome 1978!' she cried and threw her arms around his neck. Antal Lazar offered her a large piece of coal and she pretended to be horrified.

'The dark man always brings a piece of coal,' Antal said presenting it instead to Ruth who stood behind Eunice. 'It is lucky.'

'It is lucky I have a black dress on,' Ruth said taking the large shining object.

'Oh is mine marked?' Eunice looked at the front of her white dress embroidered with little pearls and sequins. She was a very good advertisement for her trade. She wore her beautiful dresses well. Frequently she only wore them once and then sold them at a fraction of their cost in her winter and summer sales. Eunice still had a hand on Antal Lazar's shoulder; it was an intimate gesture. Her arm seemed so comfortable and at ease there as though she were completely familiar with the contours of his sturdy frame.

'No there is not a trace of dirt on your beautiful dress.' Antal's tone was slightly mocking. 'It is as unmarked, as pure as your soul.' He looked at Ruth over Eunice's head and smiled.

'Mrs Harrow. I haven't seen you for months.'

'I didn't know you were coming tonight. Where's Bella?'

'In bed. She hates this kind of thing.'

'But you were expected?'

'Oh yes.' He pecked Eunice on the cheek. 'I am the dark stranger. It was all plotted beforehand.'

'But I didn't know he'd bring a piece of *coal!*' Eunice looked at her dress again in mock alarm and took Antal's hand. 'He is the spirit of New Year.'

'May it be a good one for you,' Antal murmured to Ruth and followed Eunice through the door into the lounge.

It was a rather drunken party. There had been dinner for the family beforehand, just the four Harrows and the two daughters of Simon and Eunice plus Paget's new fiancé, her second in a year. No one thought it would last, but Paget liked to be engaged. She didn't keep her fiancés long, but she made good use of them. This was her third one since she had turned eighteen, the previous year. Eunice had a strict rule that her daughters couldn't contemplate marriage before they attained their majority. Dorcas couldn't wait to be eighteen and get engaged.

This new fiancé of Paget's was a very nice, serious young man who happened to be a lecturer at the university. Paget liked serious men because she felt they made her seem not just a pretty face. She hoped it would just possibly indicate that she had brains too. Paget Harrow did in fact have brains but few people thought so; she concealed them well.

Her new fiancé, Dr Laurie Matrecht, lectured in French and Ruth vaguely knew him. She tried to put him at ease in the rather terrifying company that the Harrows had collected for their after dinner New Year party – several senior businessmen, assorted lawyers, accountants and doctors of varying degrees of eminence. The Pines, Lower Warford, was a very large house and up to fifty were assembled in the drawing room.

Eunice had been drinking all evening – sherry, champagne, more champagne. Her eyes glittered like small hard diamonds. Inside the drawing room everyone was singing 'Auld Lang

Syne' as Eunice ushered Antal Lazar in accompanied by the few that had followed her when the loud banging began on the front door.

'1978!' Eunice shouted waving her arms above her head after propelling Antal through. 'Welcome to 1978!'

The dancers broke formation to admit Antal, Eunice, Ruth and the others. Ruth found herself next to Laurie Matrecht. He still looked rather frightened. Paget was on the other side of the room, clasping hands firmly with two rather elderly but very rich clients of her father. She seemed to have forgotten all about him.

'Should auld acquaintance be forgot . . .' In and out the wobbly circle went, in and out. 'And never brought to . . .' More quickly in and out, in and out, forwards and backwards. 'Should auld acquaintance be forgot . . .' Now they rushed towards one another, the ring converging and merging and breaking away again. Ruth found herself momentarily eyeball to eyeball with Antal Lazar. He smiled at her. All she could see was his hand clasping Eunice's.

Afterwards corks popped, streamers were thrown and they all drank more champagne. Someone put all the lights out and there was a lot of scuffling and exclaiming. Then a small solitary light in the corner of the room came on. Someone tried to put it off, but the tall figure of Simon hovered protectively over it.

Geoffrey leaned heavily against Ruth, turning round and round in a slow shuffle, his hands linked round her back. His chin rested on her shoulder and his eyes were closed. She thought any moment he would start to snore. Her eyes roved among the couples. She knew what she was looking for and then she saw it. Eunice and Antal were draped round each other, stationary in a corner, engaged in a passionate embrace. Their bodies just swayed backwards and forwards to the music but their feet stayed still. Ruth almost stopped and Geoffrey opened his eyes.

'Christ, that bastard is kissing Eunice,' he muttered. 'If I was Simon I'd knock him down.'

'Simon is kissing Jordine Smith-Shaw,' Ruth said.

'Don't you think it's time I kissed you?' Geoffrey aggressively put his lips on hers, his mouth open, wet with saliva, reinforced by copious quantities of booze, so very wet. He stuck his tongue as far into her mouth as he could get and it swivelled round the inside of her cheeks. It wasn't a loving warm embrace, it was an aggressive assault, a demonstration of possessiveness.

'You're drunk,' she spluttered, pushing him away, his tongue still lolling out of his mouth. His eyes were wet and gleaming, his expression stupefied.

'I am *not* drunk,' he said trying to seize her. Rather than face a scene she submitted reluctantly to him, but kept her mouth closed tight. He pressed his loins against her. She knew that if he was capable he would want to make love when they got home, whenever that was. She suddenly hated the whole idea of New Year and parties, the false hilarity and fatuity of the whole thing. Geoffrey went to sleep again on her shoulder and they continued to shuffle round the room. Someone put the light in the corner off and someone else put it on again. It went on like that for some time.

'May I dance with your wife?'

Geoffrey started, his eyes focusing with difficulty.

'Oh s'you.' Geoffrey looked for a moment as though, in his bemused way, he was wondering whether he should hit Antal. In the end he clearly decided against it and lumbered away from Ruth leaving a clear field. She saw him slump onto a long sofa and put his head in his hands.

'I am not sure whether parties are a good thing when they get to this stage.' She slipped into Antal's arms as though he were a familiar. She felt his cool hand on her back and thought of Geoffrey's moist clammy one. It was really fantastic how

124

Antal managed to keep his cool, his poise and his head. Almost alone of all the men present he was not at all drunk.

'Unfortunately people always drink more than they need.' Antal steered her expertly between the lurching couples.

'Do you never?'

'Hardly ever.' Antal smiled at her. 'I like to know what I'm doing.' He came slightly nearer to her and she felt the pressure of his hand on her back. His evening dress was immaculate, his shirt still crisp and his tie dead centre. His hair was brushed straight off his brow and his smooth saturnine face managed to combine friendliness with an impression of mastery. She thought that he was very sure of himself. She had seldom known such a self-controlled man. He came even nearer and she saw the firm impress of his lips. As he was about to kiss her she tilted her head.

'Are you kissing all the women tonight?'

He gazed at her without smiling. 'All?'

'I thought you and Eunice were rather intimate.'

'Well if you include yourself that is only two. And I have not kissed you yet.'

She noticed the way he lingered on the word 'yet'.

'Are you having an affair with my sister-in-law?' She kept her voice muted, but her eyes on Antal's face so as not to lose any nuance of expression.

'If I were I would not say, and if I were not I would not admit it, in case you thought she had spurned me.'

'But you did try?'

'I think any man has a chance with any woman. Or do you not, Ruth?'

She didn't know how to answer that and as she was thinking of a reply he kissed her very gently. It was the merest touch, more a salute than a kiss. His lips were as she knew they would be – firm, sensual but very cool, like the rest of him. They were lips that made her want to give and to know

125

more; but she did not return their pressure and as he lifted his mouth he smiled.

'You can't blame me for trying.'

The music finished and there was a pause while someone changed the tape. Antal bowed and led Ruth back to where Geoffrey sat slumped on the sofa, his head back, his mouth open. She didn't know whether she felt spurned that he was returning her to her husband; she didn't really know how she felt or what she had expected.

'Thank you,' he whispered and merged into the gloom.

She sat beside Geoffrey's overweight clammy body thinking of Antal's cool slim one.

'I think we should go home.' She nudged Geoffrey but he slumped even further onto the sofa; a moment more and he would be on her shoulder. She got up and wandered over to the music centre and began sorting through the tapes.

'Dance, Mrs Harrow?'

She turned and saw Laurie Matrecht looking down at her, his arms slightly apart invitingly. She slid into them and he steered her into the throng.

'I hear you're at the university.'

'A mature student. I've attended some of your lectures on contemporary French philosophy. They were very good. The one on Camus was brilliant.'

'Are you doing philosophy?'

'Humanities, specializing in History. I took the first part of my degree nearly twenty years ago.'

He looked surprised. 'And since then?'

'I've been a wife and mother. You know I'm Paget's aunt by marriage?'

'Of course.' His tone of politeness altered and he looked rather anxious.

'How long have you known Paget?'

'Not long. About three months.'

'Only that long?'

'Maybe a bit more. We met at a party given by mutual friends, the Sunderlands. I just fell for her hook line and sinker.'

'Her looks *are* very striking,' Ruth said carefully. 'Both the girls look a lot like their mother.

'Oh Paget has great class. I think I am very lucky.'

He looked around; so did Ruth. She wondered where Paget was and why she wasn't dancing with her fiancé. Indeed he had spoken of her as though she were some sort of rather precious, slightly strange object – not a human being at all.

Suddenly there was a commotion at the far end of the room and the sound of breaking glass. The small light went off and the room was plunged in darkness. A woman screamed and the main light came on, harshly illuminating the chaotic scene around. Some couples were slumped together leaning on one another and some slowly gyrated. One or two were in frenzied activity on the chairs or sofas scattered about and now looked up sheepishly as the light came on. Several were asleep like Geoffrey, inert bodies stretched out. But in the corner by the music centre Simon Harrow had Antal Lazar by his immaculate tie, their chins almost touching. Paget Harrow huddled in the corner, her hands clasped anxiously in front of her, mascara streaked down her beautiful face – surely a rare sight.

'You leave my daughter alone, you lecherous swine. You've already kissed my wife *and* my sister-in-law this evening. Who's next, my *youngest* daughter?'

Simon towered over Antal. His teeth were bared in an ugly rictus. His grip of Antal's tie tightened. Antal regarded him with, in the circumstances, great poise, one hand trying unsuccessfully to dislodge Simon's from his tie. He was slowly turning puce and it was evident that the pressure on his wind pipe was increasing.

'Oh Simon, for Christ's sake.' Eunice moved swiftly across the room and seized her husband by the arm. 'This is a party, *our* party. You're insulting one of our guests.'

'He's insulting my family!' Simon roared. 'He's *molesting* them. I will not have this sort of intimate kissing going on in my home under my very eyes.'

Simon lurched and staggered and his grip suddenly relaxed. He was very drunk and the front of his shirt was wet. Eunice's mascara also was streaked and her blonde hair fell over her left eye. Her beautiful white dress was stained with red wine and it was doubtful whether it would appear in the sales at Chez Estelle that year. Eunice was drunk too, but with the controlled drunkenness of the practised inebriate. Antal carefully adjusted his tie, smoothed back his hair and straightened his jacket.

'Please forgive me. I am sorry if I gave offence. It was not my intention I assure you. I did not intend to insult the honour of your wife and daughter.'

'Or my sister-in-law,' Simon bellowed clearly beginning to lose his grip on himself.

'Of course.' Antal bowed. 'Nor her either. A good many kisses have been exchanged this evening Mr Harrow. I thought it was the custom.'

'Oh it *is* the custom,' Eunice said. 'Simon just doesn't like anyone doing it but him, do you darling?' Jordine Smith-Shaw had left with her husband Arthur ten minutes before. Eunice shaded her eyes as though the light was hurting. 'Oh for God's sake will someone switch off that main light . . .'

Someone switched it off obediently. Another came on by the window. Simon and Eunice stared at each other. Paget was wiping her mascara carefully with a lace handkerchief and looking about her.

'Excuse me.' Laurie Matrecht squeezed Ruth's hand and went quickly over to Paget who clasped him and burst into tears. He put his arms about her and looked as though he didn't know what to do next. Paget sobbed on his shoulder.

'I am sorry to have disturbed the evening and I will go.'

Antal bowed and made for the door but Eunice grabbed an arm and held him back.

'Not until Simon has apologized for disturbing your evening.

'Oh Eunice.' Antal's voice was deprecating, his eyes pleading. 'It is just a party, let's forget it.'

'No, I want Simon . . .' She linked her arm possessively with Antal's.

'Mummy, for God's sake . . .' Paget began to scream hysterically.

People moved further away from the protagonists as though fearful of becoming involved. It was impossible to tell what would happen.

Ruth looked at Geoffrey, the obvious person to help; but he was insensible. She turned off the cassette which all the time had been keeping a jarring background of discordant sound which proved remarkably suitable to the drama. She felt nervous and her hands were sweating. She wiped them on her handkerchief as she slowly walked across the room to the far corner. She spoke very gently as one does to frightened children or animals.

'I think this is all very silly and quite out of keeping with New Year. It has got out of hand. We have all had too much to drink and it is very late. It is nearly four. Please, Eunice don't insist . . .' She looked at her sister-in-law who, in turn, gaped at her; but she let go of Antal's arm. Antal straightened his jacket once again, his crumpled tie, and bowed to Ruth.

'Thank you, Ruth. That was well done. May I drive you and Geoffrey home?' She looked at Geoffrey who was snoring, his mouth open.

'I'll drive thank you Antal,' she said coolly, rather enjoying her role. 'It is only Geoffrey who has had too much to drink.'

'Then I'll say goodnight.' Antal smiled fleetingly at Ruth and Eunice, ignored Simon, and walked swiftly to the door.

Someone put on a tape again. Laurie began slowly to dance with Paget and Eunice turned her back on Simon. Ruth suddenly felt very tired and went over to shake Geoffrey. Simon saw them to the car, waving uncertainly as Ruth drove round the circular drive and out into the dark country road. Over in the east the sky was lighter, streaked by dawn.

On the whole the evening didn't seem a very promising start to the new year.

11

The Edgerton University Dramatic Society was split right down the middle in its selection of its summer production. It was a simple case of traditional versus modern. The traditionalists wanted to do *She Stoops To Conquer* and the modernists *Waiting For Godot.* It was felt by the committee that the Goldsmith comedy would attract a larger audience from among those worthy townsfolk of Edgerton who patronized the arts. The Society was always short of cash *ergo* the larger the audience the greater the takings. Sometimes, financial considerations had to take precedence over art. Tradition was the victor.

Ruth found herself cast as Mrs Hardcastle, a role she attributed to her age. Although most of the students knew she had teenage children they nevertheless behaved with cheerful informality and camaraderie towards her. Ruth realized that the difference between now and her undergraduate days was that youth today had no hidebound attitudes towards their elders, neither of respect nor of distance. If they mucked in they got on well, if they didn't they were ignored. They treated the staff the same as they treated themselves, and Ruth enjoyed the atmosphere. She knew that how she got on socially was up to her and had nothing to do with her age – except in the matter of casting. Along with certain other female members of the academic staff, she was always landed with the interesting 'character' parts.

Ruth had occasionally seen Laurie Matrecht since the

terrible New Year's Eve party, usually from a distance to wave. Now he was cast as Tony Lumpkin and she found herself seated next to him at the first read-through of the play. She kept on looking at him surreptitiously; she wasn't even sure if he was still engaged to Paget.

'Are you a regular member of the dram soc?' Ruth said as the cast put down their scripts and relaxed at the end of the reading.

'Oh yes. I think I'm a bit old for Tony Lumpkin though. I should have been Mr Hardcastle.' He smiled at her. 'Care for a coffee?'

'I'd love it.' She took off her glasses and put them in her briefcase together with the copy of the play. The briefcase had been Geoffrey's Christmas present. It was very sleek, made of the best calf with her initials engraved in gold. She really preferred to dump her books and papers in a large bag where she could also carry make up and her purse; but she didn't want to offend Geoffrey by not using the briefcase. She slung her coat around her shoulders and crossed the quadrangle with Laurie Matrecht to the canteen in the new building.

For a while they talked about the play and the work she was doing. They enthused about Camus and Sartre, Ruth with more qualifications about the latter.

'You surprise me for a mature student, Mrs Harrow.'

'Oh do call me Ruth. Why do I surprise you?'

'I would have thought you belonged to the Edgerton social set, like your sister-in-law.'

'Well you can belong to the social set and be a student you know; but I do very little socializing now, not nearly as much as I used to. I simply haven't the time.'

'It must have made a big change to your life.'

'It has; but it was worth it.'

'Didn't your husband mind?'

'*Didn't?*' Ruth gave an ironic smile. 'Does.'

'He still minds?'

'Oh yes. I've many times thought of giving it up. At first I was so engrossed I rather neglected the family. Now things are better. I am more organized. At first it was a strange new life; but I have to remember I'm a wife and mother *and* a housekeeper as well. That kind of thing doesn't change. It goes on. Everyone has been thrown more on their own. They don't really like it.'

'But you won't give up?' Laurie stirred his coffee and looked at her. She thought he was about thirty. He had blond crinkly hair and a very young face which looked beardless but wasn't. It simply didn't show and his skin was very fair with pink cheeks.

'I suppose your family came from Holland?' Ruth sipped her coffee and bit into a Kit-Kat. She'd had no time for breakfast.

'Belgium. My grandfather was a Belgian. My father settled in England after the war. He married an Englishwoman who'd been in the WAAF. Belgium was in a bad way after the war and her father employed him. Furniture. Doing quite well.'

'To return to your question,' Ruth said carefully. 'I don't think I'll give it up; but if my results at the end of the year aren't good enough I might. I can only justify this sacrifice if I get a first. I'd rather like an academic life. I don't just want to get my degree and then return to bridge afternoons. I want to change my life. Are you still engaged to Paget, by the way? I'm afraid I hardly see Eunice these days.'

'Yes. Just.' Laurie's expression looked pained.

'It doesn't sound very hopeful.'

'I don't think it is. I didn't realize Paget collected fiancés. I'm the third.'

'I know.' Ruth tried to compose her features into an expression of sympathetic detachment.

'I don't think she's serious about marriage. I think she thinks having a fiancé makes sex legal.'

Ruth felt herself start. She hadn't thought of sex. To her

Paget was still a young girl like Olivia and she couldn't imagine her daughter having sex for a long time. The thought was repugnant to her. Paget by now was probably quite experienced. Ruth wondered if Eunice knew.

'We cooled a bit after the New Year party,' Laurie went on. 'I'd seen her kissing that bloke too and it was all I could do to control myself. She said it was to make me jealous; but I regard that kind of behaviour as childish.'

'Yes I'd never have thought you were going through an emotional strain when you danced with me.'

'It helped me discipline my thoughts and emotions.'

'You *are* a philosopher.'

'What is the use lecturing if we don't try and practise what we preach? Paget says her mother is having an affair with that fellow.'

Ruth kept her eyes on the rim of her cup and she felt her pulse quicken. She counted up to ten and then spoke very slowly. 'Antal Lazar?'

'The one who caused all the fuss. That Hungarian fellow. I'm sorry if I've goofed. I thought all the family probably knew. She says her father has affairs too. She's quite used to this sort of carry on, apparently, and I think that's what makes her so casual about her relationships with men. I shouldn't think our engagement will last the summer, but I like going to bed with her and if being a fiancé is a condition I'll stay affianced. I hope I'm not offending you.'

'Not at all.' Ruth glanced at her watch. 'Oh dear, I have a class.'

'I don't really like Mrs Harrow very much, Eunice that is. I think she's terribly superficial and one sees it in her children. That's why you are such a refreshing surprise.'

Ruth got up and fumbled under the table for her bag and briefcase. She felt embarrassed.

'I'm not the family though, not a real Harrow. Sometimes I think that is an advantage. Thanks for the coffee, Laurie.

I'll see you at the next rehearsal.'

Laurie stood up as she left. He had lovely manners; but she doubted whether that aspect of him would appeal to Paget Harrow.

Geoffrey's body had gone very heavy as it did after they had made love. Sometimes she felt she could hardly breathe as he lay on her, and she shifted so that the pressure was off her heart. Geoffrey's head hung limply over her shoulder and he gave little snores. She began to wriggle from under him and then he lurched over and fell onto his side of the bed. She reached for a tissue and wiped herself. Then she put her hands under her head and stared through the darkness to the top of the window where the street lamp showed above the curtains.

Their love life was very poor. She hadn't had an orgasm for weeks. Geoffrey really didn't seem so concerned about pleasing her any more. He didn't try to arouse her sufficiently and then he completed when he felt like it whether she had or not. She didn't know whether he assumed that she did have a climax or whether he simply wasn't very interested. It had not always been that way. She would have called Geoffrey a tender, considerate lover; but since their marriage it had not changed much – neither better nor worse. Now since October it was worse.

It had started to deteriorate when she went to the university. But why? She was still a woman; she still felt the need for sex even though she had attained her thirty-seventh birthday and by some people's standards was past it. Only she didn't enjoy it very much with Geoffrey any more. She turned on the lamp at her side of the bed and went to the lavatory. Then she washed herself and put on her nightie. She went back into the bedroom and smoothed moisturizer on her face. It was one o'clock and she was going to be terribly tired the next day.

135

Nowadays she wanted to go to bed with a book at ten and lights out at eleven. She didn't want Geoffrey to start groping for her once the light was out. She didn't feel strong enough to refuse him. Because of the guilt she felt about going to the university she felt she had to placate him as much as she could. But when she wasn't aroused or stimulated she felt irritated and she wished he would get it over with. What puzzled her was that he didn't seem to notice her lack of response. Or did he?

But in the morning Geoffrey groped for her again.

'Oh no,' she said and swung her legs out of bed.

'Oh Christ, you *are* my wife!'

'But it's nice when I feel like it too and I don't now. It is nearly seven. I've had six hours' sleep and that's not enough. I have a tutorial at nine-thirty and two lectures during the day as well as a rehearsal for *She Stoops*. I don't feel like sex and that's it. I'm sorry, Geoffrey.' She had made her stand, at last. A kind of desperation drove her to it. It had nothing to do with being a good wife; she was exhausted.

'I'm sorry too.'

She could see his hand moving under the bedclothes and reckoned he was trying to soothe his irritated and aroused member. She thought it was too bad that men woke up in the morning with erections. It really was their bad luck. She went to the Teasmade and put it on. The alarm had not been due to go off for half an hour. She'd lost half an hour's sleep. A nice half-hour for them to make love, Geoffrey had probably thought. She brushed her teeth, made the tea and brought it back to bed. She passed Geoffrey his cup. She put on her glasses and picked up a volume of Comte. She was getting very interested in sociology.

Geoffrey's hand strayed over to her crotch. He looked up at her appealingly, like a small boy who is being winsome in order to get a favour.

'I said no. I'm sorry, but no.'

'But why?'

'Because I don't feel like it.'

'That doesn't seem to stop you these days.' So he had noticed. She stared over her glasses at the drawn curtains. It was already quite light outside. 'Everything has gone to pot since you went to the damn university – our sex life, our home life, our relationship, our marriage if you ask me. It's all going down the drain.'

'That's an exaggeration. It might have gone anyway.'

'Why should it?'

'You found me conventional and boring. You said so. If I hadn't done this I might have just got worse – more conventional, more boring.'

'I think what you're reading is very dull.' He sat up and sipped his tea glancing at the running head of the book she was reading. 'What the hell is logical positivism? You think philosophy helps to save a marriage?' He had no pyjamas on and the hair hung damply from under his armpits. His chest was flabby and he almost had small breasts covered very obscenely with matted greying hair. The hair in his groin was thick and black and would now be rather smelly. He hadn't washed since making love the night before and now he wanted to do it again. She shuddered involuntarily. Yet she had always thought of Geoffrey as a rather fastidious man. Or had that been when she saw him with different eyes? When she didn't care if he washed or not because she loved him so much she couldn't remember even noticing? Now she noticed these things all the time. Had she fallen out of love with Geoffrey? The thought made her pause. She removed her glasses and her book lay on her lap. Geoffrey got out of bed and went to the bathroom. The noise he made sounded like a waterfall. She realized that all his bodily functions were beginning to disgust her. She was looking at him critically all the time, no longer with the eye of love which is blind to these things.

It was the same at breakfast. He ate too quickly, one eye on the clock. He stuffed his toast into his mouth and washed it down with the coffee. She had always taught the children that they shouldn't eat and drink at the same time; but she'd never thought of whether Geoffrey did or not. Surely he hadn't? She'd never observed him as closely as she did now, not just in food and sex and going to the lavatory; but in everything he did. Geoffrey had changed. Or was it she? He pecked her on the cheek, grabbed his half read copy of *The Times* and went out of the kitchen telling George to hurry up or he'd be late for school.

George looked under the weather. His eyes were red and he sniffed a lot. Altogether he appeared low and dejected.

'George, are you all right?'

Ruth felt a tremor of unease. She had such a busy fortnight ahead with rehearsals and work. She couldn't afford to take time off if George came down with the flu.

'I'm fine,' George mumbled, finished his orange juice and slunk out of the kitchen wiping his nose on the back of his hand.

Ruth restrained her criticism and instead looked witheringly at his back. She sighed and poured herself another cup of coffee. 'More coffee?' she said to Olivia.

Olivia shook her head; she seemed to be engaged in some inward wrestling match and Ruth decided it was now her daughter's turn to be the object of her concern.

Olivia was getting more womanly, prettier; her breasts were fully developed. Ruth realized with a shock that she hardly ever looked carefully at her daughter. The same way she hardly seemed to look at her husband. Or was it that people with whom one lived changed so subtly from hour to hour, day to day that the process was immeasurable? Olivia had Ruth's thick auburn hair and her peach complexion, but large amber coloured eyes. She looked very much like Ruth had at her age except that she was more sophisticated, more assured.

Ruth at fifteen had been the complete schoolgirl, Olivia was a young woman. Olivia was hugging her cup, her elbows resting on the table. Her pretty mouth was transformed into ugliness by a downward turn.

'Darling, are *you* all right?' Ruth tried to keep the note of exasperation out of her voice. She looked at the clock. If she didn't hurry up she'd be late for her nine-thirty lecture. Olivia was the last child to leave home because she walked to school. Joe left early on his bike – he was furthest away, and Geoffrey gave George a lift because the comp was near his office.

'It's about time you noticed me, mother. And George has been looking peaky for ages.'

'And have you been looking so bad tempered and sulky?'

'It is true, mother, you don't notice us any more.'

Ruth noticed with concern that Olivia's voice was shaky, her expression that of one close to tears. The inner crisis with which she had been so obviously struggling was at hand.

'I hadn't noticed being called "mother" either. It has always been "Mummy".'

'Oh "Mummy" is so babyish.'

'But it is still "Daddy" and not "Father".'

'That seems right somehow.'

Ruth gulped her coffee; it was too hot and scalded her throat. Tears came into her eyes and she blinked them away in case Olivia thought they were because of her.

'Darling, are we going to have a scene?' Ruth glanced at her watch. 'If so . . .'

' "Could it be another day?" Is that what you are going to say, Mummy.' The formal 'mother' was dropped and Olivia spoke from the heart, her voice ringing with passion. 'Because you are busy. Because you have a lecture and a rehearsal and a tutorial and Christ, Mummy, I never ever thought you'd be like a schoolgirl again. *She Stoops To Conquer!* What an idiotic play! Now if you did Pinter or Eliot or even Anouilh; but *Goldsmith.* What sort of relevance to today has

139

that for Christ's sake? It's your second childhood. I thought you were going to university to progress? You're going back, Mummy, back all the time.'

'Is it just the play that irritates you?' Ruth knew her voice was hoarse, was aware of the slow even beat of her heart. She clasped her cup and gazed at her wedding ring. She hardly ever wore jewellery these days except for that. The gold was rather dulled after seventeen years. She scarcely ever took it off. In fact she doubted if she could. She put down her cup and started to twist it off her finger.

'It is everything that irritates me.' Olivia, visibly trembling now, seized a spoon and started bending it. Ruth was grateful it was one of the kitchen spoons. Still it was symptomatic. It bent quite easily. It would soon break at the rate Olivia was going. 'There has been a terrible atmosphere in this house ever since you started this university nonsense. And I do think it is nonsense, Mummy! I think it is childish. We spend all our childhood wanting to grow up, to be like our mothers and fathers, to have their status and their privileges and then we see our mother become like one of us again.'

'I didn't realize you felt so badly about it. You never said.'

'How could I say it? What could I say? We tried to say it all before you went. We protested strongly enough didn't we, Mummy?'

'Yes, you did; but I felt I had a right to my own life. Not so long ago you were telling me about all the girls whose mothers went out to work. The successful psychiatrists and dentists, the mothers who had jobs in shops and offices.'

'That was different,' Olivia looked sulky and ran a finger along the kitchen table.

'I don't see how. Oh I think I do; you mean they already had careers, status, they didn't make fools of themselves prancing around in jeans and tee shirts and carrying text books? If *I* was turned out as a perfectly respectable teacher that wouldn't be too bad, would it?'

140

'It just seems unnatural, for you. It doesn't seem to suit you; I can't explain really. The other life was *you*. What was wrong with it? You had everything you could possibly want; your own bank account . . .'

Ruth raised her eyebrows. 'Oh I think this part of the conversation could only have been had in connivance with your father. Is it all planned?'

'Of course it's not *planned*,' Olivia snapped. 'But Daddy and I have discussed it. Of course we have. We had lunch together the other day and he said he was utterly bewildered. He said it was as though you had decided to leave the home without letting us know why or what we had done wrong.'

'But you've done nothing wrong! That's ridiculous. It was simply . . .'

'Daddy said the Lazars influence you too much. Not only you, Mummy. I think Christopher is the reason George looks so peaky and as for that Irena . . .'

'What about Irena? You never go out with her do you?'

'*I* don't.' Olivia leaned heavily on the pronoun and raised her eyes expressively.

'Well then . . .'

'*I* don't. You should get that.'

'You mean *Joe* sees Irena?'

'Of course.'

'Why of course?' Ruth began to feel close to panic.

'It is just another of the things you never notice. That your own son is sleeping with the girl next door.'

'Olivia!' Ruth's heart began to pound and she sat back. 'Oh that's never . . .'

'It is.'

'But she is only sixteen.'

'I don't care how old she is. And he's not her first boy, either.'

'But how do you know all this?'

'Everyone knows, except you.'

'But how?'

'The boys pass contraceptives around; they tell one another where to get them. I've seen contraceptives in Joe's drawers.'

'You've *looked* in Joe's drawers.'

'Yes. I heard that he had them and of course I couldn't ask him. So I looked. He has a packet of de luxe silk Durex under his shirts in the bottom drawer. Go and see.'

'I take your word for it. I don't know what to say.' Joe; to her the idea was horrifying. Joe sleeping with Irena Lazar! 'When do they get the opportunity?'

'When do you think? When you're at university.'

'You mean they do it *here!*'

'Yes. In his room. They dash home from school and . . .'

'Oh please Olivia, spare me the details. I shall have to talk to your father about this at once!'

'Yes, but what can you *do*, mother? How can you stop them? There'll be the most awful fuss, and in the end everyone will blame you because they'll say you should have kept an eye on your children instead of prancing through *She Stoops To Conquer.*'

Ruth got up and went to the emergency packet of cigarettes that stood on the dresser. Unsteadily she lit one and as she drew on it her heart raced even faster. She felt quite lightheaded and thought again about the Pill. She really should stop using it. When she turned round Olivia was gazing at her with a cynical detachment as though enjoying every minute of what she was doing.

'You're going to be late for school,' Ruth said. 'We'll have to talk about this again. I feel I must have time to think.'

Olivia got up without a word and with the same self-satisfied smirk went out of the kitchen. She banged the front door as she left and Ruth put her head in her hands and lay like that for some time on the kitchen table.

12

Yes, *She Stoops To Conquer* did seem a very silly play, quite out of touch with reality. As the rehearsal progressed Ruth remembered Olivia's words and she saw herself as a sad, ridiculous figure trying to recapture her lost youth, as relevant to the present age as Goldsmith. She thought about the contraceptives which were under Joe's shirts, and she thought of her son making love to the girl next door in his own home while his mother was cavorting in the great hall of the university pretending she was young again.

'You seem very out of sorts today.' Laurie Matrecht put a hand lightly on her shoulder in an intimate gesture when the rehearsal was over.

'She even forgot her lines.' Janet Harrison, the play's producer, started picking up discarded scripts. The rest of the cast had dispersed.

'Let's have a drink in my room,' Laurie suggested. Ruth looked at her watch. If she went home now she might catch Joe and Irena together. Did she want to?

'Let's have a drink,' she said.

She liked Janet Harrison, a maths lecturer of about her own age; the sort of woman she would never have known but for becoming a student again. A clever, intelligent, pretty woman who was married but had no children. Her husband was a consultant at the hospital.

Janet looked tired; she was putting every effort into the play and had not wanted to do it in the first place. She had been firmly on the side of Becket. Janet was the sort who would have put her contraceptive problems in order a long time ago, Ruth thought. And if she had a son she would certainly know what to do about his sex life.

'It is going well.' Janet accepted a sherry from Laurie when they were settled in his room at the back of the old building. 'You have a gift for comedy, Ruth.'

Ruth gave an ironical laugh which made the other two look at her. 'Sorry,' she said. 'It's just that . . . oh skip it.' She toasted them with the sherry. 'To *She Stoops*. May it be successful. My last performance here, I'm afraid.'

'What do you mean?' Janet sat next to her on Laurie's comfortable leather sofa and crossed her legs.

'I am going to pack it in.'

'Pack what in?'

'The whole thing. The university. I may not even take my exams in the summer.'

'But why on earth . . .' Laurie came over to her and refilled her glass. 'I think I know. It's the family. Right?'

'Right.' Ruth's voice, she knew, was flat and hopeless.

'What is it now? General disapproval?'

'No. My son who is only seventeen is sleeping with the daughter of our neighbour. It's very hard for me to take.'

'But what is your being here to do with that? I don't understand.' Janet moved supportively closer to her. 'Isn't it the sort of thing all young people are doing these days?'

'Is it?' Ruth stared at her. 'Is it really as common as that when they are so young?'

Janet shrugged and glanced at Laurie. 'Well they're all at it here.'

'Yes, but . . .' Ruth put a hand on her brow. 'I don't know. Maybe it is because he is *my* son; but it seems so awful at his age. I simply can't take it in.'

'You only just found out?' Janet lowered her voice in sympathy.

'My daughter told me. It was part of the continuing lecture she gives me about my childish behaviour whenever she gets the chance. The home is going to pot; my son has sex when we are out. My husband eats at his club. I held the house together and now it has fallen apart. I suppose they're right.'

'Oh that *is* absurd.' Janet made an impatient gesture. 'Many many women have families and careers. I have no children but we have a largish house. John likes to entertain a lot.'

'Yes but you've always done it,' Ruth explained as patiently as she could. 'For donkey's years I was the door stop, or perhaps the cornerstone would be more flattering. The prop of the family.'

'But your son might have gone to bed with the girl next door whether you were out or not. They always find a way.'

'I suppose so. But if I can explain it to you, it is *all* part of the same thing. My family simply do not understand. They do not accept it. My marriage has suffered and my children are resentful. I no longer feel I love my husband as much as I did. I am always finding fault with him, in my mind comparing him unfavourably with other men.' In her mind's eye she saw Antal Lazar. The Lazars seemed at the bottom of everything that had gone wrong; but, yes, she did compare Geoffrey with Antal and she did blame Irena rather than Joe for what had happened. 'It is too late to change your life when people still depend on you. I just haven't successfully made the adjustment. If I had been cleverer I might have; but I didn't have enough foresight.'

'You're certainly clever.' Janet finished her sherry. 'I hear glowing reports of you at staff meetings. I think you'd be awfully silly, Ruth. Try and persuade her not to, Laurie. After all you are peripherally one of the family.'

'Is he still engaged to Paget?' Ruth said with mock levity. 'Good Lord!'

'Believe it or not I think she is going to marry me.' Laurie smiled. 'It is real love, at last.'

'Oh I'm delighted, Laurie.' Ruth made an effort to sound sincere. 'She would be very lucky.'

'I'm lucky too.' Laurie looked happy. 'I happen to love her; whether I love her mother is another thing, but I'll get used to her.'

'You're not marrying her mother, as the comedians say.' Janet began getting her things together. 'But if you really are going to marry a Harrow you must exercise your influence on Ruth to complete her degree.'

'There is little I can do.' Laurie avoided Ruth's eyes. 'I don't know her husband terribly well. I don't know how he took the news about Joe.'

'He doesn't know. I only found out myself today. I just don't know how I can tell him. He will condemn me, you see. He will say it is my fault. It will be another thing to blame me for.'

'Of *course* it's not your fault darling.' Geoffrey sat on the edge of the bed looking troubled but calm. The sight of his sturdy, familiar, comforting face nearly brought tears to Ruth's eyes and she sat next to him. He put his arm round her waist and pressed her.

'I just didn't have the courage to tell you.'

'But how long have you known?'

'Olivia told me one day last week. It's been hell keeping it to myself.'

Geoffrey tenderly kissed her cheek. She was trembling.

'It shows how far apart we've grown; that you found it so hard to tell me. It makes me feel bad that I haven't tried to understand you better.'

'Oh Geoffrey, if you go on like that I will cry.'

'No, it's true.' Geoffrey got up and padded across the bedroom to get a cigarette. He looked like a comfortable teddy bear with his loose pyjamas flapping about him, his hair ruffled and sticking up from his shiny, bald pate in wisps. He exhaled smoke and came back to the bed. 'You know I've shut my eyes to a lot of things too. I've just thrown myself in work, jobs of all kinds, committees on this, that and the other. Why do I do it? It certainly wasn't because of you. I did it long before we had this university business.'

'Maybe you haven't been really happy at home for a long time.'

'Of course I have! What more can a man have wanted? So why did I do it? Why *do* I do it, because I know I will go on. Is it to be self-important? Is it to have power? Why is it?'

Ruth shook her head. This introspection was unusual in Geoffrey. 'I do think you do have a strong sense of duty. It is important to you to be of use to the community, help it to run.'

'Yes but I don't drag myself about reluctantly. I *like* doing it. I thrive on it. Yet I didn't see my wife was restless and unhappy, and my son ready to fall into bed with the first girl who was willing.'

'I'm glad you're being like this,' Ruth sniffed in self pity. 'It does help a lot. I felt *I'd* failed.'

'Why you? If anyone has failed we both have, if it is failure. I don't know. I just don't understand people today. I don't think anything could have interested me less at the age of seventeen – Christ *seventeen!* – than going to bed with a girl. I just never gave it a thought. Now it's all over the place; on the telly, in the newspapers. You can't begin young enough and you're too old at thirty. He probably thought he was an awful failure unless he did. But there is one thing, Ruth.' Geoffrey looked at her gravely shaking his head. 'It can't go on. It will have to stop. Now that we know we simply cannot allow it to continue. It's absolutely out of the question. We can't condone this kind of thing. We can't.'

'What can we do, short of moving?'

'Well if we must, then we must move.' He kissed her and

his lips moved from her cheek to her mouth. 'I do fancy you you know,' he murmured.

Antal Lazar looked casually elegant. He had a white polo neck sweater and well pressed grey flannels with the creases dead centre. He was freshly shaved and smelt of some pleasing, masculine after shave lotion. Somehow he looked out of place in this comfortable, but untidy, sitting room with the deep, well worn armchairs and sofa, the coffee table stained with cigarette burns, the papers tossed casually on the floor. He didn't seem at home here; a man who didn't belong. Yet nor did he seem a visitor like them; he fitted and he didn't fit. He kept looking at the door as though any moment he would have to leave. Ruth decided he was a very restless, unsettled man; no wonder he unsettled everyone else.

Bella sat curled up in a chair, self-effacing as usual whenever Antal was around, head in the Sunday paper as though the proceedings didn't concern her at all.

Geoffrey, wearing a casual shirt and jeans, took the whisky Antal held out and lifted his glass. He looked like some sort of overworked, overfed lumberjack with his red face and strands of his thinning hair drifting untidily over his brow. He was sweating again, whether with heat, nerves or an incipient heart attack Ruth didn't know. Inevitably he was puffing at a cigarette. His life was in danger and hers hung by a thread so long as she persisted with the Pill. And now that their children were beginning to go off the rails what on earth was going to happen to them all? Visions loomed of a FOR SALE notice outside 45 Lawnside.

'Well we called this pow-wow,' Geoffrey thrust out his stomach, 'because we have some disquieting news. Ruth wanted to have a quiet chat with Bella but I thought we should all be in on it, as parents.'

'I *thought* it was to do with the children.' Bella sighed and turned the pages of the *Sunday Times*.

'Do sit down, Geoffrey.' Antal indicated a leather chair. 'Sure you won't drink, Ruth?'

Ruth shook her head.

'Now what is it about the children?' Antal sat down and folded his hands into a church steeple, the two forefingers going up and down. He looked grave and thoughtful; the concerned – but at the same time vaguely uninterested – parent.

'Well I'm afraid it concerns Joe and your Irena. It appears they are sleeping together.'

Bella put down the *Sunday Times* and took up *The Observer*. Ruth couldn't decide whether it was a sign of unconcern or despair. One thing good about Geoffrey was that he came straight to the point. His training as a lawyer was an asset in this sort of situation. No beating about the bush.

'I thought as much,' Bella said from behind *The Observer*. 'They're always together.'

'Mmm,' Antal went on looking thoughtful, his brow puckered by a slight frown. He glanced at his watch, then at the door. 'How did you discover this?'

'My daughter told me. It is common knowledge.'

'Had you any idea, Bella?' Antal's tone was impatient, authoritative. 'Really my dear, I do wish you'd put the paper down. You'd think you had news of this nature every day.'

'Olivia said that Irena *had* had experience,' Ruth said in a level voice.

'Oh I see, *she* is supposed to have seduced Joe?' Antal's tone was hostile.

'No one is casting any blame,' Geoffrey interrupted smoothly. 'It is not a question of who is at fault, but of what are we to do?'

'I suppose it *is* true?' Ruth looked at Bella still casually flicking over the pages of *The Observer*.

149

'What do you mean, "is it true"?'

'It sounds like hearsay to me. Did anyone ask Joe or Irena? Well look at this, for heaven's sake,' she said staring at the page in front of her. 'The European Court of Human Rights has ruled against birching in the Isle of Man. Why don't they do it in England too? Corporal punishment is still permitted in the schools of this country.'

'Bella, do let's keep to the point,' Antal said curtly. 'I think it is a very good point that you make, by the way – not about using the cane. *Did* anyone ask Joe or Irena? After all Geoffrey, as the legal man you should be sure of your facts.'

'But I am sure. That is . . . I was *presuming* Olivia knew what she was saying was the truth. She says they come back to our house and make love after school.'

'Has she seen them?'

Bella put *The Observer* down and picked up the colour supplement.

'Oh Bella you're being obstructive.' Geoffrey glanced at Ruth for support. 'If you imagine your little girl can't . . .

'I think my little girl *is* perfectly capable of it, and your little boy for that matter – much as Ruth might not like to admit it. But, *do* they? As an empiricist I feel they should be asked before we decide what to do about it.'

Bella threw the paper aside and sat nervously on the edge of the chair. 'Do you know, Antal, I think I'll have a drink?'

'A drink?' Antal stared at her. 'I don't recall you drinking alcohol for years.'

'I haven't; but I will now. Maybe I am at a stage in life where I shall need alcohol for support.'

'You mean you need a drink to ask Irena if she is sleeping with Joe?'

'I?' Bella stared at her husband. '*I* am not asking her. You know that Irena and I can't talk about things like that. With my elder daughter it is possible; but with Irena, no.'

'But I can't ask her.'

'Why not? Oh I see you feel the same too, do you? Well I certainly am not, and that is that.'

'And I can't.'

There was a pause while Antal hurriedly poured drinks. Ruth was gazing at Bella who stared at the floor and Geoffrey did his caged lion act by the window, pacing back and forth.

'We shall simply have to ask Joe. I can talk to Joe man to man.'

'Excellent.' Antal gave Bella a very small whisky and smiled at her as a doctor might possibly smile at an anxious, fragile patient.

'I would like to talk to Joe too.' Ruth balanced her tone of voice carefully. 'I want to know the truth.'

'But I can get that for you, dear.'

'I want to see Joe's face. Besides I believe that this thing should be shared between parents.'

'Oh really,' Geoffrey said tetchily. 'This women's lib thing is ridiculous.'

'It's nothing to do with women's lib.' Ruth stared angrily at Geoffrey. 'It is to do with my rights as a mother.'

Bella gave a shout of laughter and leapt up from the chair. She was wearing denim dungarees and one of her husband's old shirts. She wore no make up and a large man's wrist watch. Again Ruth was reminded of a young-looking middle aged man.

'It seems that you want to assert your rights as parents and we want to avoid them.'

'I do not want to shirk my rights or duties,' Antal said equably, looking at Ruth. 'But I don't think that to question my daughter about her sex life is my duty, or my right.'

'You think a sixteen-year-old girl should do as she pleases?'

'To answer your question,' Antal said with the manner of one choosing his words with care. 'I do think that, whether we like it or not, a sixteen-year-old girl does have a sex life, or the potential for one. She is a fully mature woman and in some countries well into marriageable age. Whether she should exercise this inborn facility is something I do not feel qualified, as a man or a parent, to answer.'

'Which is why he doesn't want to talk to her,' Bella said. 'He doesn't know his own mind.'

'It's not at all the same kind of thing. I do wish you'd shut up.'

Antal's tone was unabashedly rude and it surprised Ruth who decided she liked him less than ever. She couldn't deny his vast attractiveness; but he wasn't a nice man. She knew that now. He was dangerous. Danger Man.

Bella was obviously used to this sort of treatment because she didn't seem perturbed by it. She clumsily bent towards the floor to get the papers together and hugged them to her chest.

'I think that's as far as we can go now before we start to hit one another. This is an emotive subject. Neither of us is going to talk to Irena, and both of you are going to talk to Joe.'

'Well what do we do *then?*' Geoffrey stuck his hands in his pockets and thrust out his stomach. It really was large.

'I don't think we can decide until we know,' Bella said. 'And I don't know what we can do about it then.'

Joe's pale face was very pink and he kept licking his lips. Ruth thought he looked very guilty indeed, yet he denied it. She let Geoffrey do the talking while she sat at the back of the room longing for a cigarette. Geoffrey smoked non-stop.

'Then why do you have the contraceptives?'

Joe went even redder and blinked rapidly several times, his tongue going more quickly over his lips. 'Oh Dad. Christ, I'll kill Olivia. Rummaging through my drawers.'

'It was rather an extraordinary thing to do.' Ruth spoke for the first time, trying to impress them both with the extent of her calm. 'But it is a separate issue which we shall have to take up with her. But still you do have the contraceptives?'

'Yes.' Joe glared at her. She thought her presence had, after all, made her son more hostile. It was so difficult to know what to do for the best. He resented her. She should have let Geoffrey do it; yet she wanted to be involved, to *know*.

'Then why should you get contraceptives . . .' Geoffrey looked genuinely puzzled.

'Because Dad in *case* . . .' Joe began with exaggerated patience. 'All the boys have them. We do this heavy petting and who knows? We've all had sex instruction at school, you know. If Irena had been willing well . . .' Joe lowered his eyes. Ruth thought they were full of tears. Was he ashamed or embarrassed? He didn't want his mother at a moment like this and she shouldn't have intruded. It was a matter for father and son. For men.

'I think that's very sensible.' Geoffrey cleared his throat in a hearty manner, the lawyer successfully concluding a case. 'Very sensible indeed, don't you Ruth?'

'I don't know what to say.' Ruth plucked at her skirt and fiddled with her pearls. In her role of pained mother it had been definitely a twin set and pearls occasion. 'I suppose you are telling the truth?'

'Of course he's telling the truth.' Geoffrey began to go red and stumped out his cigarette. 'Christ what do you *want* to believe Ruth? The boy is telling the truth. He is being rational and sensible.'

'But he still might have sex with her at any time, if the opportunity presents itself. It is only Irena's refusal that stops him. It's the same thing.'

'It isn't!' Geoffrey snapped. 'It is *not* the same thing at all. The relationship has not advanced that far and I am going to ask Joe to promise me that it won't. You do see, Joe, don't you, what an awkward state of affairs it would lead to? We just can't have you sleeping with the girl next door. It would completely alter our relationship with the Lazars. Can't you see that?'

Geoffrey was very reasonable, man to man. Every inch the father, the caring, concerned parent, the lawyer, man of affairs, treasurer of the Conservative Party.

'Yes Dad, I do see.' Joe looked sheepishly at his father. 'Now that you put it like that. I'm glad you know. I'm glad I didn't. I . . .'

'That's enough son.' Geoffrey went over to Joe and Ruth slipped quietly out of the room.

'I can't understand why you should tell such a lie.'

'I thought it was the truth. You only have his word.'

'Irena denies it too.'

'They could both be lying.'

'We don't think they are. You've stirred up a lot of mischief, Olivia, and caused friction between our two families.'

Now it was mother and daughter. But there was alienation between Geoffrey and Ruth too. For the past week they'd resented each other, grown apart again. Naturally there had been no communication between the Lazars and the Harrows. Nos 44-45 Lawnside seemed rent with confusion.

Ruth was preparing for her summer exams. There were final rehearsals for *She Stoops*. Geoffrey had wanted to believe Joe and drop the matter. He hadn't wanted to confront Olivia; but she had. She knew she was putting her best neither into her revision nor the rehearsals, but she had to know. Was Olivia genuinely mistaken, or a deliberate mischief maker? It seemed important to find out.

'Everyone *thinks* they are sleeping together. That's all I can say.'

'But did you actually hear them? See them? Here?'

Olivia went very pale and pursed her lips. She gazed at her mother with hatred. 'I knew they were upstairs. I could hear them messing about, giggling . . . I knew what they were up to.'

'It isn't the same as having sexual intercourse,' Ruth said clinically. 'You know that don't you, Olivia? You have learned the facts of life at school. You can carry on and play around, petting it's called, but not have actual penetration which constitutes the sex act. That is the point. You know that don't you?'

'I think it is the same thing.'

'It is not the same thing. Not at all. You should be very sure of your facts before you make so much mischief.'

'Well everyone said . . .' Olivia's lower lip was trembling. 'Irena has a reputation. She was supposed to be sleeping with the Head Boy at the Royal.'

'Oh *supposed* . . .'

'Well I didn't *see* them mother, but even he admitted it.'

'That doesn't mean she's done the same with Joe. It was a bitchy and spiteful thing to do, with your own brother, to cause so much trouble. Anyone would think you were jealous.'

'Or anyone would think *you* were jealous Mother. You don't like the thought of anyone sleeping with your precious Joe, do you?'

Ruth stifled an impulse to slap her daughter. She saw streaks of light in front of her eyes and the blood pounded in her ears. She breathed very deeply before replying, aware that Olivia was frightened by what she had said.

'It is nothing to do with jealousy, Olivia. Both your father and I think Joe is too young. We happen to believe in the old fashioned virtues and that sex is best within marriage. That it gives the security and love that people need when embarking on something that is really quite complex and fraught with difficulty. It is not simply physical, but emotional too. We think so about Joe and we would feel the same about you. We think you are both far, far too young for physical sexual experience and we are against it whatever else anyone thinks or does. We think that about Irena Lazar too; but she is not our concern. Joe is.'

Ruth stopped abruptly. She had always left sex education to the schools who were supposed to do it well. She had never in her life spoken like to this to any of her children. Why not? Why was there such a barrier between parents and children in sexual matters? The Lazars obviously had it, and her mother had been the same with her. Now she was re-enacting all the wrong, old-fashioned attitudes with Olivia. Never a word about the purpose of menstruation, about love or intercourse in marriage or out of it. People were simply expected to know, or to find out the best way they could.

But looking now at her very hostile daughter Ruth knew that she could not break the barrier that divided them. She could not sit down and put her arm around Olivia and explain how it was and what it was like. And she didn't think Olivia wanted her to either.

The gulf. Had the gulf grown wider since she had been at the university? It was so difficult to know. There was no pity or sympathy in Olivia's eyes, only trouble and dislike and embarrassment.

She knew that it was partly because she was talking about her son, Olivia's brother, that the matter was so embarrassing and difficult. Neither of them liked to think of Joe in the act. 'Penetration' was a vile word. It was too carnal. It had not the beauty of people who love each other making love.

Was sex between her and Geoffrey beautiful? Not often.

All this business had been too painful, revealed too many open wounds. She wished they had never heard of the Lazars.

'I think I had better get tea now,' Ruth said. 'I have a rehearsal this evening. Are you coming to the play?'

'No. I don't want to see my mother cavorting around, making a fool of herself. All the girls at school are sorry for me. They think you're ridiculous. You're ridiculous, Mummy, *ridiculous!*'

Olivia flung open the kitchen door and slammed it so hard

behind her that the sturdy neo-Georgian house shook to its foundations.

Ruth rushed to the kitchen sink and retched. The bile rose in her throat and came streaming out of her nostrils while water filled her eyes and made tears run down her cheeks. She shook her head over the basin and when the nausea passed dabbed her brow with water, her hands shaking.

Patting her face with a tea towel she sat unsteadily on a kitchen chair and tried to calm herself. She had been quite wrong to have it out with Olivia, to act against Geoffrey's advice. In the space of a week she felt she had completely alienated three of the people she loved best, her eldest son, her daughter and her husband. Whatever else she had learned at the university it wasn't wisdom.

She couldn't blame the Lazars for that.

13

Paget Harrow was a dazzling bride and Laurie Matrecht seemed appropriately dazed by his good fortune. He valued her the more, Ruth decided watching his expression during the reception, because of her reputation. How unfair it was that people prized only things which were hard to come by, fraught with unsuspected pitfalls and potentially disastrous – in other words thoroughly unsuitable. Paget Harrow was a beautiful girl, but she was not at all the sort of wife for a serious minded university don. She couldn't possibly enhance his career. In its very nature it was bound to fail.

Paget's family also seemed unprepared for the happy event, quite overwhelmed at this acquisition of a son-in-law.

'I wonder how many I'll have,' Eunice observed, tipsily standing on tiptoe and pouring champagne into Geoffrey's glass.

'Many what, Eunice?' Geoffrey immediately raised his glass to his lips as though he'd just been rescued from the desert.

'Sons-in-law. You don't think she'll just stop at poor Laurie?'

'That is awfully cynical, Eunice,' Ruth observed putting her hand firmly across the rim of her glass. 'No thanks, no more. He is a very nice boy.'

'He is too, oops,' Eunice hiccuped. 'Too nice. Paget needs a rotter. Someone like him.'

Ruth followed the direction of Eunice's gaze. Antal Lazar, urbane as always, dressed in morning suit and carrying a grey topper, was deep in conversation with Simon on the far side of the marquee that had been erected on the lawn of The Pines. No one had cared to trust the mild early September weather sufficiently to hold the reception completely out of doors.

'I did wonder what he was doing here,' Ruth said, 'and Bella too. Simon and he actually speak after the New Year affair?'

Eunice threw back her head and gave a bark of mirthless laughter. 'Oh very much so! Simon apologized. I made him. When Simon came to his senses he realized he couldn't offend someone who was such a good client of the firm. Isn't he, Geoffrey?'

'Mmm?' Geoffrey had been talking to someone else and turned round at his name.

'Isn't Antal Lazar a good client of your firm?'

Geoffrey frowned. 'I believe so. I have no dealings with him, thank God. I can't abide the fellow.'

'Oh we all know that, Geoffrey.' Fred Leadbetter, who was the chairman of the local Chamber of Commerce, screwed up his nose. 'It's your chauvinism.'

'How do you mean my chauvinism?' Geoffrey thrust out a jaw aggressively. The sole button on his morning coat strained across his large corporation and he now had two folds of chin covering the knot on his tie, not one. His face had a greyish tinge and his eyes were very bright and rather watery. Ruth turned away. Sometimes she could hardly bear to look at him. He didn't seem to be her husband, the father of her children, the man with whom she shared a bed every night; but some absolute stranger encountered, like today, at a party and to whom one took an immediate and irrational dislike.

'Dislike of foreigners, darling,' Eunice said leering at him. 'He says you don't like Antal because he is a wog.'

'It's nothing to do with that,' Geoffrey growled. 'I just don't like *him*, or his family, his lazy wife, his sexually precocious daughter or his layabout son.'

'Bella isn't lazy,' Ruth said quietly. 'She's just permanently ducked for cover. I wouldn't wish Antal Lazar on anyone for a husband.'

'Why, what do you know about him?'

Eunice's apparently innocent smile hovered on the verge of being dangerous.

'He is very charming, urbane, totally unreliable and a lousy husband and father. Other than that I know nothing. I think Laurie Matrecht is a good, nice boy; I only hope Paget doesn't trample all over him.'

'Oh she will,' Eunice said as though the thought rather pleased her. 'She will make mincemeat of him; then eventually she will land up with someone like – *him*.'

Eunice stared at Antal again and he raised his eyes from talking to Simon and looked at her. He waved a hand in greeting. There was something rather peremptory about the gesture; derisive and dismissive as though he couldn't quite make the effort to come and talk to her.

'Then you don't like him either?' Heather Leadbetter looked maliciously at Eunice. All the Bridge Club said she was having an affair with Antal Lazar.

'I think he's an absolute bastard.' Eunice looked towards the house. 'Ah here come the happy bride and groom. They're late out. Maybe they were having a quickie upstairs.'

Paget was dragging Laurie, shyly holding her hand, across the lawn. She had insisted on full bridal rigout with a long train and a veil over her face during the ceremony. There were those who said she wore it to hide her blushes when she had to make all those vows about fidelity. She also promised to 'obey' which seemed a joke to everyone who knew Paget. She now had the veil tossed back, and her clear peach complexion, twenty years younger than Eunice's, enhanced the difference in their ages. Beside her daughter Eunice looked positively raddled. Laurie wore a grey morning suit and a dark grey cravat. His curly blond hair shone in the interval of sunshine they were now enjoying. It was the sort of day when clouds scurried about the sky and the sun disappeared for minutes at a time when it became very cold and windy, and everyone either shivered or hurried for cover until it came out again.

Paget put her cheek out to be kissed by Ruth and Geoffrey and the Leadbetters, and Laurie followed her example, shaking hands with the men. Ruth could tell that he was already preparing himself for his role in life to be two paces behind her, to follow in her wake wherever she led. She smiled at him and, seeming to sense her sympathy rather than her congratulations, he frowned.

'I hope you'll be very happy, Laurie.'

'Thank you. I am.' His voice was low and firm, as though to give the lie to any doubts he may have admitted to himself or others.

'Paget looks absolutely lovely. You're a very lucky man.'

'I know.' His voice grew even lower.

'Oh congratulations,' Geoffrey boomed seizing his hand and wringing it. 'I wish you all the joy in the world. Come now we're related. Let me see, you are my . . .'

'Nephew-in-law!' Paget threw back her head and showed her splendid teeth sparkling to advantage in the sunshine. She wore no make up except for a pearl matt glow on her lips and mascara on her lashes. Her very blonde hair showed beneath her veil, the ends curling on either side around each ear. 'Darling you're a nephew-in-law!' She drew Laurie, now blushing furiously, forward and kissed his cheek. 'Isn't he a pet, Uncle Geoffrey? I ummm *love* him!'

Paget flattened her nose against Laurie's cheek and then she playfully bit his ear. 'He's awfully good in bed,' she said turning to the gaping concourse.

'Paget, please!'

'You *are*.' Paget looked at him, standing back as though to admire this paradigm of masculine virility. 'It is something to be proud of, not ashamed. Isn't it, mother?'

Eunice's eyes glinted more with anger than maternal joy and a high colour on her cheeks shone above the carefully applied make up. 'I don't think it's the way to talk on your wedding day, darling.'

'Oh Mummy don't be idiotic!' Paget gave her mother a very unbridal glare. 'It's only a joke. Can't anyone take a joke?'

'Well it's a funny thing to joke about, that's all.'

'What's funny about sex?'

'You're being very irritating, Paget, and even if it is your wedding day I don't mind telling you so.'

'I'm just saying . . .'

'I know what you're saying. You're trying to tell me that you're a big girl now and grown up. I think you're being silly that's all.'

Mother and daughter were sharply contrasted as they looked at each other. Although Eunice was a handsome woman and had worn well her looks did not stand comparison with Paget's almost ethereal, fey type of beauty.

Laurie clasped Paget's hand as though he wanted to take her away. But she pursed her mouth looking mulish and remained where she was. A look of exasperation came into Laurie's eyes and Ruth knew he was licked already within an hour of being married. A large wedding band, identical to Paget's, gleamed on his finger. He had plighted his troth.

'Oh I see, mother. A wedding is not all about sex then? Well, you should know.'

The Leadbetters smiled mirthlessly and began to drift discreetly away. Geoffrey made rasping noises in his throat.

'I don't think this should turn into a family brawl,' Ruth said, 'whatever the reason.'

'Too much champagne in my opinion.' Geoffrey looked at

her with approval. 'You can't go round saying this kind of thing to everyone you know, Paget. It isn't done.'

'I don't want to say it to everyone, Uncle,' Paget said in clear silvery tones. 'Just to Mummy. And I am not at all drunk. Ask Laurie.'

Laurie looked at the sky as though pleading for help. It came, but not from above.

'May I congratulate the bride?' said Antal.

Paget, in a rapid transformation of mood which made Ruth wonder anew about her sobriety, gave him her dazzling smile and leaned forward. He kissed her lightly on the lips. When he finished he stared at her and she stared back at him. Geoffrey again cleared his throat loudly and Bella took a step forward filling the space vacated by Antal.

'I hope you'll be very happy, Paget. Congratulations, Laurie.' She shook Laurie's hand.

Ruth breathed inwardly a sigh of relief. Bella, looking rather incongruous in a wide-brimmed hat and a silk dress a size too small, seemed to have saved the situation. Except for the green caftan for evenings, Ruth had never seen her in anything but jeans.

'You look very pretty, Bella.'

'Thank you, Ruth. Isn't Paget exquisite?'

'She is lovely,' Ruth murmured apathetically, glad to see more guests come up to the bridal pair.

'I can imagine what Eunice must have been like at her age. The spitting image I would imagine?'

'I didn't know her quite at that age,' Ruth said. 'Geoffrey is a little bit younger than Simon and the two girls were already born when we were married; but Eunice was and still is very lovely I think.'

'She drinks too much,' Antal murmured. 'It's affecting her skin.'

Ruth stared at him. 'What a cruel thing to say.'

'It's perfectly true. Women who want to keep their looks

should not drink. I shouldn't imagine you're a drinker, Ruth? Nor is Bella. If she didn't neglect her complexion so atrociously it would be lovely; but she doesn't drink.'

'*Does* Eunice drink a lot?' Ruth, puzzled, looked from one to the other.

'Oh yes.' Antal nodded. 'You can tell.'

'Well I've known her for nearly twenty years and I wouldn't say she was a heavy drinker.'

'Maybe he knows her better than you?' Bella smiled sweetly.

Ruth felt embarrassed and plucked at her gloves.

'I hardly know her at all.' Antal teetered on his feet. His shoes, with pointed toes, were expensive and beautifully polished. 'I just said that anyone could tell by her complexion that she drinks.'

'Oh there is Bernice Leighton. Excuse me.' Bella gave them a friendly smile. 'I want to have a word with her. She is typing my new book on macro economics.'

Bella sped off and Ruth gazed after her.

'She is awfully clever. I do admire her.'

She could feel his presence almost tangibly.

'I hear you're doing very well at the university; I'm sorry I missed the play. I hear you were excellent.'

'You do hear a lot don't you?' Ruth looked at him without smiling.

'People talk, you know.'

'Which people?'

Antal shrugged. 'Now that I am a citizen of this community I hear a lot of things. But I'm so delighted to hear about your progress. I'm sorry we don't see more of you.'

Ruth noticed the 'we'. It was true that ever since the episode with Joe she had hardly seen any Lazar. Joe had been away most of the summer on a scholarship trip to America.

'I've left the university anyway.' Ruth's glance was cold His presence was alien. He was an enemy.

'I beg your pardon?'

164

'I'm surprised your "sources" didn't tell you that already.'

They both knew she was talking about Eunice.

'But I haven't heard . . .'

She supposed Eunice had been too busy with preparing for the wedding, or too indifferent, to tell him. 'I didn't do well in my exams. I was referred in sociology and that was becoming my favourite subject.'

'But surely . . .'

'I didn't do well because I had too many things on my mind; too much guilt. I shan't ever do well while I feel like that. I'm wasting time and Geoffrey's money. We have to pay full fees.'

'Guilt?' Antal sounded as though the word was new to him.

'About the family.'

'How do your family make you feel guilty?' He clearly didn't understand.

'I was very upset about Joe.'

'But nothing happened with Joe!'

'I am still not sure. I don't think they'd confess it. Do you?' Antal gave his familiar continental shrug.

'I don't understand young people at all. Of course we never discussed it with Irena.'

'That must have pleased her.'

'Ruth, you sound so bitter, so hostile.'

'Do I? I'm sorry.'

'You sound as though you blame me.'

She smiled at him without humour. 'Perhaps I do.'

'But why?' His concern appeared genuine.

'You started the whole thing. You suggested I should go to university to improve myself, to save my marriage. My marriage didn't need saving then. It does now.'

'*Really?* I'm sorry.'

'My daughter hates me.'

'But that is nothing to do with me!'

'It is in a way. Everything seems to be to do with you.'

Antal shrugged. His blue eyes and very white teeth seemed

so odd with his dark hair and swarthy complexion that she sensed that here was the core of his attraction. He did attract; but he repelled. At that moment she felt she hated him.

'I do protest, Ruth. We hardly ever see you. Bella says you never run in as you used to and chat. We gathered it was because you were so busy. I doubt if I have met you a dozen times since we came here nearly two years ago.'

'But still, you have affected my family. Your family has affected mine. That is all I can say. It is because of you that I went to the university and because of you that I've left. It has been quite disastrous. I could never have believed it could have done so much harm.'

'I'm terribly sorry; but I don't really feel I am to blame.' Now he looked angry. He bowed and clicked his heels and walked quickly away leaving her alone.

Dorcas caught Paget's bouquet which everyone interpreted as meaning that she would soon have her first fiancé. Already a number of young men were in tow. Paget and Laurie drove off in his vintage M.G. They wore old clothes and there were two large rather battered suitcases tied up behind. It appeared they didn't want anyone to know they were newly married. But still Paget managed to look lovely; even old clothes on her looked as though she had grown into them and made them part of her. They became her because of her natural elegance. She had a new headscarf over her head to keep her hair in place.

'Something new,' she called and tucked her arm through Laurie's as he engaged the gears. He kissed her and gently shook her hand away. They both laughed into each other's faces.

They looked so happy. Ruth hoped they always would be. It would be cynical to doubt it, but unrealistic not to. Maybe such an incompatible pair would hit it off. She and Geoffrey had appeared so well suited. She took her hat off and followed the others into the house. She felt very hot and tired and ashamed of herself. Why on earth had she been so histrionic with Antal Lazar? She'd spoken like someone out of a B movie and been aware of it too. It was terribly dramatic and stupid.

Only she and Eunice were left as evening fell and the long shadows on the smoothly kept lawns drew near to the house. Geoffrey and Simon had seen off the last of the guests and then disappeared, probably to do some more serious drinking in Simon's study. Dorcas had gone off to London with several friends to celebrate the wedding and George had gone home with the Lazars. Olivia was on holiday with the school in Germany and, like Joe, due back for the new term at the end of the week.

Eunice wriggled off her shoes and put her feet on the sofa. 'Christ what a day! He's a nice boy but what a slut that girl is.'

'Who are you talking about?' Ruth leaned her head back on the cushions. She ached all over.

'My daughter, who do you think? The married one. Trying to get at me.'

'I think daughters are like that. I've had a terrible summer with Olivia. Sometimes I think either she will have to go or I shall.'

'Let's have another drink.' Eunice swung her legs off the sofa.

'No thanks. Not for me.'

Eunice poured herself a large whisky and steered an erratic course back to the sofa. Ruth wondered if what Antal had said was true. She hadn't really had a good talk with her sister-in-law, or observed her behaviour, for six months.

'She's a perfect little bitch. Didn't I think sex was for marriage or marriage for sex or whatever she said.' Eunice sat on the side of the sofa and slurped her whisky into her mouth. The angle at which she was sitting made Ruth realize just

167

how drunk she was. A little of the whisky trickled down her chin and onto her bare chest. She wore a very low cut short dress of *broderie Anglaise* with a matching coat. Her bosom nearly burst out of her tight bodice.

'She was getting at me that's what,' Eunice continued. 'I'd have slapped her face if it hadn't been the occasion it was. Just wait until she comes home.'

'I'd forget it,' Ruth said. 'I don't really remember what she said or why she said it; but I would forget it. Everyone else will.'

'I won't. She's telling me I'm on the shelf; that I'm past it. That she is a beauty and I'm an ex-beauty; that she has an active sex life and I don't; that she can have babies and I can't. What she's bloody well saying' – Eunice lay flat on the sofa with her knees up and slightly apart – 'is that it's all washed up for me and it's beginning for her.'

'Did she really say all that?' Ruth tried to hide her concern behind sarcasm.

'Well not in so many words; but I got the message. Oh I got it all right. Little whore. He's a bloody nice bloke, but he won't keep her. I pity the poor sod. Oh I pity him.' Eunice yawned and closed her eyes. For a moment she gave a little snore then jerked herself awake again. 'God I'm drunk, aren't I? What a fucking awful day. Wasn't it an awful day, Ruth?'

'I didn't altogether enjoy it to be honest.' Ruth studied her nails. 'I also made an awful fool of myself in front of Antal Lazar.'

Eunice gave a hoot and threw her glass, empty now, onto the floor. It smashed into small pieces.

'So *you've* done it too have you? Who hasn't made a bloody fool of herself, note I say *her*self, in front of Antal Lazar? Half the women in Edgerton would cheerfully prostitute themselves for Antal Lazar. Not that the mean bugger would expect to pay a penny. Now you've fallen too.'

'I don't mean like *that!*' Ruth said hotly. 'I'm not at all interested in him sexually. Anyway I don't think he has all that much of a come-on. You're exaggerating.'

'Oh no I'm not! He likes to tease. He's an absolute swine. I nearly died when I saw his name on the wedding list. No one can stand him, yet everyone sucks up to him. Simon's firm won't fall to pieces if he doesn't come to our daughter's wedding yet Simon asks him!'

'I thought you liked him at New Year.' Ruth looked at her slyly.

'That was New Year.' Eunice avoided her eyes. 'Well what did he embarrass *you* about?'

'I said I had left the university because of him.'

Eunice leaned over on her stomach in what appeared to be a paroxysm of mirth. She beat her hands against the cushion.

'Ohh-ohhh-haaa. Because of him. You bloody fool. You told *him* that!'

'I mean he was to do with me going there. You remember he suggested it?'

'Yes I do.' Eunice was groping in the recesses of her drink-befuddled mind. 'At that dinner party. He said you had a fine mind. What a joke. He's not interested in any women's minds; he's only interested in their c . . .'

'Eunice! I do think your language is unnecessarily coarse today.'

'Oh do you?' Eunice tried to mimic Ruth's tone, making it sound ultra refined. 'Oh fancy that. It's coarse is it? It's like my mind, coarse and crude. That's what we're all like underneath you know, savages. So are you if *you'd* let yourself go. Oh this veneer of civilization . . .'

Eunice groped round for her glass and encountered shattered fragments. She got to her feet, careful to avoid the bits, and tottered over to the bar.

'And how did Monsieur Antal make you leave the university? Did he promise you an affair? Because if so I warn you . . .'

'Oh don't be so absurd.' Ruth got to her feet and looked for her bag. 'You know we've had trouble with Joe and his daughter. Then George always tags round after Chris and is invariably up to no good. Olivia can hardly speak a civilized word to me; she is so full of resentment. I feel I should be at home keeping an eye on my family.'

'They can always do it behind a tree you know.'

'Crude again, Eunice.'

'That's me, Crude Eunice.' Eunice wove out into the middle of the floor clutching the whisky bottle. She waved it above her head and then she unscrewed the cap and put it to her mouth. In this elegant drawing room surrounded by expensive furniture Eunice looked incongruous, like a chorus girl at a palace party. She looked nasty, crude and rather violent. Ruth felt pity for her, but also disgust. 'So you really have given up the university?' Eunice sat on the nearest chair, the open whisky bottle in her hand.

'Yes.'

'And you're going to play bridge again?'

'Yes.'

'And help me in the shop?'

'From time to time if you want me to.'

'And run the Conservative ladies' functions?'

'Yes.'

'And be secretary of the Sports Club?'

'Yes.'

'And have coffee mornings and meet up in Town?'

'Yes.'

'All for your bloody family?'

'Yes.'

'And are you going to be happy?'

Ruth didn't reply. Eunice stretched out her arms, her legs splayed in front of her, a ladder running up one side of her tights. She leaned her head back and opened her mouth and began to snore. Her hair was tangled and her mascara ran

170

down her cheeks through little crevices by the side of her mouth.

Ruth wondered how Antal Lazar, the Edgerton stud, would feel if he could see her now.

Part 3

The Mistress

14

Ruth pushed her way through the pre Christmas shopping crowd to the food store at the back of Selfridges. She thought she'd buy some smoked salmon, and then have a coffee and a sandwich at the snack bar. Her arms were full of parcels and her feet ached.

She climbed the stairs from stationery into the food hall and looked at the pâtés. Geoffrey loved pâté. But with so much time on her hands she was now able to make it for him. Salmon one didn't smoke oneself. She wished she could drop the parcels and have a good lunch, even put her feet up. The salmon was terribly expensive. However she wouldn't be in town again before Christmas. She took out her purse and stood in the short queue looking at the varieties of beautiful fish arrayed before her on the ice covered slabs.

'Fish for supper, Mrs Harrow?'

She didn't know where the voice had come from, the store was so crowded. It seemed to be disembodied and float upwards as though it came from within her, as though it was subconsciously something she wished to hear. Then she knew by an awareness of his presence, even before her eyes travelled up his blue mohair overcoat with the warm muffler at his throat and she saw his face. He was smiling down at her.

'Antal Lazar! Whatever are you doing here?' She tried to keep her voice normal.

'I could ask you the same thing.'

'Shopping for Christmas, buying smoked salmon.'

'I'm passing through. I use the store as a short cut to get to my office.'

'Which is?'

'In Bruton Street.'

'You have an office in Mayfair *and* Edgerton?'

'And Birmingham and Edinburgh.'

'No wonder one never sees you.'

'Yes I'm very busy, though flattered you should miss me.'

'I don't actually. I just said I never see you.'

'Not since the wedding.'

'No.' She edged forward in the queue. Should she have a pound, or half a pound?

'How are the bridal pair?'

'I think they're very well. A pound of salmon please. Yes the best. Oh my goodness is it as expensive as that? Well it is Christmas, nearly.'

A ten pound note was proffered.

'Please let me pay.'

'Oh no, I couldn't.'

'But I want to.'

'But I can't let you.'

The assistant, quite immune to the altercation, took the note and gave the sparse change to Antal and the salmon to Ruth.

'Next?'

Ruth fumbled with her purse.

'I feel terribly embarrassed. I knew quite well how much it was and I can afford to pay.'

'I know you can. I wanted it as a peace offering present.'

'Why peace offering?'

'Because you told me at the wedding that I'd ruined your life, or words to that effect.'

'Oh that was stupid. I regretted it afterwards.'

'No. I think you meant it. You said it with great sincerity. It impressed me and upset me. It really did. I wanted to say

176

I was sorry but I didn't know how. Now I do. Have lunch?'

'Lunch?' Ruth looked at him as though he had suggested a trip to New York. She felt excited and a bit worried. She loathed him, yet he was fascinating. He made her feel immediately on another level of existence.

'Yes, something to eat.' He made a gesture putting his hands to his mouth and smiled. He smiled so easily and confidently aware of his charm; no not aware of it so much as full of it. His charm was part of him and unconscious; yet he must know when he exercised it and its effect, particularly on women.

'I simply couldn't!'

'Why not?' He looked at his watch. 'It is just lunch time. Or have you eaten?'

'No; but I have a lot to do. I thought I'd go to Harrods and maybe just have a snack here. We could have a coffee?'

Antal looked at the Brass Rail where people were standing munching snacks, and grimaced.

'I'm sure I could use my influence to get us a table at Genevieve. It is only five minutes away. Please?'

There seemed no question about it. To go on arguing would be to behave like a schoolgirl. She followed him obediently out of the store and he lightly took her arm along Wigmore Street, through Manchester Square and into Thayer Street.

'Yes of course Mr Lazar, always a table for you.'

They showed him upstairs. There was a little corner table for two overlooking Thayer Street. The whole place was delicious, warm and inviting, full of people discussing business or having love affairs. She looked at him.

He shook out his large starched linen napkin, his eyes sparkling. 'This is nice.'

'Yes it's a lovely place.'

'No I mean it's nice to see you.'

She didn't reply but crumbled a roll while studying the

177

menu which the waiter had brought. She knew Antal was looking at her, not the menu; she was aware of his gaze but she was not going to let him fluster her with all this show of incipient sexuality. She raised her eyes and stared at him.

'I think I'll have the giant prawns and the tournedos.'

'An excellent choice. I'll have the pâté and Dover Sole. And we can have a bottle of red and a bottle of white and change around.'

'Oh I couldn't possibly drink as much as that!'

'Then I'll drink what you can't.'

He smiled at her reassuringly and ordered with care asking Ruth how she liked her steak and what vegetables she wanted with it. The waiter knew him well; he smiled a lot and paid elaborate attention to Ruth.

'I see they know you well.'

'Yes I eat here a lot. It's near my pied-à-terre.'

'Oh? You have a flat in London?'

'A small one, up the road.'

'How convenient.'

'For what?'

Ruth ignored his question and sipped her cool white wine looking at him over the rim of her glass. She felt a different person. Here she was sipping wine in an elegant restaurant with a good looking man who was not her husband. It hadn't happened for years and even when she and Geoffrey had been engaged they had been too gauche and certainly too poor to eat in a place like this. Geoffrey would never have known how to order anyway, or what wine to drink with what. He hadn't much of an idea even now.

'You look very lovely today, Mrs Harrow.'

'Thank you.'

He leaned over towards her. 'You have the most beautiful colouring. Has your husband ever told you that?'

'Frequently.'

'Really?' He lifted an eyebrow.

'Why do you say "really?" in that tone of voice?'

'Geoffrey doesn't seem to me the sort of man to pay compliments.'

'Well he does.'

'I'm glad to hear it. You deserve them.'

'And do *you* compliment your wife?'

Antal sat back and scratched behind his ear. 'What is there to compliment in Bella?'

'She has a good figure; she is a nice person. She has a very nice face. I think you once said she had good skin but she neglected it.'

'She does. She neglects herself.'

'I think it is probably deliberate.'

'Oh it is. To show me how asexual she is. Now you, Mrs Harrow, dress so carefully and take such pains over your appearance. You make up well and your hair is beautiful. It enhances you as a woman. Bella doesn't want to be enhanced.'

'That must be your fault.'

'Why is is?' He began eating his pâté while Ruth tried to remove the shell of the Dublin Bay prawns as delicately as she could, with a degree of expertise she didn't possess.

'I don't know. If she ceases trying to please you there must be a reason.'

'Maybe it lies with her. She ceased trying to please me after our children were born. I had done my job as the procreator and I was expendable.'

Ruth rinsed her fingers in the bowl of warm scented water and dried them carefully on her napkin. 'I'm sure it's not as simple as that. These prawns are delicious.'

She looked at him again, more aware than ever of the feeling of excitement. She felt poised and sophisticated, womanly and desirable. She felt somehow that at this moment she ruled him, and could determine what happened next. Their destiny was in her hands, not his. She was glad she'd worn her beige Hardy Amies dress with her fur, her high suede boots and her little fur hat. She was glad she'd had her hair and nails done the day before and that she always made up carefully every day regardless of what she was doing.

Antal looked masculine and elegant. He had on a dark grey suit, a pink shirt and a deep red tie. His hair was brushed straight back. A few inches of shirt showed beneath his cuffs and his nails were well pared and beautifully clean. He had little tufts of black hair just above his knuckles. She thought of Geoffrey's pot belly and his gleaming red face with the increasingly sparse blond hair. But even if Geoffrey shed a couple of stones could he ever look like Antal Lazar?

'Tell me how you like not being a student any more?'

They had started the main course. She had broccoli with her tournedos and he had his fish without vegetables. She supposed he ate carefully so as to take care of his figure.

'I like it. I feel I'm in control. Before I didn't.'

'So I did the wrong thing advising you?'

'Yes.'

She hadn't tasted anything as good as this steak for years and the wine was delicious, a crisp clear Gamay, quite light. Antal had assured her it would be.

'But you told me at one time you were transformed.'

'I was, into a careless thoughtless slut.'

'Oh come!'

'I ignored my home, neglected my family, dressed like an eighteen year old. My hairdresser could hardly remember me when I went back to see him.'

Antal smiled and she laughed. Then he burst out laughing. They paused in the act of eating and looked at each other, knives and forks poised in their hands. She wondered if people were looking at them and thinking about them as she did in restaurants. Did people wonder if this was a business lunch or, perchance, if they were lovers?

She knew that word had been at the back of her mind ever since he'd greeted her in Selfridges by the fish counter. This whole new feeling of anticipation, of being different was like someone on the verge of a love affair. Even their talk was charged, though it was pretty mundane; everything was calculated and special. She knew it was for her and she knew it was for him – but for her it was unique. How many times did he chat up a woman as he was chatting her?

'I don't think you were a thoughtless, careless slut. Besides, you said your mind had atrophied.'

'You can read good books and also dress well, look after your home, without doing a university course. I do read quite a lot of philosophy now, actually, and enjoy it.'

'And please your husband?' Antal leaned over and stared at her.

'Of course. Naturally.'

'*Do* you please him?'

'I think so.'

Antal put his fish bones on the side of his plate and joined his well cared for hands. 'Tell me, I like to know because my marriage is so abnormal; but do you . . . make love frequently?'

'Why do you like to know?' She gazed at him, half smiling, still aware of her power.

'Really it's not prurience. I'm interested sociologically.'

'Of course.'

'How many times married couples do it . . . you know, once a week, twice, that sort of thing? I'd be interested to know.'

'I could only speak about my marriage and not in general.'

'Naturally.' Antal sipped his wine. He looked very eager and interested.

'And I'm not saying.'

'Oh you're teasing.' He lightly touched her hand. The act was like an embrace and she felt a tremor go through her body.

'Why do you get onto this intimate level, Antal?'

'Why do you think?'

181

She lowered her eyes. The thing was beginning to get a little out of control, not quite as she had anticipated.

'You know that you attract me a good deal, Ruth?'

'Isn't it that you just like women?'

'Not all women.' She avoided looking at him. She didn't trust herself, didn't know what her response would be. 'I know you seem to think I am a first class seducer and woman-izer – I don't know what lies Bella has told you – but this impression of me always gets around. It's false. I have no mistress or anyone I'm currently going to bed with.'

'What about Eunice?' She met his eyes. It helped her to externalize this relationship – to try and remember how loath-some she found him, or thought she found him up to an hour or so ago.

'Eunice?'

'My sister-in-law.'

'Of course I know Eunice is your sister-in-law; but what has Eunice to do with me?'

'I clearly understood you were having an affair.'

'From *her*?'

Ruth thought for a moment. 'In a way.'

'Maybe it is what she wanted you to think. In that case I will not give her away. It wouldn't be gentlemanly.'

'I'd like to know.'

'Why? Ah because of what I've just said. Fair enough. I suppose I was making some sort of proposition. The opening gambit as it were, that you attracted me and I had no mistress. I was telling you that I was available and that I hoped you were too, because I want you. You are telling me that you are a woman of the world and you know what this sort of conver-sation leads to.'

'I'm not saying anything of the sort. I'm asking you about Eunice because I had the very definite impression that you were having an affair.'

'Well we're not. Oh I won't say she didn't want to. She was

182

very flattering in that respect; rather obvious, if I might say so without being offensive. It was so obvious that it put me off. She is a very attractive woman; she is very sexy. But she wants it so badly that it's off-putting. I like people who are hard to get. Like you.'

'How do you know I'm hard to get?'

Her heartbeat quickened because she was so excited.

'Oh you aren't hard to get? I see.'

'I'm impossible to get actually. I haven't the slightest intention of having an affair with you.'

'I know that really. That's why I knew we would be safe lunching together. After all, you are a neighbour. How would you feel chatting to my wife? What would you do when you and your husband saw us together, or when I saw you two together, that sort of thing.'

She felt deflated, let down. 'The lunch has been delicious,' she said, putting the emphasis firmly on the food. 'I would like to go to Harrods now.'

'May I take you there in a cab?'

'If you wish.'

'First a coffee and brandy at my flat? It is literally on the other side of the road.' He pointed out of the window. She followed his long white finger with the gleaming nail and saw that the hairs finished half way up the back of his hands before starting again beneath his watch strap. His face was very close and he looked at her meaningfully. 'Seeing that we are *not* having an affair; that the whole idea is impossible, there is nothing to be afraid of is there?'

She drew in her breath. The excitement was almost overwhelming. 'I must get to Harrods though.' She kept her voice very level and controlled.

'Of course.'

It was a small modern block built above two of the shops that lined the High Street on both sides. There was an old fashioned grocer's underneath and a tobacconist's. The entrance to the block was between the two, a discreet black door with six nameplates on either side of an entry phone.

The flat was made up of a living room and a bedroom, a small kitchen, at the back like the bedroom, and a tiled bathroom. There was very little furniture in the main room, a three piece suite, a dining table and a colour television set. In the bedroom there was just the large double bed, a chest of drawers with a mirror and a wardrobe.

The whole place exuded an impersonal air like a hotel; it was clean, clinical and detached. The ceiling was low and there was no central light, a table lamp on one side of the bed. There were net curtains at the window and through them Ruth could see the back of the building that faced on to another street with a tiny yard in between. Because of the proximity of the building opposite the room was rather dark.

Antal's chest was covered with a neat mat of small dark hairs that spread over his nipples, came to a point by his umbilicus and proceeded in a neat single line to his pubis where it positively burst into a thick black wiry mop. He lay on his back, his left cheek touching the pillow, giving her a profile of his face, his hair, no longer sleek, his eyes closed, his sensual mouth slightly open as he breathed evenly in sleep.

Ruth glanced at the thin gold watch which was all she wore and looked through the net curtains at the dusky building opposite again. She would never get to Harrods now.

'Can't you stay?' Antal's eyes were wide open and she wondered if he had really been asleep.

'What do you mean "stay"?'

'For the night? What time is it?'

'Five o'clock.'

'Not worth going home. We could have dinner at Odins and . . .'

'I can't possibly stay.' Ruth pulled the sheet over herself as though to hide her nudity. Antal reached up and pulled it away.

'Don't do that. I want to look at you.' He leaned over on his side, his blue eyes staring at her. She had not realized they were quite so blue but then she had never seen them so close. He put a hand on her breast and she felt herself quiver. 'You've got a most beautiful body, Ruth. Your proportions are perfect.'

'I always think my bust is too big.'

'Well it isn't.' He kneaded her breast and she saw the nipple harden, felt an erotic quiver in her loins. His touch was exquisite, light, delicate and very expert. His body was lithe and lissom and agile. It performed gyrations that even a slim and youthful Geoffrey had never been able to. When Geoffrey lay on her he covered her body with his flab; he was too heavy for enjoyment; one supported him, put up with him, endured him. Antal was so light she couldn't feel him and his trim athletic body lay comfortably and naturally between her legs as though it belonged there, the hairs of his chest tickling her breasts as he supported his torso on his hands. Even when he bore down on her, his hands clasping her back, he wasn't heavy; yet he was a big man, he wasn't small. Geoffrey was gross.

She hadn't made love twice in an afternoon for years, or thought she could enjoy it the second time as much as the first. He knelt up on the bed and looked at her. Again she glanced at the thin gold watch.

'Stay.'

'I can't. It's nearly six.'

He looked like a victorious satyr kneeling there looking at her, his penis still half erect springing from the black bush at his groin.

'Are they expecting you home?'

'Of course.'

'Ring up and say you're staying with a friend.'

'I can't. I can't think of anyone we actually know who lives in the centre of London – except you.' She smiled mischievously. He threw himself beside her and covered her with his arms.

'You're absolutely gorgeous, Ruth. You know I wanted you from the very beginning?'

'No I didn't know.'

'At the dinner party that night, you remember?'

'That was an awful long time ago.'

'It was when I gradually intruded myself inside you, so to speak. I made you want to do what I suggested.'

'Go to the university?'

'Yes it was like making love to you; to get you to do my bidding.'

'That sounds awfully Freudian. I think it's only occurred to you now.' She tried to struggle up but his arms restrained her.

'No I wanted you and I knew I'd get you. I didn't think it would take so long.'

'You don't seem to have tried so terribly hard. I mean today was a chance encounter; or were you following me?'

'No I wasn't following you; but it was meant. I knew it would happen one day and today was the day. I hoped that it would happen when you were at the university.'

'Why?'

'You would be able to get away more often; but probably you wouldn't have. Maybe this is best. You can come up to London.'

'I never come up very often. Three or four times a year.'

'You will have to come up every week.'

'I can't. Besides . . .'

Ruth tried to push him away and at last sat up and smoothed back her hair. He still lay sideways looking at her, his eyes on her breasts. They felt heavy and full as when she had had children. She had certainly not made love with such intensity

186

with Geoffrey for years. She felt milked and drained and full of Antal's essence. He had come inside her twice. Her pubic hair was wet and sticky and the area throbbed slightly as though she had somehow been massively used.

'Besides what, Ruth?' His soft accented voice was very deep and gentle. His hand caressed her waist.

'Besides . . .' She looked at him and saw his trusting, amorous almond shaped eyes. 'I mean we can't continue this.'

'Good God, it isn't just a one afternoon stand?' Antal sat up with an exclamation and folded his hands, staring at her.

'Well what else is it?'

'The beginning of an affair.'

'I don't see it like that.'

She swung herself off the bed and sat on the side finding that her legs were trembling slightly. She would have to have a bath. 'I can't have an affair. I have a husband. This was . . . well an accident. You might have planned it but I didn't.'

'But you wanted it, didn't you?'

'I didn't just want sex. No.'

'You wanted me.'

'No. I didn't. I still don't like you very much and I certainly don't trust you.'

'I don't believe you, Ruth. Every time I've met you in the last two years, since we moved to Edgerton, you've given me some sort of come hither sign. Subtle but unmistakable.'

'It wasn't conscious.' She lowered her head and bit her lip. She realized she had thought of very little else but Antal Lazar since she had first met him. He had always been there at the back of her mind, like a shadow hovering, menacing but infinitely alluring. Dangerous.

'No, but it was there. I knew it was a matter of time.' He sat beside her; she was aware of the contrast of their bodies, the male and female, the hair, the protuberances different in each, the quality of the flesh. He put a hand on her thigh and she looked at his well kept nails, the fine dark hairs showing off her pale skin. It was an intimate familiar gesture. They were lovers; whatever else happened she and Antal Lazar knew each other with the greatest intimacy possible between human beings. 'I have to see you again Ruth.'

'We are neighbours.'

She tried to sound flippant but her heart was full of foreboding. This afternoon had changed her life. How in fact *would* she feel when she saw Bella, Geoffrey, her children, Eunice? But with the foreboding the excitement was still there too. The pulsating, inextinguishable excitement of sexual attraction. He put his mouth to her ear.

'I want to see you here. Very soon. You must come back to me soon. You must.'

'I don't know . . .' She looked at him and he put a hand through her thick hair letting it spring back to the sides of her face. To her at this moment he looked the embodiment of a heroic god, even though she knew he was Antal Lazar, the husband of her neighbour, a rather sharp, cunning Hungarian who bought and sold and could get you almost anything you wanted from Coronas at half price to Liberty materials at cost. The sensual smell of him assailed her nostrils and she knew if she didn't tear herself away she would want to go on and on and on. She stood up, consciously parading her body for his inspection. His admiration thrilled her and she stretched up, aware of her full breasts, her narrow waist and her rounded thighs. She was so glad she'd kept her figure. His eyes glinted and he ran his tongue round his lips moistening them. She saw the gleam of his teeth.

'Well, I suppose I could say I haven't finished my Christmas shopping,' she said with a deliberate hint of enticement in her voice. 'After all, I didn't get to Harrods.'

15

After the chaos of the New Year's Eve party the previous year the Simon Harrows decided to give a decorous Christmas party, seating twelve people for dinner – to symbolise the twelve days of Christmas – and with twenty to thirty coming in afterwards for drinks and buffet.

Ruth thought it had exactly the same formula for disaster whenever it was held, because too much drink always seemed to flow in the household of the elder Harrows; but she wondered if she mentally attributed the reason to the presence, or expected presence, of Antal Lazar. Everything connected with him seemed to bring disorder and chaos, though looking at his neat, well preserved and cared-for person you would never think it.

They had decided to start dinner half an hour late without him. Eunice was clearly in a furious mood and sat simmering at one end of the table, the empty place to her right. Simon suggested they should close the table up and remove the twelfth place but Eunice refused. She seemed so edgy that her disquiet affected Ruth who didn't know how she herself would react seeing Antal in public for the first time since they had become lovers. She had found a number of occasions to go up to London for that pre-Christmas shopping since the lunch in November. She still hadn't been to Harrods; it was really quite far from Marylebone High Street when it came to the point.

'I don't know why you invited him,' Simon said truculently,

carving the roast beef. 'The fellow has absolutely no conversation.'

'Oh I don't know, I think he can be very amusing.' Paget Matrecht spoke from the centre of the table.

'Only with women,' Laurie said. 'He clams up entirely when speaking to me. I've tried him on any number of topics but without success.'

'Have you tried him on a cheap fur coat or strawberries from California in the heart of winter? I believe we have them for dessert.'

'A gift of course,' Eunice said going an ugly colour of red and glaring at her husband. 'I do wish you wouldn't talk like this about a guest in front of others, Simon. They might wonder what we say about them when they're not here.'

'Oh we know.' Paget smiled at Laurie.

'You're not a guest, darling,' Eunice corrected with a sweet smile. 'You're family.'

Ruth closed her eyes and prayed that there would be no irritated riposte from the prickly Paget. But no, marriage appeared to have mellowed her. She did in fact look very settled and happy, and so did Laurie. Paget had a job and commuted daily to London. Their house was half way between London and Edgerton. It seemed a very amicable, harmonious arrangement.

'The fellow is a deadly bore.' Geoffrey put a large helping of mustard on the side of his plate. 'Why do you invite him, Eunice? It's so embarrassing that he never brings his wife. What if I went everywhere without Ruth? I think it's very odd.'

'Oh *she* is the bore,' Eunice replied sipping her Burgundy. 'The wife, I mean, not Ruth. I find Antal Lazar very good company. If he is a ladies' man well so what? He is far more entertaining than some men I know.' She looked at Simon, but he was having his work cut out carving beef for eleven people.

Suddenly Antal Lazar appeared at the door, his usual

immaculate self, in a crimson velvet evening jacket with black satin lapels. His hair was a little longer than usual and curled slightly around his ears. His sidewhiskers were thick and neatly trimmed, just parallel to his high cheekbones. His dark, well shaved face shone with cologne. Ruth felt her heart lurch. She stared at him, noting every movement he made, the slightest gesture and she knew that she was hopelessly obsessed by him.

Antal went rapidly over to Eunice, bent low and kissed her hand. 'Forgive me, my dear. I had an early shipment at Southampton. I . . .'

'Oh spare us your excuses you naughty boy.' Eunice patted the chair beside her and smiled at him flirtatiously. 'You have already missed a course. You eat your prawn cocktail as quickly as you can before Simon finishes carving the beef or he mightn't give you any. He is so cross with you.'

Eunice had rather a good knack of shifting the onus of discomfort on to other people. She was especially adept at making her spouse feel awkward.

'Now do you know everyone . . .' Eunice started going round the table and Ruth felt a sensation of panic before she got to her. She clasped her hands under the table and cracked her knuckles. 'Ruth you know, and Geoffrey. Do you know John Harrison and his wife Janet? They are . . .'

His eyes had only briefly rested on her; not a muscle in his face moving. She thought of how his face looked when they made love, the corners of his eyes screwed up, the veins bulging on his forehead and then afterwards that beautiful limpid look of peaceful repletion in his blue eyes.

'Tell me what you have been doing since you left the university.' John Harrison next to her tried once more to engage her in conversation. To begin with she had been too distraite wondering how she would feel about seeing Antal; now she was equally distraite because she knew.

*

'He really does chat up the women,' Geoffrey said glancing over his shoulder. 'I can't think what they see in the oily bastard can you?'

Ruth hadn't been paying attention. She moved round the room in a state of emotional emptiness. The little dinner she had eaten seemed to weigh very heavily on her stomach.

'Why are you so interested in him?' She grasped Geoffrey's hand and stared at him.

'I'm not; but he does have a way with the ladies. I've never discussed anything else with him but business in my life. I don't think he really can talk of anything else; but look how he chats to women, especially Eunice.'

Especially Eunice. Did he do it deliberately? His eyes had hardly ever left those of Eunice at the table; he danced with her immediately after coffee when the carpet was rolled back and the tape recorder started in the drawing room. He had scarcely glanced at Ruth at all. She felt like a schoolgirl ignored at her first date.

Geoffrey, never a very good dancer, fell over her foot. His watery eyes swam in his red face and he breathed heavily. He was terribly out of condition. She guiltily wondered if she was helping to kill him by not insisting on a more healthy regime and a diet of some kind. But she felt such total indifference to Geoffrey that she hardly ever thought about him, or worried about him, at all.

The room was getting crowded and couples pressed in on them from all sides.

'I think I'll get a drink,' Geoffrey said mopping his brow. 'I could do with a whisky.'

'I think you could do without a whisky,' Ruth said. 'You're horribly out of condition, Geoffrey. Let this be your resolution for 1979, to slim.'

'And let it be yours to mind your own business.' Geoffrey left her abruptly and lumbered through the crowd.

'May I?' Laurie was by her side smiling, alert, happy. Ruth

glanced at him gratefully. 'I haven't seen you for such a long time,' he said. 'We've been awfully busy with the house.'

'I hear it's lovely.'

'You must come and see it.'

'And Paget has a job?'

'Yes; she travels quite a bit; but she loves work. It is essential for her. I don't mind. We're very happy.'

'I'm so glad.' Ruth felt empty inside; she was too unhappy herself really just now to wish happiness for anyone else. She kept looking around for Antal. There were more people now than she remembered at New Year's Eve but the atmosphere was different. If only Antal would ask her to dance and reassure her.

'I'm very sorry you gave up the university. I became a member of the family too late to do anything about it.'

'You couldn't have. I had made up my mind. I think I was there for all the wrong reasons.'

'But you still think it was the right decision to make?' His handsome friendly face looked at her with concern.

'I don't really know.' Antal was dancing with a woman she didn't know. He held her close and was talking nineteen to the dozen, moving expertly, his blue eyes gleaming, his white teeth flashing. What was he saying? 'I'm sorry, I'm very preoccupied,' Ruth said. 'I think I'm getting the flu.'

After Laurie she danced with a number of men but always looking in vain for Antal. She began to feel sick and rather dizzy and she decided she must go home. Geoffrey was asleep on the sofa and, as usual, she would have to drive. She saw Eunice and she thought she saw Antal; but she couldn't be sure. She went over and shook Geoffrey beginning to haul him to his feet. A hand touched her lightly on the shoulder and she froze.

'Just one with me before you go?'

She let Geoffrey sink back, still slumbering. The smile was for her and the laughter in the eyes. The cool hands that controlled her body with such precision held out their welcome. She was speechless and let him fold her in his arms, nuzzle his head against hers. He'd been dancing like that with all the women so no one would notice.

'Why did you leave it for so long?' Her voice was shaking.

'I didn't want people to get suspicious. That's what you want too, isn't it?'

'I suppose so; but I began to feel quite ill.'

'You silly goose,' he murmured. 'I thought of you the whole time.'

'You needn't be so animated with the other women, especially with Eunice.'

'Oh Eunice is my standby in case you get tired of me.'

'Don't joke. I can't bear it.'

'But don't be so serious. How can I think of anyone but you?'

'I wish I knew you were telling the truth.'

He pressed her close and she knew what his body looked like; she wished they were naked together on the bed in the room in Marylebone High Street, rolling and falling, tumbling and stretching, arching and thrusting, clinging. He seemed to know what she was thinking because he pressed her even closer. She wanted to kiss him but she didn't dare.

'How soon can you get up?' he said.

'The January sales.'

'I can't wait.'

She spent a lot of the time that holiday looking out of the window, hoping to see him. The Lazars didn't invite them in and they didn't invite the Lazars, though she and Bella, meeting at their gates, had each said they 'must come in for a drink' over Christmas. There was too much hostility from Geoffrey and, officially, the families didn't get on since the incident involving Irena and Joe. The children behaved as

194

they normally did, but not the parents. Ruth also felt guilty about confronting her lover's wife. She thought the guilt would show in her eyes. She was glad that she and Bella were no longer close, no longer popped in for chats. She wondered sometimes if Bella knew.

After Christmas the weather was terrible; the worst English winter for sixteen years. Whole areas of the Home Counties were cut off, places like Kent and parts of Berkshire and Hampshire. In the north many cattle died and isolated farmhouses were without supplies for weeks.

Ruth battled determinedly through the weather to get to the January sales. Geoffrey couldn't understand it and said she was a masochist. Sometimes she took the children because they seemed to give verisimilitude to her double life; but she trailed round the shops with them thinking of Antal. London now to her was a taxi from Waterloo to Marylebone High Street, sometimes lunch at Genevieve or Odins. It was a fairyland, another world, quite cut off from life. It was like being cast adrift and isolated in the snow and she wished they were.

'You can use the weather not to go back tonight,' he said looking out of the window. 'The roads are absolutely icy. Edgerton will be cut off by now.' He drew the curtains and poured himself a drink from the whisky bottle that stood on the bedside table. She eyed him critically.

'If you drink too much whisky you'll get like Geoffrey.'

'God forbid.' He tossed it back and lay down beside her. Despite the fact that the central heating was turned up high she was cold.

'Geoffrey's not too bad,' she said.

'Geoffrey is awful. He typifies everything I detest about the average middle-class Englishman. He is a snob, he is self important, he is vain, he is narrow-minded, he is . . .'

She felt herself getting colder and her body stiffen. 'He is my husband,' she said knowing that she sounded too middle class for words. 'There are some things he is good at, for instance, he is a very clever lawyer, and he is kind. Basically he is very kind.'

'Well he is certainly kind in letting me have you; but then again I'd call that incompetent. If my wife was having an affair I'd know it and I'd put a stop to it.'

'Even Bella?' She gazed at him half smiling.

'Of course I wouldn't like Bella to have an affair. It would make me look a fool.'

'But you enjoy cuckolding other husbands?'

'I don't enjoy it. I think they're idiots. Married to a woman like you . . . I'd be making love to you the whole day long.' He began to lick her stomach gently, soft little caresses of the tongue that made her tremble.

'You wouldn't. You'd get tired of it.'

'I could never get tired of you. You know that, Ruth.' He paused and raised his head. Her stomach was wet and she massaged it with her finger. 'But when did you last make love with Geoffrey?'

'That's none of your business.'

'It is my business, now that I am your lover. A jealous lover. I do not make love to Bella.'

'She said you did. A few times a year.'

'Well not this year. I haven't touched her this year and I don't want to.'

'Doesn't she?' She wondered how a woman could sleep in the same bed as Antal and not want him to touch her all the time.

'I don't know. She never makes any overtures and neither do I. What about Geoffrey?'

'I think if we ask these kind of questions of each other we will only have trouble.'

'He *does* make love to you?'

She took his hand and kissed it. 'Don't ask.'

'I want to know damn it!' Antal sharply withdrew his hand and pummelled the bed. 'I bloody well want to know.'

196

She felt the tears come into her eyes. 'How can I say "no" to Geoffrey? What would I give as an excuse?'

'Say you bloody well don't like his big fat body. My God the very thought gives me the shivers. I hate a man who lets himself go as he does.'

Antal did an hour's exercises every day, the kind approved by the RAF to keep their men fit. Often, after making love, he would start press-ups on the floor as if he hadn't pressed up enough already.

'You just hate Geoffrey. You aren't each other's kind of person.'

'He doesn't like me does he?'

'Not much.'

'He thinks I'm a toady foreigner?'

'He certainly is chauvinistic; he thinks everything good begins and ends at Dover.'

'I've got his wife though.' He lay against her and kissed her breast along by the side and up towards the nipple.

'That should make you happy.'

'But I still can't bear the thought of him making love to you.'

'It's not the same. I do it because I have to; it's like submission; but I don't want to.'

'Don't,' Antal said digging his face into her flesh, biting her hard. 'Don't, don't, don't.'

'Who was it you stayed with?' Geoffrey looked at her over *The Daily Telegraph*, which he now read because of the suspension of *The Times*.

'A girl I was at school with. Joanna Forbes.'

'I've never heard you mention a Joanna Forbes.'

She felt guilty and rather shaky. She and Antal had hardly slept all night and she felt the effects. Leaving London on the morning train was like setting off to prison – a prison without any remission. 'She has a small flat in Finchley.'

'Well, I've never heard you mention her before. The line all right this morning?'

'Yes. It seemed fine.'

'George isn't well.'

'Oh?' She felt alarm, an increase of guilt. 'What's the matter?'

'He looked as though he'd been drinking last night. He was tottering about the place. Olivia says he's been odd for weeks. You'd think, Ruth, that you'd notice this kind of thing being his mother, now you're at home. You seem to be awfully apathetic to me. Sometimes I'm sorry you left the university.'

Rage welled up in her heart, rage, despair, guilt and shame. She flung her handbag down and rushed up the stairs to George.

At first she didn't know whether George was asleep or awake and then she saw his eyes flicker. There was a peculiar smell in the room; a chemical smell that she had vague recollections of having smelt before. She sat on the bed and looked at him closely.

'George?'

'Mm?' He gazed at her sleepily.

'What is the matter, darling?'

He ran a hand across his brow. She saw that his lips were very red as though he had been licking them. There was also a nasty ugly patch that looked like a sore of some kind.

'Have you got a cold, George? Your lips are terribly sore.'

George shook his head and then he started to cry. As she used to when he was a small boy Ruth took him in her arms and leaned her head on his. He was trembling.

'Tell Mummy, darling?'

George trembled even more and wept copiously but said nothing. Ruth began to feel seriously alarmed. She went slowly downstairs. Geoffrey was still absorbed in *The Telegraph.*

'I think we should call the doctor.'

198

'But what is it?'

'I thought he had a cold; but I don't know. His lips are very red and he has a sore by the side of his mouth. But it is his demeanour that worries me. He is so listless and weepy and fearful. I wonder if he's having some sort of nervous breakdown.'

'A breakdown? At his age? Nonsense.' Geoffrey lit a cigarette and blew out the match shaking it with irritation. Added to her worry about George Ruth felt her repugnance for Geoffrey mount to such a point that she felt she could scream.

'I think you can have a breakdown at any age, Geoffrey, if things aren't going right.'

'And they aren't going right here for a start.' Geoffrey shook the paper and glared at her.

'Geoffrey, could we postpone the brawl until later? I'm going to call Doctor Marlow.'

'I don't want to brawl, why should I? All I want is a contented normal happy life at home to cushion me against the worries of my work. It's all I want and I don't think it's much to ask, seeing that I provide a lovely home for you and give you all you could possibly ask for. I . . .'

Ruth went out of the sitting room and banged the door. She went upstairs to the bedroom to use the extension phone to call the doctor. It was three o'clock. His wife said he would try and be round before nightfall.

Ruth lay on the bed for ten minutes. She felt desperately tired. She knew that Antal was coming home too for the weekend. He would be next door and the thought tantalized her so much that she had to stifle an urge to tear out of the house into his arms. What would he say if she came running through the door? He had driven home, probably arriving before her as she had taken the train. He had run her to Waterloo and they'd enjoyed a long lingering lovers' kiss in the car park outside.

How long had George been like this? What else was going

on in the house? How long had *The Times* been suspended? She really didn't know. She only knew it was Saturday because Geoffrey was at home dressed in his cords and the thick fisherman's jersey that made him look enormous. The shirt Antal had put on that morning she had given him, a very fine blue poplin with a dark blue stripe. She had paid the earth for it – far more than she had ever spent on a shirt for Geoffrey. But Antal looked so beautiful in it, so handsome in his well cut grey suit, his highly polished brown slip-ons. She loved watching him dress and she loved being seen with him in the street, being driven about in his new black Porsche, being his woman.

She slowly undressed and looked at herself for a long time in the mirror. She had a very small love bite just below her collar bone. Geoffrey would never notice it; but she always asked Antal to be careful. He was such a biter that she frequently feared he would bite off one of her nipples. She sometimes cried out with pain and it pleased him. The savagery of their lovemaking was not the least attractive aspect of it.

She knew she didn't smell of him any more because she had bathed carefully before leaving the flat. She wished she did; she wanted something of him still. She had just finished putting on clean underthings, slacks and a grey sweater, when Dr Marlow came. She combed her hair and went down to greet him.

After a preparatory talk in the living room they went upstairs leaving Geoffrey watching sports on TV. The first thing Dr Marlow noticed was the smell. He stopped inside the room and sniffed. Then he looked at Ruth.

'How long has there been this smell?'

'I have smelt it before,' she said looking round vaguely. 'On and off. Never as definite as this.'

The doctor went over to George and took his pulse looking carefully at his face. He bent down and examined the sore. He took his stethoscope out of his bag and sounded the boy's heart and lungs. Then he sat back on the bed.

'George?'

George said nothing but his eyes flickered. The doctor held back his lids and examined his pupils. 'George, it's Doctor Marlow. You know me don't you? Ruth felt fear clutch at her heart and sat down abruptly on the chair by George's desk. 'George how long has this been going on? You've got to tell me.'

'Has what been going on?' Ruth sat on the edge of the swivel chair.

'Glue sniffing,' Dr Marlow said. 'It is the current curse of Edgerton, especially but not exclusively at the comp.'

'*Glue* sniffing?'

The doctor got up and walked over to George's desk, riffling through the things on it. He finally found and held up a well known proprietory brand of glue.

'This.'

'That? What on earth does he do with that?'

'Squirts some of it into a polythene or plastic bag and sniffs it. It makes them high. It also makes them very drowsy and lethargic, irrational. If he's been doing it for a long time it will take him a long time to get over it.'

'My God! Is it like drugs?'

'That sort of thing but not as dangerous, thank heaven; although it can lead to tragedies in young people who are too dopey to take care.'

Ruth was shocked. The doctor went back over to George and sat again on the bed.

'George, I know you can hear me and I know you've heard what I've told your mother. I'm going down now to talk to her and your father. I'll give you some medicine that will relax you and make you sleep properly and we'll decide what to do to get you off this habit. It is only a habit and you must stop it or you'll be really ill. Do you hear me, George?'

201

George nodded and some tears stole out of his closed lids; but he didn't open his eyes.

16

Christopher Lazar hung his head; he was sitting in the centre of the room rather like the scapegoat surrounded by accusing members of the tribe. Ruth felt sorry for him. She had never seen such a display of temper as that to which Antal had just given vent. All the passion of his Magyar forbears seemed to rise up inside him and froth out of the top. He literally spat and sizzled with rage. Even Bella seemed impressed. Mindless; stupid; insufficient to do; boarding school; all the words and threats came out until Antal paused breathless and glared at his son.

'Well, what do you say?'

Christopher mumbled and Antal looked as though he was going to start all over again when Bella intervened.

'George is only a year younger than Chris. I'm sure you can't blame Chris exclusively for what George does.'

'It's his wicked, pernicious influence,' Antal howled, his face mottled. 'Of *course* you can blame him, especially as it was obviously making George ill.'

'It wasn't obvious to his mother.' Bella glanced at Ruth.

'*I* certainly didn't think he was ill,' Ruth said. 'But there have been symptoms. I thought it was puberty.'

'You think everything is puberty.' Geoffrey looked at her contemptuously. 'You don't seem to notice a thing.'

'Neither did you.'

'But I'm not at home all day, and you said you smelt that chemical smell.'

'I thought it was a chemistry set or something. I thought his lethargy was late nights. I thought . . .'

'You *thought* . . .' Geoffrey was withering.

'You can't blame yourself, Ruth.' Antal spoke softly. 'Bella didn't spot a thing with Chris.'

'But Chris wasn't affected.' Geoffrey edged closer to Bella as though tacitly offering his support.

'But still Chris *did* know the glue sniffing was going on and that George was into it more heavily than him.'

'But Chris is *not* George's keeper.' Bella's tone was patient but not resigned. Ruth thought she had lost even more weight, grown more ascetic looking.

'Of course he's not.' Geoffrey lit a cigarette.

Ruth realized it was Geoffrey and Bella versus her and Antal. The thought made her smile inwardly, but outwardly she remained grave. She wished she could put her arms around Antal and lean her head on his shoulder. The display of bad temper had been primitive, exciting; she wondered how much of it was deliberate, to impress her. She was so aware of him that she thought the other two must see it. Even being with him in the same room, despite the circumstances, made her want to sing. Poor Chris.

'I think Chris should go now,' she said. 'He has told us all he knows.'

'And just mind, you young so and so,' Antal advanced on him waving a menacing finger, 'if I so much as *hear* . . .'

Chris scuttled out of the door.

'I think we all need a drink.' Antal went to the sideboard and sorted through the bottles. 'I must say I am terribly sorry about Chris's part in it.' Chris had admitted getting George involved in sniffing glue and then becoming scared himself.

'I think you overdid the shouting,' Bella said in a tired voice. 'He's going to hate you, more than he does already.'

Antal paused in the act of pouring whisky. 'What do you mean "more than he does already"?'

'He thinks you don't take enough interest in what he does.'

'What the hell . . .'

'That you never take him out or come to school functions. He's quite right, you don't. This is his way of rebelling, or telling you you aren't doing what you should be doing.'

'Oh don't give me all the psychological stuff.' Antal passed Ruth a sherry first, smiling at her; then he resumed his frown as he turned to Bella. 'All that Freudian wish-wash. I am as good a father as I can be, a hard-working father and if you think you're the ideal mother then you're fooling yourself.'

'Chris hates the way you're always late or not turning up. He really feels it. It shows him up in front of the other kids. Our other children didn't seem to mind so much as he does.'

'Hard luck on him then. Time he became adjusted.'

'You'll have to keep an eye on Chris, Antal. He'll become a delinquent.'

'*I'll* have to keep an eye . . .' Antal stared at Bella. 'What the bloody hell are *you* doing to stop him? Sitting all day in the garage writing books. For Christ's sake. We have a filthy house, a delinquent kid and you . . .'

'I just said he *might* become delinquent.'

'Well, see that he doesn't.' Antal downed his whisky.

Ruth thought of the bottle on the bedside table in Marylebone High Street. She could see him standing by it naked, pouring a shot after they'd made love. She thought he did drink a lot, but not as much as Geoffrey. She wondered if her eyes revealed her thoughts because Bella was looking at her in a strange way.

'We're all to blame,' she said quickly. 'I don't think any of us really understand our children.'

Shortly afterwards they left. Bella said they really must come to dinner and she would get down to thinking about it. Ruth knew that as long as she did that the invitation would never come. She looked over Bella's head and saw Antal

205

standing in the hall. She lowered her eyes and she was sure that Bella knew.

Ruth had left the lunch joint in the oven, asking Olivia to baste it and do the vegetables. When they got back there was no sign of the vegetables having been done or the table laid. The joint had obviously not been basted either. It was nearly one o'clock. From upstairs came the sound of the pop group, Abba. Ruth raced upstairs and found Olivia lying on her stomach kicking her heels in the air listening to the record player. She seized her from behind and dragged her to her feet. She wanted to hit her.

'Do you know that *nothing* has been done?'

Olivia affected an air of surprised innocence. 'You're back? I thought there was loads of time.'

'Well there isn't. We've been gone an hour. I could hit you.'

Olivia leaned her right cheek towards her mother. 'Go on then.'

Ruth drew back her hand, felt a choking sensation and ran downstairs. In a great fury she began to do the vegetables.

'I don't suppose you could lay the table?' she called to Geoffrey through the hatch.

'No I couldn't.'

'Thank you very much.'

'Not at all; but it's not my job. Where's Olivia?'

'She thinks it's not her job either. It's obviously only my job.'

She went into the dining room and threw the cloth on the table. She spilt the jug of water on it and had to get a fresh one. She felt if she didn't calm down she'd join George on tranquillizers. She stood making gravy and taking deep breaths.

The meat was overcooked.

'I like it like this,' Joe said chewing steadily.

206

'I don't want your sarcasm.'

'I'm not being sarcastic, Mum. I do. What happened this morning to put everyone in such a bad temper?'

'You mean you don't know?' Olivia gazed at him. Joe blinked innocently. 'What were you *doing?*' Olivia leaned meaningfully on the verb.

'Out.' Joe went rather red and lowered his eyes. Ruth wondered where Irena had been as she hadn't noticed her at the Lazars. She had the distinct impression that, but for them, the house had been empty.

'Where were you, Joe?' Ruth helped herself to gravy. She tried to keep her voice level and her eyes calm.

'I just went for a walk.'

'Alone?'

'With friends.'

'Which friends, may I ask?'

'No you may not.'

Geoffrey looked up and rapped the table.

'Don't you be rude to your mother, Joe!'

'I'm not being rude, Dad. But I'm nearly eighteen and if I want to go for a walk I think I can do so without asking my mother.'

'Technically you're still a minor.'

'Then I do have to ask Mum every time I want to go out?'

Geoffrey drank from his glass. He had brought a large whisky to the table to have with his lunch. He looked absolutely choleric, Ruth thought; perhaps today would be the day of the heart attack.

'Of course you don't; but she asked you a civil question. Who were you with? If you asked me who I was with or your mother who she was with we'd tell you.'

'Would you?'

Ruth thought there was an odd note in Joe's voice. She froze with terror. Did Joe know something about her and Antal? Supposing someone had seen them kissing outside

Waterloo Station? After all, many people used the train. However his eyes looked angry but not shifty, not accusing.

'Yes we would. It is quite a usual, civilized thing in families to ask what the other members were doing. Unless you have anything to hide you wouldn't mind.'

'He was with Irena Lazar,' Olivia sang, going a-a-arr at the end of Lazar.

For a few moments there was silence round the table.

'Were you?' Ruth's tone was polite.

'Yes.'

'Why didn't you say?'

'Because you're all so bloody funny about her since the fuss that summer. We have to meet in secret.'

Ruth's heart felt really heavy, palpably, as though it was carrying a large weight.

'You *do* meet then?'

'Yes. No one said we hadn't to.'

Ruth looked at Geoffrey. He got up and refilled his glass. She had never known him drink all through lunch like this.

'Well of course we didn't say you hadn't to.' Geoffrey sat down heavily at the table. 'We just hope you're being sensible about it.'

Joe looked at his plate and blushed. Ruth knew he was sleeping with Irena. She felt sick and put knife and fork neatly together. There was a feeling of panic, of nausea as though everything that was stable and orderly was tumbling down. She was sleeping with Antal and her son was sleeping with his daughter. It was almost worse than incest.

'I'd better take George's dinner up.' Olivia had gone rather pale. 'He didn't eat any breakfast.'

'The doctor said he mightn't feel hungry. He's given himself a bad shock.'

'What are you going to do about it?' Olivia stared at her mother. Ruth realized she had not seen a tender or even friendly expression on Olivia's face for weeks, or was it

208

months? She felt totally and completely isolated from her family and realized they were from her.

'We thought, your father and I in consultation with Doctor Marlow, that he might see a psychiatrist. The doctor thinks it is not a deep-seated problem but a few chats with a qualified person might help.'

'It's adolescence,' Geoffrey said gruffly. 'I don't go along with this psychological rigmarole myself; but I have to bow to Marlow's judgement. We might also take him away from the comp and send him to the Royal. Or we may send him to boarding school. It depends how he gets on with the shrink.'

'There was nothing wrong with George until the Lazars came to live next door.' Olivia's voice – was it her imagination? – seemed to Ruth to have a note of menace.

'I think that's a very silly thing to say. Chris Lazar wasn't even heavily involved in the glue sniffing.'

'He's a toady little bastard though,' Geoffrey said. 'Like his father.'

Ruth blushed. She saw Olivia look at her, her eyes narrowed. She felt that Olivia knew, everyone knew that she was sleeping with Antal. She got up and started to remove the dishes.

'Can I help you, Mummy?'

'If you don't think it's too onerous.'

'Oh *why* must you talk like that when I try and help.' Olivia stamped the floor. The dishes in her hands fell and two plates broke. Olivia burst into tears and her father got up and put his arm round her.

'Here, here, here, what's going on? It was an accident.' He looked at Ruth.

Ruth shrugged her shoulders and walked into the kitchen to fetch the brush and pan. She was trembling.

Ruth sat by the mirror for a long time doing her face. Geoffrey was already in bed, pretending to read. She could hear him riffling through the pages too quickly for someone who was as slow a reader as he was. She cleansed her face very thoroughly, put lotion on it, then spread a thin layer of night cream. She brushed her hair and watched it spring back into place. It was very thick and kept its set well. Her clear green eyes peered at her from under her carefully arched brows. Her nose was long and narrow, delicately flared at the end, her chin firm. Was it sagging a little underneath? She felt it and resolved to get throat cream.

She had on a flowing nightie that concealed her figure; it hung in graceful folds and she wished Antal could see her like this. She knew she was desirable and she felt desire. Her loins absolutely ached for him; a physical need that she wondered if he could ever sufficiently assuage.

'Aren't you coming to bed? I want to put my light out.'

'Put it out then.'

She went into the bathroom to brush her teeth. It was always the last thing she did.

Geoffrey's light was out as she got into bed and looked at the clock. She wondered if she should read. Her mind was too active to sleep.

'I'm sorry if I was a bit hasty,' Geoffrey said turning clumsily towards her. 'It has been a bloody awful day.'

'It hasn't been pleasant.' She took up the book and looked for her place. The bookmark fell out of it.

'You say that in a very detached way.'

She rested the book on her lap.

'Geoffrey, I am awfully tired. If you want a long talk, could it be tomorrow?'

He sat up leaning his heavy body on his hands. The bed quivered. 'You're always too bloody tired. Too tired to talk, too tired to read, too tired to make love!'

'Maybe I'm having an early menopause?'

'Menopause. Rubbish.' He sat upright and lit a cigarette.

'You are going to kill yourself you know.'

'Isn't that what you bloody well want? You can get rid of me and have the insurance and . . .'

'Oh for God's sake *Geoffrey*.'

'Well look, Ruth, we've got to have a talk sometime. You never want to talk. It's never convenient. Tomorrow won't be convenient or the next day. I want to talk now.'

Ruth replaced the bookmark and put her book down. She took the Pill with a sip of water. 'Talk then.'

'What I want to say is this.' He wriggled himself into a comfortable position, propping up the pillows. 'This household is, in my opinion, falling part. It is bloody awful living here.'

'You're saying "bloody" a lot.'

' "Bloody" is how I feel. I feel bloody. The whole place is like a wound; the kids are all sick or unhappy. I'm unhappy. I . . .'

'But I'm happy, you suppose?'

'No I do not suppose! But I don't think, you don't seem . . . to care Ruth. You just seem indifferent to what is happening here.'

'I'm not. I just don't know what to do. Olivia seems to hate me and I can't communicate with Joe. Now George is slipping away. O.K. Geoffrey, I'm a failure as a mother. You're going to tell me I'm not even a good wife.'

'But *why?* That is what I don't understand.' Geoffrey stubbed his cigarette out and coughed. 'I simply don't understand what has gone wrong. I'm not saying you're a bad mother, or a bad wife. It's probably just as much my fault too. But I want to know, *why* is all this happening. To us? Why?'

'Well things do go wrong in households. Children grow up and parents don't understand them. It's happening to us. We must make more effort to understand our children, though I doubt if I'll ever understand Olivia. She's so hostile.'

'Not to me.'

'You're a man.'

'We must make more effort to understand each other Ruth.' He put an arm round her and moved closer. She knew all this was going to end in sex. 'I do love you, you know. I want you very badly. I want to be close to you as we used to be.'

She turned and looked into his watery eyes. It was all she could do to stop herself shivering. Why did she dislike him so much? Was it because of Antal? Or was Antal a symptom? When had it all really begun?

'I think people grow apart too, Geoffrey.'

'You're saying we have grown apart?'

'Of course we have.'

'But I don't want to, my darling. I love you and I want to make things go right. I really do. Tell me what I must do. I know I go out a lot, O.K., I'll stay at home more. I don't see enough of the kids. O.K., I'll take more interest in them. We'll go out together as a family and I'll drop some of my activities.'

He stopped talking but she said nothing. There was a lump the size of a tennis ball in her throat, panic rampant in her breast. 'No Geoffrey, I want less of you not more,' she was shrieking; but the words were silent. Only she could hear them.

'What *can* I do, Ruth? Do you want to go back to the university? They said you could. You can register for next year. We'll get a resident housekeeper. I'd do anything, anything at all to make you happy.'

'We can both try,' she said at last. 'For the sake of the children. We must.'

'But for each other too. Christ, we don't want to get like Eunice and Simon. What a battle there is going on all the time there! And look at the Lazars, always bitching. We don't want our household to break up do we, Ruth?'

'No.' She threw back her head and gazed at the ceiling. How could you argue with someone who was being so reasonable? How would you forgive yourself if you refused the olive

212

branch, however clumsy the hand that held it? 'Also, I don't think I want to go back to the university, Geoffrey. It was a phase. It's past. There are things for me to do without behaving like a teenager. I think that's what Olivia disliked most; she saw me as a rival to her and hated me for it.'

She smiled wanly at her husband and he stretched and relaxed as though he had won a victory.

'You look terribly sexy in that outfit.'

She sighed and leaned back on the pillow sensing the inevitable, knowing that to refuse him was tantamount to a fresh declaration of war. They were married; it was called conjugal rights. His right, and her duty, not a pleasure like making love with Antal. He drew her nightie up to her waist, his eyes on her pubic hair. It was dark and springy, fresh from her bath, a darker red than the hair on her head, like brown rust. Antal said the contrast with her fair skin turned him on. Unfortunately it turned Geoffrey on too. He began to unfasten his pyjama trousers.

'I'm bloody lucky to have a wife like you. Many men would give their eyes to be me. Why we row I don't know.' He threw his trousers on the floor. 'Did you ever do anything about the Pill, darling? You were awfully worried about it some time ago.'

'I still am, but what can you do? I got a lower dosage. There doesn't seem much alternative. You could always have a vasectomy.'

She looked apathetically at Geoffrey, but he was too excited, taking off his pyjama jacket. She wondered what he'd think of her if she looked as repulsive as he did naked. Would he expect her to feel desire for him? It was an insult to offer yourself to someone looking like that. Perhaps he thought he was still handsome; people seemed to have an infinite capacity for self deception.

She fumbled with her nightie to take it off but he eased it over her head and threw it impatiently on the floor next to his pyjamas. His hand began travelling slowly over her body; he was breathing very heavily.

'Vasectomy to hell! I sometimes think you want me to have it off!' He saw her expression and his bellow of laughter faltered. 'Sorry, silly joke; but I don't want you to go on taking the Pill if it's dangerous. Let's try the cap or the old sheath.'

Ruth shuddered. What the aesthetic Antal would think of such crude contraptions she couldn't think. She stayed on the Pill for him, even if it killed her.

'And I will do something about my weight,' Geoffrey continued virtuously. 'You're absolutely right; and this smoking is killing me. I'll go on a diet and stop the fags. For you my darling, I'll do anything; but I don't want anything to harm you. I love you too much. Give the Pill up if you want.'

'I'm not dead yet.' Ruth switched off the light, lay back and closed her eyes. She felt like a ritual sacrifice on the altar of marriage.

17

Ruth sat in the coffee bar opposite Antal's flat. She had already had three coffees, a toasted sandwich, and smoked three cigarettes. The lunchtime crowd had come and gone and there were only a few stragglers like herself. The woman standing behind the bar by the coffee machine kept on giving her glances of sympathy. If Antal didn't turn up in ten minutes she would have to go.

Antal was invariably late for their dates. It was difficult enough to make them. She either waited for him to call her at home during the day or, if she hadn't heard for some time, she left a message on the answering machine in his London office which she took to be just a room. She never dared call the warehouse in Edgerton in case someone recognized her voice. She had resumed her place fully in the social life of the town and, if anything, did more than before.

So it was not easy for her to fit in these trips to town; and to have to sit in a coffee bar for an hour and a half waiting for Antal made her resentful, indignant and increasingly desperate that she was so involved with a man who had such little regard for other people that he always made them wait for him.

She had bought lunch at the supermarket, cold meats and salads, a bottle of wine and cheese. They had it in bed before or after they made love, and these love feasts constituted one of the most delightful parts of their encounters. Food and wine and sex went together in a way she had never thought of before. It all lay now in a carrier at her feet. She got up to pay as a taxi stopped outside and Antal emerged. As she paid she kept the smile fixed on her face and turned to greet him with all the freshness of someone who had just arrived. The woman behind the counter who knew her fairly well by now gave her a conspiratorial smile and a meaningful glance in Antal's direction.

'I didn't think you'd still be here. There was no way I could let you know.'

She didn't reply, but crossed the road and he followed her. She stepped back to let him open the outside door. She was simmering with rage and anxiety and her relief was an anti-climax. They climbed the two flights of stairs and he let her into the flat. It seemed very cold and impersonal and she shivered.

'Did you buy any food?'

'I've eaten.'

He put his hands on her shoulders. 'Darling, I do hope we're not going to have a scene. If so . . .'

'Yes?' She turned towards him, her face quivering.

'Well I had just better get back to the office and do some work. It's a very bad time for us at the moment; a disastrous winter of strikes, goods not getting through and payment for them delayed and now a general election. If Labour get in I'll slit my throat.'

'Antal, I come up from the country for these meetings. It is not easy for me. I have to lie, explain, make arrangements and then sit for an hour and a half waiting for you.'

'Surely it's not as long as that.'

'One o'clock you said. It's now two-thirty, two forty-five actually. I have to get back this evening because I have a meeting.'

'Oh you can cancel that.'

'No I can't. Why should I when you don't bother to alter any of your arrangements? Why are you always late, Antal, antagonizing everyone?'

He sat down and ruffled his smooth hair. He still had his coat on.

'I don't know. Ask a psychologist. I just have so many things to do, so many pressures. You don't know what it's like.'

'If you have an appointment you can say you have to go.'

'It's not as easy as that. I can't say I've got to meet a woman and walk out.'

'I don't think you've really time for this affair.'

'Oh yes I have! It's just that I wish you'd be more patient and understanding with me.' He got up, came over to her and tilted her chin. 'Please?'

She stepped back to avoid his embrace. 'But I haven't the time either, Antal. I cannot waste a day and then be left hanging around.'

'Oh it's a waste is it? Seeing me?'

'No, you know what I mean.' She gestured helplessly. 'I really have to work hard to fit this in, to justify it. My frequent trips to town are already the subject of comment by Olivia, needless to say.'

'You don't think she knows?' The alarm in his voice impressed her.

'Oh no. At least I don't think so. No there is no way she could know. She just criticizes everything I do.'

'How's George?' Antal took off his coat and rummaged in the bag of food.

'The psychiatrist says he is more deeply disturbed than our doctor thought. It seems he's nursed a deep-seated resentment with me for going to the university. He felt I'd deserted him. This was how he took it out on me.'

'Oh what rubbish these people talk.'

'You think it's rubbish?'

'Of course it is. Things like that blow over. He needs a good hiding.'

Ruth swallowed. 'Geoffrey wants to send him to boarding school.'

'Well that would be one off your hands.' Antal looked at her cheerfully and began to take off his shoes.

'But I don't want him off my hands.'

'Oh come, darling. Don't give me this perfect mother bit. Take off your clothes for God's sake and let's go to bed.'

She could walk out and perhaps not see him again, or she could succumb. She wanted him, and her body needed sex with him. She wanted both so badly and she decided to succumb. She began to undress.

The sight of her excited him and he quickly took his clothes off folding them neatly on the chair. When they were both nude he clasped her body and stood behind her looking at themselves in the long mirror on the wall. He put a hand between her legs and caressed her and the sight of it made her blood pound. She turned to him and they embraced, their bodies merging, their genital parts interacting where they stood. He pushed her quite roughly to the bed and she lay on it her face downwards clasping the pillow, her rump slightly arched so that he could enter her from behind. He lay the length of her body, his arms wound round her clasping her breasts, his head buried in her hair. His warmth and the sensation of his body hair on her back excited her so much it was almost unendurable. Yet even more important than the excitement, was the feeling that they were united, acting as one person, perfectly in tune.

They had their lunch at five; the tension was dispelled and the wine tasted very good. They sat up with the covers over them and the food on plates by the side of the bed. Ruth sat propped up against the pillows drinking her wine; she wasn't very hungry but Antal ate as though he were starving.

'This room *is* terribly impersonal,' Ruth said gazing round. 'I can't really believe you ever live here. Do you?'

'Not really; I sleep here occasionally.'

'Do you mainly keep it to bring women to?'

He glanced at her, taking a bite of a soft roll. 'If you want to use that interpretation you're welcome to.'

'It's so odd, really odd, to think we actually live next door and yet we very rarely meet.'

'Only when the children are in trouble. I'm not really at home all that often either. I'm peripatetic. There's nothing at home to interest me. Bella has her own life and the kids have theirs.'

'Where *do* you belong, Antal?'

'I don't really know,' he said quaffing wine. 'Inside you. That was one of the best sessions we ever had.' He leaned over to kiss her cheek. He was so adept at changing the conversation. 'It gets better and better. Worth waiting for, Ruth?' He glanced slyly at her and she tossed back her hair.

'Is that why you do it, to increase the sense of anticipation?'

'Of course, anger is a good breeding ground for desire.'

'You are an absolute swine.'

'You know it's not true.' He put a hand on her arm gazing into her eyes.

'I don't actually. I still don't really like you, even if I'm obsessed by you and you know I'm always jealous of you, wondering what you're doing, where you are, who you're seeing. It's cruel to make me wait as well.'

'But surely you didn't think I was seeing another woman?'

'No, but I think it could be so important to you to see me that you turn up on time. It would flatter my ego.'

'You should feel flattered enough that I desire you so much. Anyway why are you jealous of me? I *know* you sleep with your husband. You've told me as much. I don't sleep with anyone else. What do you think I feel about that?'

'I have to sacrifice myself with Geoffrey because I want you.'

'Yes but I hate to think of him penetrating your body.' Antal's face grew dark and angry. 'How many times does the swine do it?'

'Oh Antal, please. Do you want me to leave Geoffrey; because if I refuse him sex I shall have to leave him. Is that what you want?'

'No, of course not.'

She expected it, but she was sad that he said it; to know that he never ever contemplated anything more permanent than what they had now.

'Geoffrey is being particularly nice at the moment. The business with George has worried him; he sees that Olivia and I don't get on. He has gone on a diet; he is cutting down his smoking. He is making every effort to make our marriage work, to improve things at home. If we split up who do you think would keep me? Not you I'm sure and Geoffrey would be vicious, and have every reason to be. What do you think he'd say if I refused him sex? It should please you that I don't enjoy it. I never have an orgasm with him now, never.'

'Does he know?'

'I pretend. It saves hurting him.'

'Do you pretend with me?'

'You should know I don't.'

'You make me wonder now. Women can pretend and men can't. It's not fair.'

'If women have to pretend they can't be enjoying sex very much. Pretending is very hard work.'

'Is it hard work with me?'

She smiled at him over the rim of the glass, silently toasting him, playing the temptress, revelling in her sexuality.

'Up you mate,' he said.

At seven she decided she must go. He was asleep and she crept out of bed. She would write him a note as they did in the films; but a hand jerked out and held her.

'Stay.'

'I can't.'

'You've already missed your meeting.'

'I'm going to ring home and say I'm on my way.'

'Say you're staying with Joanna thingmy, that you've got a headache.'

'Supposing he asks for her number?'

'Give him this one. Stay. Please stay. It means an awful lot to me.'

She had a sudden feeling of apprehension. 'Why?'

'No particular reason. It just does. We'll go somewhere special for dinner and then I want to make love to you again tonight and in the morning. Then you can go.'

Ruth felt it was important. She felt she ought to stay and went into the sitting room to phone home.

As they stood at the door preparing to leave for dinner she fumbled in her bag and gave him a small box.

'Just a little present.'

He took it exclaiming with surprise. 'But darling you shouldn't. You're always buying me things.'

It was true. It was never reciprocated; but there was something delicious about buying secret gifts for her lover. He took out a pair of plain gold cuff links with his initials delicately engraved. A.L.

'Oh darling they're beautiful.' He kissed her. 'What a thoughtful gift. I really must buy something for you. What would you like?'

'Surprise me,' she said, knowing that the surprise would be if he gave her anything at all. But she didn't really mind because she didn't think of Antal in terms of giving her anything other than himself.

Neither of them had been to the restaurant before, Miranda, newly opened near Antal's office in Bruton Street. It looked very expensive and there were no prices on the menu. She wondered why he should take her to such an expensive place and she felt an ache of foreboding when he ordered champagne.

'What *is* the occasion?' She smiled nervously.

'You.' He took her hand. 'Just to be with you is an occasion.'

'There's something that makes me uneasy about all this. You wanted me to stay; coming here is obviously costing the earth. Are you doing very well?'

'On the contrary, but it's not a business occasion. I'm toasting my mistress.' He held up his glass. 'Thanking her for being herself, for giving me herself. I love your body, Ruth. I worship it.'

'What about my mind?'

'Ah now that is another thing. I can't make love to that but, yes, a woman with a mind is more interesting than a woman without one however beautiful her body.'

'You make me feel jealous again. It's as though you had years and years of experience.'

Antal tried to look modest. 'Well I have known, as the Bible says, a good few women in my time. I will not deny it; I am not ashamed of it.'

'Were they all frustrated wives like me?'

'You're demeaning yourself. You think I'd take advantage of you?'

'It makes me feel I'm just another.'

'How could you feel that? I have never made love so wonderfully with any other woman as I have with you. I am quite obsessed by you. I wish you could stay more often.' She was relieved to hear him refer to the future. 'What did Geoffrey say when you phoned?' His tone altered slightly every time he mentioned Geoffrey's name.

'He wasn't there. He's very busy with the election. I spoke to Joe and left a message.'

'Will you have to explain things to Geoffrey?'

'Probably. I don't think he'll probe though because he's trying to be nice.'

'And Joe wasn't curious?'

'Oh no. Joe . . .' She looked at him and stopped. 'Joe doesn't know anything does he? I mean Irena?'

'Don't be absurd.' He placed a hand over hers. 'You don't suppose I discuss my sex life with my children?'

'Irena is very like you.'

'You mean sexually or in looks?'

Ruth felt annoyed. 'I know nothing of Irena sexually; but she is like you to look at.'

'In temperament too; she is the most like me.'

'So she is sexy?'

'Possibly.' He smiled at her. 'You should ask Joe.'

The colour sprang to Ruth's face. 'What an awful thing to say.'

'Why?' He looked surprised.

'He's my son, can't you understand?'

'She's my daughter. It doesn't prevent her having a sex life.'

'You think she and Joe . . .'

'Of course. Don't you?'

'You *always* thought that?'

'Yes.' His grip on her hand tightened. 'Don't mind so much. Youthful love is very beautiful. I imagine they have a pretty good time.'

'Did Irena say so?'

'Not in so many words; but I don't have many doubts that they are lovers.'

'I think it's horrible.' Ruth sat back taking her hand from under his.

'But why is it horrible? Sex is beautiful.'

'Not at that age! Your daughter and my son? I think it's awful, like incest.'

'Oh you've slept with your son?' His tone was deliberately irritating.

'Don't be disgusting, Antal! That's where you're so primitive. There are a lot more things to life than sex at their age. Such as A levels.'

'I think you can have sex and get your A levels.'

'Well I mind even if you don't.'

'I don't know for sure.'

'You spoke as if you do.'

'Darling, don't spoil the evening.' He kissed her cheek, took her hand and bent over it. His arm slipped familiarly round her waist. She'd seen the movement in the far corner as the new couple arrived. It was only a small restaurant and it wasn't until the flurry of waiters had dispersed that she was sure. Paget Matrecht was staring straight at her, an odd little smile on her face. It was no use pretending she hadn't seen. Ruth's face cracked into a smile and she raised a hand. Antal felt the gesture and looked up.

'What is it?'

'Paget and Laurie, over there.'

'Oh my God.'

Antal looked in the direction Ruth was nodding and raised a hand. Laurie and Paget got up and came over to them.

'Hello!'

'Hello!'

'What a surprise!'

'Isn't it just?'

Antal got up and bowed, kissing Paget's hand. 'Won't you join us?' He indicated the table for two.

Laurie shook his head. 'We've got friends coming thank you. How nice to see you. Fancy you knowing this place. We hear it's very good.'

'It's just round the corner from my office.'

Paget still smiled at Ruth; but unquestionably her eyes were enigmatic. She must have seen the little quarrel they'd had, heads earnestly bent together, Antal putting his arm round her waist, kissing her cheek then her hand. Ruth knew that her expression as she gazed at her niece was quite vacuous.

Antal was looking at Paget's stomach. 'Am I mistaken . . .'

'Oh you don't know! Aunt Ruth didn't tell you?'

It seemed ridiculous to be called 'aunt' when you were with your lover.

'Paget's about five months pregnant. Is it five, Paget?'

'Yes, aunt. We've opted for domesticity.'

'I'm delighted,' Antal said. 'Let us at least drink to it.'

Paget was looking at the champagne as he signalled for two more glasses.

'And another bottle please.'

Bollinger '62. Quite expensive.

No one attempted to ask Ruth what she and Antal were doing. All the talk was about the Matrechts and the baby. Laurie looked blooming. Ruth had been astonished to hear that the ambitious Paget was to have a baby.

'We thought we should have our family while we are still young.'

'But you are very young,' Antal said. 'Not yet twenty I think.'

'Oh I'm nearly twenty-one, flatterer!' Paget opened that delicious mouth and laughed, showing all her teeth. If anything she appeared more beautiful than before and the rounded stomach looked seductive rather than maternal. She looked large for five months, as some women do who are eager to proclaim their condition to the world. Laurie was obviously very proud of her and kept on touching her.

After a few minutes the friends the Matrechts were expecting arrived, a glamorous looking showbiz couple, were introduced and then they all departed to their table at the rear of the restaurant. Despite the heat Ruth felt shivery.

'Who on earth would have expected to find them here?'

'It's quite fashionable. Paget's a fashionable girl isn't she? It's the "in" place.' Antal shrugged. 'It doesn't matter.'

'It *does* matter. It matters terribly. They never once asked what we were doing.'

'They guessed!' Antal gave a short laugh. 'They didn't need to ask.'

'What can I say?'

'To whom?'

'Well what can I say to Paget?'

'Say nothing. I must say Paget is very beautiful. I bet Eunice was a knockout when she was younger. She's still tolerable.' Antal looked reflectively across the gloom.

'Do you think she'll tell Eunice?'

'What if she does?'

'Oh Antal, sometimes you can be very tedious. Do you *really* not care or are you pretending?'

'Don't let them see us rowing.' Antal smiled across the restaurant where the sharp-eyed Paget kept on glancing at them. 'You don't want them to see how much they've disturbed you.'

'Us.'

'I'm not disturbed. Let them make of it what they like. We are a couple having a meal.'

'And I'm Paget's aunt. Geoffrey is her father's brother.'

'Well from what I've heard he carries on.'

'I'm not worried about Simon, I'm worried about Geoffrey.'

'My dear if you start an affair with a married man and you are a married woman . . .' Antal looked at her with mock severity, 'You can't expect everything to go right.'

'But in the middle of London!'

'I once met the husband of a woman I was having an affair with on a business conference in Manila. It is a very small world.'

'You don't really care do you?' Ruth looked at Antal, busy with his *escargots*.

'Not much.' He stared back. 'Things are never as bad as you expect them to be or, if they are, what can we do about it?'

He shrugged his elegant shoulders and drank some more champagne.

226

18

She could see the quadrangle between the old and the new buildings of the university behind Laurie's shoulder. He sat at his desk like a tutor conducting an interview with a student. The trees in the quadrangle were full of buds and rows of daffodils neatly lined the central lawn. Ruth felt at a disadvantage sitting in a low chair in front of Laurie's desk. She wished she were higher up.

'It's a terribly awkward thing to have to ask,' she said, 'but I've never been able to talk to Paget, in that way.'

'Neither can her mother,' Laurie said. 'It's a pity because there is an awful lot to Paget, she is a very sensitive person and quite profound.'

'I'm glad you're so happy.'

'You didn't expect it by the sound of your voice at the wedding, the look of doubt on your face.'

'I thought you were very unalike. As you say I probably didn't know Paget very well. First she was a little girl, and then she seemed to grow up very quickly, to develop a veneer I found hard to penetrate. But could you explain it to Paget do you think?'

'You're sure you don't want to?'

'I simply couldn't.' Ruth crossed and uncrossed her legs looking at her high patent leather black boots. She had dressed with care to ask this favour of Laurie. She wanted to appear poised and sophisticated, rather insouciant, as though it really didn't matter very much.

'It may be too late,' Laurie said. 'She sees her mother quite often now that she has given up work. Eunice is very good at interior decoration.'

'What did Paget say afterwards?'

'After we'd seen you?' Laurie began to fill his pipe in a leisurely academic way. He wore a thick tweed suit, a tweed tie and a check shirt. His blond curly hair was becomingly tousled and he now seemed to wear spectacles all the time. She saw that his fingers were broad and well kept. 'Well Paget didn't say much. I mean there wasn't very much to say. It was quite obvious that, well . . .' Laurie dug the tobacco firmly into the bowl of his pipe.

'That we were intimate?'

'Exactly. I mean you wouldn't be having dinner with Antal Lazar to talk about the weather; or even your mutual family problems I would have thought. You looked much too intimate for that. Anyway Paget said she wasn't surprised.'

'Oh?' Ruth felt irritated for some reason. She undid the large buttons of her light black woollen coat which had been fastened to the neck, her pearls on the outside. She wore no hat, just a black bandeau round her freshly dressed hair. She had taken great pains with her appearance; spent hours rehearsing what she would say. Now, as with most rehearsals to do with real life and not stage plays, things weren't really going according to plan.

'She thought Antal had rather obviously made a play for you, whenever she saw you together. I must say I never noticed it myself. He always . . .' Laurie went slightly pink.

'He was always after all the women?'

'Well. Not my kind of bloke really.'

'Do you think Eunice knows?'

'Now? I really don't know. We didn't talk of it again.'

'Wouldn't Paget have told you if she'd mentioned it to her mother?' Ruth felt a note of desperation coming into her voice.

'I don't think she would have. She might have forgotten. All she can think of is the baby and having the house ready in time.'

Not about me and my predicament, Ruth thought. Typical of Paget to be so self-centred, so selfish. She hadn't changed at all.

'Laurie, it's cost me a lot to come and ask you to ask Paget not to tell Eunice. It's very humiliating for me.'

'I appreciate that, Ruth.' Laurie smiled kindly and pushed his swivel chair away from his desk. 'I really am sorry.'

'Sorry about what?' Ruth knew her voice bordered on hysteria. She felt close to tears which was quite ridiculous, but somehow the contrast between her misery and the happiness of Paget and Laurie seemed more pronounced at this moment.

'Well sorry about everything.'

'You mean sorry for me because I'm having an affair with the local lady killer, or sorry because you saw me in the restaurant with him and caught me out?' Ruth got out her handkerchief and blew her nose.

'I'm just sorry that . . . well yes.' Laurie blew out the match with which he was trying to light his pipe and came over to Ruth. 'I'm sorry about both. Paget said she thought you and Geoffrey were very happy, unlike her own mother and father. She said she thought you got on and had a happy family life. That's why you going to the university was such a shock. They all thought you were very happy at home.'

'I was,' Ruth's lip trembled, 'until *they* moved next door.'

'The Lazars?'

'They disrupted all our lives, upset our children. He suggested I was bored, flattered me by saying I was misusing my great brain and made me discontented and yes, I was attracted by him, right from the beginning. I suppose Geoffrey and I had been going a little sour. For instance he criticized me a lot, called me conventional and I began to notice his appearance, that he was getting fat and smoked too much. I began to carp at little things that seemed O.K. before; things you wouldn't notice with someone you loved.'

'But you'd notice if he was getting fat! There is all this emphasis on diet and health.'

'Yes, but I found it repulsive. Instead of wondering how I could help him reduce I began to find *him* repulsive. He irritated me in a way he never had before, the things he did and said. I suppose all the time I was falling in love with Antal; falling physically for Antal, comparing him with Geoffrey.'

'You can't blame yourself for that. He has great charm and a sort of sympathy that I could well see women would fall for. Paget agrees he is a very attractive man. But weren't you friendly at one time with Bella?'

Ruth nodded her head, blowing hard again. 'Yes that petered out when I came here. I was so busy. Also I suppose we didn't have a lot in common. Then when I started with Antal I felt very guilty and didn't want to see her. Oh but you've no idea . . .' Ruth succumbed to the tears that she had known were there and buried her face in her hands. From time to time Laurie patted her back and made little soothing noises as though she were a child.

'I'll get some coffee,' Laurie said at last, and Ruth was grateful when he left the room so that she could pull herself together and try and compose herself before he came back. She got out her compact and started to repair the damage to her face. By the time Laurie returned with two cups of coffee and a plate of biscuits on a tray she had fresh powder, fresh lipstick and fresh mascara on. She tossed back her head and smiled, taking off her coat to show her new purchase from Eunice, a grey shirt-waister dress in shantung with pink facings and a large pink bow tie. It looked very smart.

'A pretty dress,' Laurie said, putting the tray down on his desk. 'Eunice?'

'Yes.'

'She's a very clever woman. She has wonderful taste.'

'She does. I'm sorry, Laurie, to make such a fool of myself; to embarrass you.'

'That's O.K.,' Laurie said. 'After all I am family. You can command me to listen whenever you like.'

'But I'm your aunt!'

'Ah but I'm not as young as Paget. I bet there's only about ten years between you and me.'

'I really lack a confidant,' Ruth said. 'Someone I can unburden myself to. It's a very superficial world we live in, I often think. I have loads and loads of friends but no intimates.'

'Not Geoffrey once upon a time?'

Ruth studied the ceiling, her hands loosely clasped in front of her. She began to feel more relaxed.

'Not really. Of course I was very happy; there was not much that worried me. I liked life, the children were relatively easy to bring up. I played a lot of bridge and had a lot of social outings. The practice, of course, has always gone well, so there were never any money worries. Geoffrey and I were happy enough without giving the matter much thought. We took ourselves, our love and our life for granted. I suppose I should be much more worried if he had an affair. Thank God he's not the type; not like Simon.'

'You're not afraid of him having an affair?'

Ruth sipped her coffee. 'Not really. I'd feel relieved in a way; it would help assuage my guilt.'

'Wouldn't you be jealous?'

'I can't say; not until I've got Antal out of my mind. I don't really care about Geoffrey at all.'

'You don't want to go away with Antal or anything do you?'

Ruth gave a bitter smile. 'He doesn't want to go away with me. The very idea horrifies him! No. Antal has affairs with married women. It's safe. He really wants no other life. It sounds sordid put like that doesn't it?'

Laurie shrugged and stirred his coffee. He had sat down in an easy chair next to Ruth. 'I'm a very happily newly married man. I can't say how I'd feel after twenty odd years of marriage. I hope the same as I do now; but I wouldn't be realistic if I was sure of it. I just think, if you don't mind me saying so Ruth, if you don't think I am presumptuous, that you are in a mess with Lazar. It's making you very unhappy. That's the point isn't it? You're not happy.'

'But I am when I'm with him; the brief times we are together. It's very exciting; it's rapturous.' Laurie said nothing but began lighting his pipe again with an air of great concentration. 'Do you find that scandalous, Laurie? Does it shock you?'

'No.' Laurie carefully extinguished yet another match. 'After all I lecture in French literature and it is what all the dramas are made of. Madame Bovary, Marguerite Gautier, Eugenie Grandet . . . You're in very good company. I think Emma Bovary suits you best. She was married to a very nice man but she was bored. You're bored Ruth, aren't you? Having an affair with Lazar was like going to university. You're simply bored being married for however many years it is, having almost grown up children and a successful but very busy husband.'

'But I should be thankful to be so well off. Instead of being a good and careful wife, a loving mother, I've neglected my home, my husband and my children's welfare. For what? For an obsession. I had everything I wanted and a busy life, lots of things to do. Why? Tell me why?'

'I couldn't explain it any more than you can. I'm not a psychiatrist. Maybe he could tell you; but I can't. I just hope that everything turns out for the best.' Laurie got up and put his cup on the tray. 'I'm terribly sorry, Ruth, but I have a class at twelve.'

'Of course I must go.' Ruth got up quickly and put on her coat again. 'I'm sorry I've taken up so much of your time.'

232

'You haven't at all. I hope I've been of help. Even to have someone to cry on often helps! Do come and see me whenever you like.'

'And you must come to me, Laurie, if at any time there is anything I can do. You're so well balanced I'm sure there won't be. But please, if there is. After all we're related.'

'Of course aunt-in-law!' Laurie smiled his attractive smile. Ruth thought that Paget was so lucky to have him. Maybe she appreciated him, after all.

'You'll tell Paget?'

'I'll discuss it with her this very evening.'

'But not everything; can you keep that secret? The tears, the confidences? Have I a right to ask?'

'Every right.' Laurie gathered up his books and notes from his desk. 'I won't tell anyone; you can count on it.'

The Angler's Arms had hardly changed in two years except the pattern of the chintz and the fact that the menu was even more expensive. The company hadn't changed either Ruth thought looking around and remembering it was here on the same occasion, Geoffrey's birthday, that she had seen Antal Lazar in that corner kissing the hand of a young blonde girl. She wondered who she was and what had happened to her. She thought her obsession with Antal had, subconsciously, started then.

Of course they'd been back several times in the two years that had passed; but this was a special occasion, Geoffrey's fortieth birthday. This time also all the children were with them as well as Dorcas Harrow who, to everyone's surprise, had not yet had one fiancé but was taking an arts course rather seriously in London.

Ruth thought how stupid it was to generalise. Everyone had always considered that Dorcas and Paget would turn out no good and that her children would be the credit to the family. Well how wrong could one be?

She looked at her children all registering various degrees of displeasure as none of them had wanted to come. George had just been told that he was leaving the comp and going to boarding school, and Joe and Olivia were worried about forthcoming O and A levels respectively.

But the Simon Harrow family seemed blooming. Dorcas, rapturously pretty, was very happy studying in London, living in digs and coming home at weekends and Eunice was thinking of opening a third shop. Harrow and Harrow were doing as well as ever and Geoffrey had become chairman of the local Conservative Party after working so hard to elect Margaret Thatcher. He felt now that the country would just surge forward with a new Tory government. He was even reconciled to having a woman Prime Minister.

'Oh yes there's opportunity everywhere,' Geoffrey was saying expansively. 'No doubt about it. A completely different spirit. Less taxation . . .'

'What about the whopping increase in VAT?' Eunice said. 'It's really making me wonder if I should open a new shop. I'm not as optimistic as you are, Geoffrey.'

'It's the education that worries me,' Joe said. 'All that money for private schools.' As befitted someone with an expensive private education behind him Joe was a member of the Workers' Revolutionary Party and had helped canvas for Vanessa Redgrave at the election. He and his father could not discuss politics without coming to blows. Geoffrey looked at him and spluttered over his *blanquette de veau* but Ruth smiled sweetly.

'Don't get upset on your birthday, darling. He only says it to annoy you.'

Olivia glared at her mother. 'He's absolutely right, mother. The Tories are set to ruin the State system. They are downgrading . . .'

'Oh for Christ's sake!' Simon seized his glass and raised

it in the air. 'Who suggested bringing the children? I propose a toast. To Geoffrey on his fortieth birthday.'

'To Geoffrey. To Daddy.' Glasses were raised and Geoffrey smiled.

'Thank you. I'll spare you a speech; but thank you for being with me on this day.' He leaned over and kissed Ruth's cheek. 'Thanks to my dear wife for tolerating me for all these years.'

Ruth felt close to tears. She saw Eunice looking at her across the table and for a moment their eyes met.

'To Geoffrey's new figure!' Eunice said quickly. 'It really is miraculous, Geoffrey.'

'Thanks to Ruth too. She made me slim.'

'How much is it now, Dad?' George said forgetting for a moment to sulk.

'Sixteen pounds. One stone and two pounds since I started my diet three months ago. I also smoke only cigars.' He thumped his chest. 'I feel a new man.'

He looked like one too. He wore a new suit and Ruth had bought him new shirts for his birthday a size smaller than before. Because he wasn't so fat he wasn't so red and his eyes had lost their watery look because he didn't drink so much. Hardly touched whisky. His hair was quite bushy at the back to compensate for being so sparse on top.

'I shouldn't be eating *blanquette de veau* of course. This is just for my birthday. But, talking of the economic situation, you know that the government *has* to make these cuts. It has to trim the economy; but a lot of the people who expected the Tories to help them are going to the wall. The small business-man isn't really benefiting yet, any way. Antal Lazar, for instance, is in very serious trouble.'

Ruth felt the happiness that she had briefly engendered evaporate. She kept her eyes on the table to mask her face.

'He's certainly in trouble,' Simon said with gusto, 'though of course we shouldn't talk about a client.'

'What sort of trouble?' Ruth raised her eyes at last, her voice level and controlled. She didn't dare take up her fork again in case her hand shook.

'Well bankruptcy if you ask me. The pound is too high to export all the things he used to deal in profitably. The dollar is weak . . .'

As he talked Ruth stopped listening. She thought of their last dinner together, since when she had scarcely seen him. Was it a farewell dinner? Had he known? She saw him once in the drive as he was leaving home and they waved. He hadn't stopped. Then he had phoned to say he had to go abroad and asking if they could meet. She was so busy after the election that she couldn't find a moment, much as she longed for him, much as she wanted to. She just couldn't find an excuse to get away.

'Oh I'm sure he'll come through it,' Eunice was saying. 'He has the knack.'

'He'll certainly have to cut down.' Simon was off again and feeling she couldn't bear it Ruth excused herself and went to the ladies. There was no one there and she sat on a stool in front of the mirror and began carefully to make up her face. Her chest and her cheeks were red and she covered them liberally with powder. The door opened and Eunice swept in in her chic silver lamé evening dress carrying her mink stole.

'I daren't leave this behind. My, it is hot in there.' She sat down next to Ruth and lit a cigarette. She blew the smoke at her face in the mirror and stared at it. 'God, I can't bear the thought of being a grandmother. Isn't Paget beastly? Fancy, a grandmother at forty-three!'

'I think it's rather nice,' Ruth said.

'Wait until it happens to you.'

'Are Paget and Laurie enjoying their holiday?'

'I don't know. We haven't heard. The post between here and Greece is terrible. They wanted to get away early before she was too heavy to travel. She's big isn't she?'

236

'She is a bit.'

'Rather her than me. God, a grandmother.' Eunice peered at herself again. 'I never thought when I had my children so young that I'd suffer for it at this age. It's terribly hot in there isn't it? I think I prefer it here. Simon is being so boring about the economy. But then Simon can be boring about anything.' Eunice exhaled smoke again and looked at Ruth in the mirror.

'I'm sorry about Antal Lazar.'

Ruth saw the colour leap back into her face and she avoided Eunice's eyes. 'Yes it's too bad. I think he thought the return of the Tories would mean better business not bankruptcy.'

'He flew too high.'

'You talk about him as though he's finished.'

'I think he is, for the time being anyway. They're putting the premises here on the market. Simon can tell you everything about it if you want to know. He's handling it.'

'Why should he tell me?' Ruth etched her lipstick round her lips again, pressing firmly to avoid her hand shaking.

'You care. Don't you?'

Ruth didn't reply. Her heart gave a frantic little run and then almost stopped. She felt it jerk in her breast. Eunice knew.

'So Paget did tell you?'

'Yes. The day after she saw you we were hanging curtains and I suppose she couldn't resist it. I know that you later asked Laurie to tell Paget not to say anything; but it was much too late, dear. You know we women can't resist a gossip. Of course I wouldn't say anything to anyone, certainly not Simon.' As she puffed her cigarette, her eyes bright with excitement, Ruth wondered how many of their mutual friends knew by now. If Paget couldn't resist a gossip Eunice certainly couldn't.

'I feel so sorry for you, my dear. Because we've always been so close I wanted to talk to you; to sympathize with you. But

237

I lacked the nerve. Now that I've had a few drinks I feel able to. Besides your face was so stricken. I felt so unhappy for you in there just now. I can see you care. I know how attractive he is. I hope you're not too heavily involved because he really is a shit. He's completely ruthless and self-centred; but he has all the charm and the push that we bored married women sometimes find lacking in our husbands. I, of course, throw all my energies in my work. Did he take you to that awful little flat in Marylebone High Street? I always thought it looked like one of those seedy hotels near King's Cross. Not that I've ever been into one, mind you, but that sort of place. Quite impersonal, with one object in view.' Eunice nervously stubbed out her cigarette rubbing it hard into the ash-tray as though extinguishing the life out of Antal.

Ruth stared at Eunice in the mirror. She opened her mouth to speak when the door flew open and about four rather drunk, excited women ran in, all talking.

She wished they'd come before.

19

Bella Lazar looked very tired. There were dark smudges under her eyes and her thin frame was almost skeletal.

'I hope you don't mind me popping in,' she said shyly pausing at the open kitchen door. It was one of the few fine days in a summer of almost continual cold and wet. All the children were away and Ruth was making a batch of pastry to freeze before she and Geoffrey left for a holiday in Italy.

'Of course I don't mind. It's nice to see you.'

'We kind of lost the habit of popping in. We used to do it a lot at one time. Remember?'

'Yes I do.' Ruth busily rolled the pastry. 'I got all caught up with the university and of course you're always terribly busy.'

'I'm sorry though. I thought at one time we would be very good friends.'

Ruth wondered why Bella was going on like this. Was it leading up to something? Not having made love to Antal for three months she could look at his wife with relative equanimity. Besides she'd made up her mind to finish, whatever happened. She just wanted to see him once more; to tell him what she thought of him.

'Of course there was that business with the children,' Bella said rather lamely when Ruth didn't reply. 'It didn't help did it? Anyway I just wanted to tell you we're leaving. We've got a purchaser for the house. Maybe it will be a relief to you. I don't know.'

Ruth stared at Bella and then wiped her floury hands on a towel. 'You're leaving Edgerton?'

'Yes. You look quite astonished. I'm flattered it should affect you so much. You know Antal has had a lot of trouble with his business; too much diversification. The change of government made things worse not better. He is cutting down to avoid going bankrupt. Simon Harrow has been awfully helpful and thinks he can just make it. He really is a financial wizard that brother-in-law of yours. Antal owes a lot to Harrow and Harrow.'

'I'm glad.' Ruth filled the kettle. 'I'd no idea it was as bad as that. I'm so sorry. I've been a bad neighbour. Shall we go into the sitting room?'

'No it's cosy here.' Bella looked round. 'You and your cooking, very domestic and cosy. You look very contented, Ruth.'

'Oh I'm not *that;* but perhaps not quite so churned up as before! Geoffrey and I are going off to Italy for two weeks and the kids are all at summer schools of various kinds.'

'You're very busy locally again, I know.'

'Yes I'm now chairman of the Ladies' branch of the Conservative Party. I didn't really want to be but it pleases Geoffrey, and infuriates my children who are all Socialists to the core. Anyway I think Mrs Thatcher is doing a jolly good job, even if it is not so good for Antal.'

'Oh he was having difficulties for the past year. We should never have come here really. The move, the cost of the house and the warehouse stretched his capacity too far. It was beyond his means. Simon says if he retrenches he'll be all right.'

'But why move from here? Where are you going?'

'Back to London. I was never happy here, you know. I miss the city. I'm a Londoner by birth and inclination. Actually we've got a flat very near our old flat in Swiss Cottage. I think it will help Antal to be settled, just to have one office and one home. Irena wants to live on her own and Chris will live with us. Maybe you won't send George to boarding school now.'

240

'Why not?' Ruth poured water on to the instant coffee she'd spooned into mugs.

'I know it was really Chris's influence you disapproved of. You thought he led him into that glue sniffing.'

'He did I'm afraid. There's no doubt about that. It was only going on in Chris's year, not George's. However let bygones be bygones. We all think George will be better at a boarding school with some more discipline. He can concentrate on his work. Joe has missed out on Oxford or Cambridge because he didn't apply himself.' Ruth glanced at Bella, but she was nervously making little patterns with her finger dipped in the flour on the kitchen table.

'You must come and see us when we're settled.'

'I'd love to.'

'Maybe we can go to some things in London. Antal will like that. He will miss the odd glimpse of you. I think he had quite a torch for you, you know.'

Ruth put milk in the coffee and went to the cupboard for some home-made biscuits. A breeze drifted into the kitchen and she was glad she'd left the back door open. She felt hot around the neck. She was quite sure that Bella was going to come out with something. This was just a preliminary. She knew. Everyone knew. All her life Ruth would be haunted by her brief affair with Antal Lazar. That was largely why she had become chairman of the Tory Ladies. Tory chairwomen never had sordid affairs of that kind. She didn't really care a rap for party politics or for Mrs Thatcher. It was the image that mattered. You couldn't imagine Mrs Thatcher having an affair with someone like Antal Lazar.

'I don't know why you thought Antal liked me especially.' Ruth sat opposite Bella and bit into a biscuit. 'We hardly knew each other.' She had to know.

'Why, I could tell. You remember that day we discussed the glue sniffing? Antal so much wanted to please you. I sometimes wish he would have affairs with a woman like you rather than some of the women he does go with. He takes them to a flat in Marylebone High Street. He doesn't pay them, though. Not even Antal goes as low as that.'

'How do you know all this?' Ruth's throat was dry and she tried to clear it. It was difficult to be detached, even now.

'Oh he was always a compulsive womanizer. He can't resist a bit of skirt; but an intelligent woman is too much of a challenge. He never liked any of my friends; but he did like you. You're very lucky to have escaped him. He can wreak havoc with women. At least two I know have had abortions and one tried to kill herself.'

'But does he *tell* you this?'

'He often tells me afterwards. He told me about the abortions at the time because the girls were young and I had to do the arranging. One was only eighteen.'

Might he tell Bella about her later? She would never know.

'But I could see Antal fancied you from the way he shouted at Chris. He was trying to impress you with all that noise. You see he is basically a very weak man and he thinks if he shouts a lot people will be impressed. The kids despise him of course but other people notice. He seems so masterly and in control.

'But because he is weak he has to appear so aggressive, banging and shouting all the time. His inability to form strong relationships with women makes him want to sleep with as many as he can. It establishes his virility; his domination over the physically weaker sex.'

'You make him sound absolutely horrible. I'm sure that's a very subjective, maybe rather prejudiced view.'

'Oh no, it's true. I know him so well. I've put up with it for all these years. Of course it hasn't been easy; but basically I like him. I'm really very fond of him. Maybe in Swiss Cottage we'll start again. It's a tiny flat. I'd like him to be happy, I really would. I've been married to him for twenty-five years and he's one of the unhappiest men I know.'

*

242

For once Antal Lazar was on time. Ruth had already ordered coffee in the bar across from the flat and sat there sipping it with composure when he came in. For a moment he stood on the threshold looking at her and it was interesting for her, this moment, in order to see how she felt about him. He looked very debonair in a lightweight tan summer suit with a cream shirt and a brown tie. His hair was a little longer at the back than usual, waving slightly.

She was still susceptible. She thought it had gone, she thought she hated him and despised him and was here to give him a piece of her mind. How could she tolerate a man who was so perfidious? So weak?

He slipped into the seat beside her, casting his beautiful smile at the waitress and asking in his soft voice for a coffee. He took her hand and squeezed it. She withdrew it hurriedly.

'I wanted to see you so badly,' he said.

'It took you an awful long time to telephone.'

'No I've rung and rung; but you're out such a lot. I went round to leave a message, but I saw Joe and thought it was risky, at this stage.'

'At any stage it's been risky.'

'You're very brittle, darling. I can feel it.'

'It's not the same, Antal.'

'I know I haven't been in touch but I've been away, and very worried. I thought I'd go completely bust. I must say Simon has been very smart. He's a clever man. Mind you *I've* paid. I've contributed greatly to your financial prosperity via Harrow and Harrow. Even if you're on the verge of bankruptcy they charge – in advance, just to be sure.'

'The business is nothing to do with me.' Ruth felt annoyed.

He took her hand reassuringly. 'I know, darling. I'm being facetious. Bella told you about the house?'

'That's why I'm here. To say goodbye.'

'Oh my darling what nonsense.' His lips brushed her cheek. 'You and I are made to last.'

243

She thought of the flat across the road and her resolve weakened. It would be so easy just to slip between the sheets and forget the whole business, who had been there before, who would come after her. The sheets were always fresh, that was for sure. She would just surrender herself to physical, carnal, lovemaking. She would forget that he was deceitful and she had a husband.

'I know about Eunice, Antal.'

'What about Eunice?' His eyes flickered as they always did when he was lying. This was one of the things she'd learned about him very quickly. He fluttered his eyelids when he was evading the truth; it was a weakness he very quickly overcame and replaced with a hard confident stare.

'I know that she was your mistress too.'

'She was never my mistress!' Ruth could almost have believed him such was the honest indignation on his face.

'She knows about the flat in Marylebone High Street. Did she just come for coffee?'

'She told you about the flat?'

'Yes, and Bella said you brought a lot of women there. Apparently it's quite notorious, that flat. Eunice said it was like a seedy hotel at King's Cross and I know what she means. Very impersonal; but not smelly. I always wondered that you hardly seemed to keep any clothes or belongings there.'

'I hardly lived there.'

'You hardly live anywhere do you, Antal? You hardly exist.'

Antal put his arms on the table and momentarily put his head in his open palms. 'I'm terribly tired, Ruth. If this is giving you pleasure . . .'

'How could it give *me* pleasure, Antal? To know I was made such a fool of?'

'I did *not* make a fool of you. Our affair is very important to me. Eunice was not my mistress.'

'But you did go to bed?'

'It was terribly unimportant. Once or twice. No more. I tell

244

you she didn't interest me. She just flung herself at me and I couldn't say no.'

'Being you, you couldn't.'

'Well it is difficult. It flatters the ego. It's so wounding to a woman if a man turns her down. As Simon is my lawyer I had to be nice to his wife.'

'And all the other women? '

'Oh that is a fantasy of Bella's. She tells everyone I go with a low class of woman, almost prostitutes. I know what she says because other people have told me. I think she gets a kick out of it. But it's untrue. I am very fastidious as you know. I do *not* go with common women. I choose very carefully. It has to be special.' He seized her hand again and looked into her eyes. 'I do need you, Ruth. Please, can we?'

'You mean to say you really desire me sexually at this moment?'

'Very much and unless I am mistaken you feel the same.'

'I thought I was free from you, Antal. I despise you so much in my heart. If I am in bondage to you physically I am hardly a free woman.'

'You're perfectly free, to make love or not. As you please. If you're going to start to talk about women's liberation I really am off. There is no such thing as a liberated man or woman. We are sexually tied up with one another, both in bondage. In our case I need you and you need me.'

'I think sex is a tyranny,' Ruth said. 'If you don't behave properly, you don't get it.'

'That goes for many things,' Antal said smoothly. 'Come on. You're off on holiday next week?'

'Yes. To Italy.'

'Then you'll be having a lot of sex with Geoffrey?'

'Probably.'

'I still hate that, you know.'

Ruth looked at him and repudiated the longing in her heart,

the physical need. 'Antal I do want to finish with you. This is a good time to finish. When you leave Edgerton . . .'

'We have not left Edgerton *yet.*' Antal got up and paid their bills. Then he went over and took her hand. 'Come on. We'll get a taxi.'

'Where to? What about the flat?'

Antal looked across the road. 'Oh that's gone, didn't I tell you? It was too expensive. I only rented the place anyway.'

'For women?'

'For convenience.'

'Well where are we going then?'

Antal spread his hands apologetically. 'Darling, the only place at the moment is the office. It is very small; but we haven't signed the lease for the Swiss Cottage flat yet.'

'I wouldn't dream of going there anyway.'

'Then it's the office.'

It was on the top floor of a house in Bruton Street. They'd stopped just outside the expensive restaurant Miranda. How vividly she recalled that night. They walked up the four flights of wooden uncarpeted stairs with the sound of typewriters clicking behind closed doors. The ground floor was the show-room of a well known couturier.

The office was really an attic, terribly small, sparsely furnished, with a high window that looked over across Bond Street and Hanover Square. She could see the top of Liberty's in Regent Street. She shivered.

'If you're cold I'll put the fan heater on.'

'It's incredibly sordid, Antal. I thought at least there'd be a couch.'

'The floor is very sexy, darling. The carpet is quite comfortable. It was a leftover remnant from the man on the ground floor and he spares no expense. I got him the whole carpet at cost through my friend who is in carpets.'

'You've made love on it before?'

'You're determined to be suspicious aren't you?' He started to fiddle with the zip at the back of her white silk dress. As usual she had dressed with care so as to get the better of Antal. As usual she had lost. 'Really I feel quite flattered that a man of nearly fifty should be supposed to have so many women. I'm sorry I can only make love to one at a time.'

If she ran out now would she feel better? Would she have won a battle, saved her integrity? Would he despise her or would he admire her? Or would he trouble to think much about it at all?

He unzipped her completely and pulled her dress over her head. 'No pearls today, I see,' he murmured into her ear. 'Something you can easily get off. No tights, or roll-ons. Saucy wench. You wanted it, didn't you?'

His words made her feel randy and she turned and kissed him. He pulled off her petticoat and fiddled with the back of her bra. When she only had her panties on he released her and started to undress.

She got a cushion from the one easy chair in the room and lay down on the floor, taking off her pants and throwing them on top of the grey steel filing cabinet. She felt incredibly excited and aroused. As he leaned over her he looked like some dark colossus, sinewy and hirsute. She reached up for him to pull him down, raising her legs and opening them wide.

The gentle warmth from the fan heater in the corner across the room played on her bare bottom.

One last time.

The pantechnicon arrived in the middle of September just after she and Geoffrey got back from Italy. It parked one day outside the Lazars' house and for moment she felt almost hysterical with some sort of irrational, unexplained violent emotion. The excitement was going out of her life with the Lazars.

247

She rushed next door and the house was in chaos, men coming and going carrying the huge old-fashioned pieces of furniture. Antal was busy shouting upstairs and Bella looked as though she was about to burst into tears.

'Can I help? I didn't realize it was *today*.'

'Oh Ruth, I should have told you; but it has all been so awful. We nearly lost the flat in Swiss Cottage and Antal is being sued over the warehouse in Edgerton. No, there's nothing you can do. In fact the very best thing would be if you kept out of the way. I simply can't cope with him and all the men. He's been raging like this all morning.'

Ruth looked at the ceiling. She didn't want to see him. 'O.K. if you're sure there is nothing. Would you come for coffee and a sandwich before you leave?'

'Oh we can't do that, Ruth. The men have got to get up to London and unload and we're late already. Did you have a nice holiday?'

'Lovely, really lovely.'

'I'm so glad. You look terribly well. You're so brown and we've had this awful summer here.'

'I know.'

'I expect you'd like to pop up and say goodbye to Antal?'

'I don't think I'd better.' Ruth gave a falsely bright smile. 'He might throw me down the stairs.'

Bella grinned at her conspiratorially. 'I doubt it, but you'd better not risk it. I'll say you sent your love.'

'I think "regards" would be better.'

'Regards then. And look, as soon as we're settled I'll give you a ring and we'll . . .'

'Yes, yes. Goodbye Bella.'

The shouting upstairs had stopped and Ruth feared he was on his way down. She kissed Bella on the cheek and squeezed her arm. Then she ran quickly out of the house before Antal came down and saw her. She couldn't get that wild scene when they made love on the office floor out of her mind. It was as though she was a third person looking on, seeing it all so clearly, being both excited and shocked by it. The chairman of the Tory Ladies that would be, the one looking disapprovingly on.

The men worked very quickly. Sometimes Antal appeared in the drive, his arms full of clothes or books or *bric à brac*. They seemed terribly disorganized. He wore jeans and a check shirt and hadn't shaved. She'd never seen him look so dishevelled. Perhaps he was a real person after all. Sometimes she wondered if only Bella saw the real Antal while she, glamorizing him, projected some creature of the imagination into her fantasy life.

She stayed behind the curtain windows in the bedroom and she remembered the day she'd seen them first arrive, nearly three years before.

Finally the back doors of the pantechnicon were closed and bolted. There was some altercation at the door between Antal and the men, but whatever it was was settled and the van drove off.

Antal had a jacket on now and stood by the Porsche which had been parked behind the van, shouting and gesticulating at the house, looking at his watch. There was no sign of any children.

Ruth saw Bella emerge in her coat, shut the front door, lock it then turn into the drive. She was clutching various loose articles and looked extremely harassed.

She ran to the car and Antal opened the door for her, shut it, looked at his watch and then glanced at the Harrows' house. Ruth thought she would probably never see his face again. She stepped back from the window as he looked at it, into the shadows of the bedroom.

Then as his car drove off, she quickly drew back the net curtain and pressed her face to the window staring after them.

She didn't even wave.